WHAT IT TAKES

HER BEST FRIEND COULD BE HER WORST ENEMY

SUSAN WILKINS

In loving memory of Jim Wall (1923-2024). Avid crime fiction fan and our biggest supporter.

PROLOGUE

A child's scream rips through the night. She jolts awake, heart hammering, and fumbles for the light switch, her trembling fingers finding only empty air.

Is it real or part of the nightmare? In this wavering borderland between sleep and consciousness, she can never tell.

Alone in the darkness, her breathing is fast and shallow with fear, her mind still caught in the dream, hearing those cries.

And she's back there. The heat that day, the burning summer heat on her skin and the phantom roar of the river filling her ears. But in the woods it was cool, running through a carpet of dried leaves, a perfect playground.

What's a recurring dream and what's a memory? Long ago, the two fused into one. It's the raw sensations that still engulf her. The choking panic. The gut-wrenching terror. And the guilt, ever-present, wrapping around her like a shroud.

All the thinking, all the work she's done since then, it makes no difference. You can never escape what you've done.

The horror lives in you, breathes with you, haunts you forever.

1

Monday. 4.15pm

Lexi Harper glances at the satnav on the dash. She hates being late. The wipers smack across the windscreen in a vain attempt to disperse the torrential rain. Next right; although in the fast fading afternoon light, it's impossible to see more than ten metres ahead. It's been sheeting down since she left the M25. The worst wettest November on record, they said on the radio. She's already fifteen minutes late.

She grips the steering wheel.

The right-hand turn is little more than a muddy track awash with puddles, but there is a sign just about discernible through the murk: Renfrew Hall.

The client will understand, of course he will. If he's a reasonable man.

Fat chance.

When it comes to dealing with the super-rich, you can never tell which way they'll jump. Lexi's been in the property business long enough to expect the unexpected. Ultra-high net worth individuals, or UHNWIs as they're known, live in a rarefied world where they assume that everyone else is there to meet their needs and anticipate their whims, because, by and large, it's true.

Roger's words when he hired her are still etched in her brain.

'Remember,' he said, 'dealing in the super prime property market is a delicate balancing act between telling a client what they want to hear in order to secure the listing, then finding a buyer who's willing and able to pay the price.'

C'mon, you're not a rookie anymore. You got this.

She slaps the steering wheel, eyes straining to see ahead through the failing light. She knows what she's doing, and she's done her homework.

As she navigates the rutted track, she gets her first glimpse of the house looming ahead through the veil of rain. Mansion would be the correct description. A Tudorbethan monstrosity, built in 1878 by Norman Shaw for a wealthy banker, it has the tall chimneys and projecting gables of his early style; a quick zip through Google told her that. The interior still shows the Arts and Crafts influence. Grade II listed, set in fifteen acres, and within an easy commute of central London. On paper, the valuation has to be close to ten million; it depends on how much work is needed, but foreign buyers will be queuing up for such a screamingly English country house. All Lexi needs to do is persuade the client to give them the listing. She's confident the place will sell itself.

A row of wind-thrashed ornamental trees on either side of the drive lead to a turning circle in front of the house. There's a fountain in the centre, the bronze figure of a nymph reaching upwards. The surrounding pool is overflowing and choked with dead leaves. She parks her car as near as possible to the front door, as she rehearses her spiel.

She'll begin with a fulsome apology and hope that he recognises the effort she's made to even turn up at all in such bloody awful weather. Best to dispense with the umbrella; looking damp and bedraggled will advance her case. But she still slips off her trainers and replaces them with heels. Dress the part. That's the second thing Roger taught her. But clothes have always been her armour.

As soon as she steps out of the car, the deluge hits her and she makes a dash for the shelter of the porch. The front door is heavy, blackened oak, matching the vertical and horizontal timbers of the building, and it's ajar.

She hesitates, then pushes it open and calls out, 'Hello?'

A quarter past four, it's nearly dark, and the interior is a mass of shadows. Someone really should have turned on a light. Lexi's boss, Gemma, spoke to the client and made the appointment. He didn't say whether he was in residence, but the place has a chilly, unoccupied feel. There's a smell to empty properties, musty and airless; obviously no one has lived here for some time.

Lexi steps into the hall and shouts, 'Hello!' Her voice echoes through the wood-panelled hall and up the wide, dark stairway.

Sod it!

There's a row of three light switches next to the door and she turns them all on. At least the electricity is working. As the amber glow brightens, she finds herself standing under an enormous metal chandelier. Medieval design with energy saving candle bulbs, it casts a muted amber glow.

The light gives her the confidence to stride across the room. She decides to do a quick recce, switching on another light as she moves down a narrow passage towards what she assumes will be the kitchen.

It's large. Unpainted wooden cabinets with hand-wrought

iron hinges and latches. The floor is natural stone. The room exudes craftsmanship and quality materials, details which matter in a premium sale. And with some updating and added high-tech accoutrements…

She stops in her tracks. There's a movement on the….

What the f…?

A shiver runs through her. A puddle of blood is creeping across the stone flags from behind the central kitchen island. And she can see a head. Only part of it, turned away from her, but definitely the back of a bald head. A man? Is he alive? There's a gurgling, breathy sound in between gasps.

Oh my God!

She stands rooted to the spot in shock and disbelief.

What do you do? What the hell are you supposed to do?

Her hand shakes. Her whole body shakes as she scrabbles in her bag, pulls out her phone, fumbles, and nearly drops it.

Should she do something? Try to help him? But what? She takes a step closer. One arm is twitching, as if he's trying to lift it but can't.

All that blood!

Her thumbs hit the buttons; she's quick, dextrous. In her game, you have to be. She does most of her business on the phone.

The emergency operator answers at once. 'Which service do you require?'

'Yeah, I…okay, I need help…'

Get a grip!

'An ambulance. He's on the floor. He's bleeding.'

A click on the line followed by a different voice. 'Is the patient breathing?'

She takes another step and peers.

'Yes, but there's so much blood. I dunno…looks bad.

Maybe he's been stabbed, I'm not sure. I don't know what to do.'

'Stay on the line. But give me your number in case we're cut off.'

Lexi reels it off.

'Can you give me your location?'

'Yes, I'm at Renfrew Hall. Just north east of Redbourn, towards Harpenden. I don't know what…I just got here. I'm a property agent. I came here to meet a client.'

My God, is this him?

Moments ago, she pulled up in her car, but now that feels like another time. Dodging through the downpour. And she was hassled because she was late.

Shit! Fifteen minutes ago…

Fear surges through her. Whoever did this could still be here. Hiding. Waiting. The place is vast, cavernous, and creepy with the light going and this stupid pouring rain. She spins round, back to the route she's just taken from the oak-panelled hallway to the kitchen. Shadows everywhere and pockets of darkness. Loads of places to hide.

Run!

The emergency operator is speaking. 'Look at the patient. Describe what you see.'

'I need to get out of here. I'm sorry.'

Better to be a cowardly, selfish piece of shit and alive.

'An ambulance is on its way, and I've alerted the police. Can you stay on the line?'

Lexi turns towards the kitchen door, but as she does so, she hears a voice. Barely audible between gulps. 'Please…'

She stops, pulse racing.

'Please…'

Don't be stupid! Get out!

She moves round the large kitchen island to where he's

lying on the floor. The blood is pulsing from the side of his neck. He's clutching at it with his hand. His eyes are wild and full of terror, but they lock onto hers, begging.

Oh fuck! You can't just...

Lexi squats beside him. 'Ambulance is coming. Police are coming.'

She has to stem the bleeding, but how? Apply some kind of pressure to that terrible gash? Isn't that what you do? She's seen it on television.

She pulls off her cashmere scarf, Vivienne Westwood, with the embroidered VW logo, but she has no choice. It's all she's got. Putting her phone down, she reaches towards him. 'Just let me...'

She presses the white scarf against his neck, gingerly at first. It turns crimson with his blood, but he doesn't resist. His gaze is both fierce and pleading as he clings to consciousness. She folds the end of the scarf over and pushes down harder. The bleeding slows.

'They're coming. Try to keep still.'

The only sound now is the gurgling in his throat. Worse with each breath. If she can just hang on. If they can both hang on.

'It'll be okay.'

Stupid thing to say. Clearly it won't.

He exhales. Almost a sigh. Then this odd thing happens. The eyes empty, turning sightless and blank. The spark is gone. It's eerie. Sends a shudder right through her. He was here, a person, a living person, whoever he was, now he's not. He's gone.

Lexi stares. It's unreal. The bile rises in her throat. She has to swallow hard so as not to puke.

She lets go of the scarf. Rocks back on her heels. The scarf is soaked. Her hands are slick with his blood.

A thick silence descends. The place is freezing. She glances around and becomes aware of the rain thrashing against the small casement windows. A door slams somewhere at the back of the house. The wind…or?

Panic crashes through her brain. What the hell has she walked into here? Who is he? Was he? The client?

One thing is crystal clear. She needs to get out of here. Back to her car. Lock herself in and wait for the police. She stands up; her whole body is shaking. What if someone's lying in wait out in the hall?

C'mon! You've been in tight spots before.

She grabs her phone and, leaving the scarf on the floor beside him, she heads for the kitchen door. The hallway is still ablaze with light from the chandelier. The front door is open. Did she leave it like that? She can't remember. She glances around quickly, strides across the hall, gets half way and bolts for the door.

The rain swamps her as soon as she steps outside, but it's a relief. A couple more seconds and she's in her car. She clicks the lock.

Safe. Breathe.

Water trickles down her face. She wipes it away and tastes blood. His blood. Her phone, her hands, her coat, she's covered in it. Her bloody prints are on the door handle.

She pulls a packet of wet wipes from the glove compartment and scrubs her hands. But it's everywhere; her fingers are stained red and it's under her nails. It won't come off. She hates any sort of mess, but this? Gross. And now the tears spill out.

She wants to drive off, head for the motorway, stop at the services, be amongst people, get a hot coffee. That would look bad, though. Like she was running away. She stares up at the house. Whoever did this could still be here. Watching her. And she's a sitting duck. Except they can't get to her in the car, can they? Unless they smash a window.

Fuck it! Go.

She starts the engine and is about to drive off when she sees flashing blue lights approaching at speed up the long drive.

2

Monday. 10.30pm

For Beth Nolan ten thirty is the beginning of her evening, not the end. She's primping her naturally honey blonde hair in the vanity mirror over the marble sink and checking her makeup as she waits for the Uber to arrive. Her phone buzzes.

Not the Uber, but an incoming call.

Lexi.

Lexi may be her best friend since forever, but she's also an old fart when it comes to knowing how to have fun. She goes clubbing about twice a year, if that. All she cares about is work. And more work.

Beth sighs as she answers.

'Hey, babe. Surely it's past your bedtime?' She tries to mask her irritation.

'I'm in a cab. I'm coming over.' Lexi's voice sounds weird. Throaty, like she's been smoking or crying.

'Oh, I was just about to—'

'Please, Beth.' The tone, the urgency pulls Beth up short.

'What's going on?'

'Tell you when I get there.'

The line goes dead.

Beth stares at the phone. She hates it when her plans get disrupted. And for what? Sounds like some stupid deal has fallen through. Lexi takes her job way too seriously. But Beth's hardly in a position to complain.

She wanders from the bathroom down a short hallway to the great room, a huge space where living room, dining area and state-of-the-art kitchen are seamlessly integrated into one. The ceiling to floor windows give a bird's eye view of the glittery nighttime city with the illuminated dome of St Paul's directly across the river. So cool. Definitely a multi-million pound vista. But the fact she's here, in this luxury apartment next to the Tate Modern, is thanks to Lexi. It's her job as a hotshot property agent that gives her access to places like this.

Truth is Beth was in a bit of spot when she and Damian split, and Lexi arranged for her to flat sit this spectacular gaffe until the rental client Lexi has lined up flies in from Dubai.

'Couple of weeks tops. You promise. And don't crap the place up.'

Beth had promised. Lexi believed her. That part of their relationship has always been easy. Trust. Lexi trusts her.

With another sigh, Beth texts the Uber to cancel. It's annoying. More than annoying. She was looking forward to her evening. A new place in Mayfair, and she's on the guest list, thanks to a friend of a friend. All the usual crew will be there. They've been rallying round to cheer her up.

She goes to the fridge and pulls out a bottle of white wine. She had a glass or two earlier to psyche herself for her night out, but there's still half a bottle left. It'll do. Lexi's not much of a drinker.

Kicking off her shoes—a relief, frankly—she plonks down on the Italian leather sofa. She tucks her feet up under her, but finds it hard to sit still. Always has. Her body is just naturally restless; it likes to be on the move. This is probably why her modelling career never quite panned out as she expected. She was rubbish at holding a pose. ADHD, they said when she was at school. Not her fault. It's a condition.

She definitely has the looks, the agency that took her on at seventeen assured her of that. But she was probably naive. Didn't realise that to get a foothold, there were people you needed to shag.

There's always a trade-off.

She's as feminist as the next girl, but when you grow up in the arse-end of nowhere, leave school with no GCSEs, and don't fancy being poor your whole life, you have to learn to use the assets you do have. And Beth has certainly figured out how to do that in the last ten years.

Sipping the wine, she grows sombre. Her thoughts drift to Damian. He wore aviator shades, drove a vintage Mustang and behaved as if he was the dog's bollocks. The trouble was he had that edge, that whiff of trouble that she always finds beguiling. He pursued her in a laid-back sort of way. Sent flowers. Very old school. In the end she gave in. Why not?

They were together for nearly nine months. It was a blast. The truth is she really liked him. He had a bit of a temper, but she could manage that. He was sweet as pie with her. Never raised his hand. She was beginning to think he was a keeper. They had a real laugh, did some crazy shit, and he wasn't mean. He splashed the cash. Liked her to look good. The dress she's wearing now was the last one he bought her. A genuine Stella

McCartney, not a knock-off. She's tearing up, which is no good. Thinking about him makes her too emotional. She jumps up, goes over to the kitchen area and tops up her glass. The bottle's nearly empty. She gets another from the chiller cabinet.

Lexi was the one to point out that she had to let Damian go. Always sensible, Lexi. Beth knew in her heart it was good advice. Her mate has her back. Always. Since they were five years old. Didn't make it any easier when she went to tell him. He was on remand, awaiting trial. He cried, that's how nice he is.

At times, she does actually envy Lexi, because when they were dishing out the brains, Lexi got more than her fair share. Loads more. She has looks too. Dark to Beth's light. When they do go out together, they make a stunning pair. Real head turners. But Lexi has a few other things that aren't so good. Most of the time she's just so uptight. Like a tightly wound spring. And she worries about everything. Getting stuff right is an obsession with her. Keeping everything in order. It's exhausting to watch.

Beth is channel hopping on the sixty inch television when she hears the front door open. Lexi has a key. She appears from the short hallway and she looks like absolute shit.

Jumping up, Beth rushes to her. 'Babe! What the fuck?' She pulls her friend into a hug. And Lexi doesn't go rigid and resist as she usually does. Holding her at arm's length, Beth looks her up and down. A disgusting cheap pair of trackies that look like they'd come from a cut price sports outlet, and this on a woman who is never less than immaculate and owns a designer outfit for every day of the week. She seems to be carrying her own clothes in a plastic bin bag.

'Lex, what the hell are you wearing? Did you have an accident.'

'Sort of. I need to wash my clothes.' She's super jittery.

Extreme even for Lexi. She heads straight for the kitchen area, and the washing machine, which is in a bank of cupboards. Beth follows, concerned and curious.

Lexi opens the machine; it's a top-of-the range Miele, obviously. All the appliances in the apartment are expensive. 'The detergent's pre-loaded, isn't it?' she says in a worried tone.

Beth shrugs. Laundry's not high on her list of priorities. 'Yeah, I think. I've used it maybe once.'

Lexi pulls a shirt out of the bin bag. Hawes and Curtis with a narrow stripe, her usual work gear. But the front is smeared with what…OMG, it looks like blood? Beth's heart leaps into her mouth.

'Fuck me, is that blood?'

'Not my blood,' says Lexi, stuffing the shirt and her Ralph Lauren pencil skirt into the machine.

Shit. This is bad.

Lexi shuts the door and pushes the buttons. 'You know the country house I told you about? Renfrew Hall?'

'Yeah.' She has no idea. Lexi tells her stuff all the time, so how's she supposed to keep up?

'Don't lie Beth. The place out in Hertfordshire, near St Albans. Worth close to ten million if we get the listing.'

Beth remembers the ten million bit. She nods.

'I went there this afternoon to meet the client. But when I got there…' She hesitates, choking on her words. She has tears in her eyes. 'I found him on the kitchen floor with his throat cut. He was still alive. He died right there in front of me.'

Beth's eye's widen. 'Seriously? That is…' She shakes her head in disbelief, '…terrible.'

'I tried my best to help him.'

Course she did. That's the kind of numbskull she is.'

'Babe, I'd've just run. How d'you know whoever did it wasn't still there?'

'I didn't know.'

'Jesus wept, Lexi. And you think I'm dumb.'

'I just…I dunno. I couldn't just walk away from a dying man. I couldn't.'

'I could.'

Beth grabs the new bottle of wine from the counter, gets a large glass down from the cupboard and more or less fills it. Lexi accepts it without comment. No eyebrow raising. No asking for a smaller measure. She just drinks. When half the glass is gone, she turns to Beth and exhales. 'I had to go to the police station, do a video interview about what happened, give my fingerprints and DNA. It took hours.'

'Had you met this client before?'

'No. Gemma set it up.' Gemma is Lexi's boss. An anorexic Sloane with a bug so far up her arse it practically waves at you out of the top of her head.

'Have you talked to her?'

'On the phone. Briefly. She's in a complete spin. She's worried about the firm's reputation. Predictably.'

'It's not your fault. You just found him. You didn't get him killed.'

Lexi sighs. She shakes her head sorrowfully. 'You don't understand, babe. In this business, it's all about reputation. You can't be associated with anything like this. We have to look squeaky clean. Always.'

'But you said you tried to help him.'

'Doesn't matter,' she says. 'Someone gets murdered, questions will be asked, won't they? Like who the hell was he? Was he dodgy? If so, why didn't we know this? Did we check him out properly? Due diligence it's called. There are all kinds of regulations we have to comply with. Gemma will be looking for a scapegoat, someone to blame, and that will be me. They'll sack me. I bet you.'

She does this. Always expects the worst.

'Yeah, but you just said Gemma set it up. He was her contact. So isn't it down to her?'

'Yes. It is. She told me it was all fine. But she's also CEO and Roger's daughter.' Lexi drains her glass. 'And she's lazy and she lies.'

'Nah, you're too good at your job. You bring in the buyers. Stupid cow knows that. They won't sack you.'

Lexi holds out her glass for a top up. 'C'mon Beth. Don't be naive. A classy upper-crust outfit like Cavendish Cooper. They'll absolutely want to distance themselves. Gemma's been gunning for me for months. Now she's got the perfect excuse. Basically, I'm fucked.'

Beth considers this. Lexi's a worrier. Still, it doesn't sound good. What if they do sack her?

She's fucked, means we both are.

3

Tuesday. 7.50am

Ewan drags each tangled item of clothing from the washing machine and arranges it neatly on the drying rack. The spinner's knackered, so it's quite wet.

The kitchen is tiny and cluttered, with little room between the rack and the table squashed in the corner behind the door. Out of the window, the slack cables on the rotary washing line are dripping with heavy droplets of water, which hang for a moment before falling onto the concrete patio. It's been raining all night and this morning it's still raining. Ewan lugs the loaded drying rack through into the sitting room and dumps it next to the radiator.

The old man is spread-eagled on the sofa, fully dressed, out cold. Ewan stares at him, waiting for some emotion to hit him. But there's nothing. Zilch. No feelings. Just the bare facts: this person is his father. He looks way older than his fifty-two years. His face is crumpled and sweaty like a broken down cage fighter. But it's all self-inflicted. He's been tipping the booze down his own throat ever since Ewan can remember.

Ewan returns to the kitchen, gets out the blender, throws in a handful of frozen berries from the freezer, and dumps a couple of scoops of protein powder and some milk on top. He puts it on its base and whizzes it up.

As he pours the smoothie into a glass, the old man appears in the doorway, scratching his exposed belly and scowling. His trousers are unfastened, flies gaping. 'What the fuck? I'm trying to sleep.'

'Want some breakfast, Dad?'

The old man farts, then disappears back into the sitting room. 'What I want is some fucking peace.'

Ewan takes his smoothie and follows. He perches on an armchair. The old man is searching, digging down the back of the sofa. 'You seen my fags?'

Ewan doesn't reply. He sips his drink.

'I'm talking to you, boy.'

'You probably smoked them.'

More rummaging, and he comes up with an empty packet. *Predictable.*

In the month Ewan has been back home, he's discovered that more or less every move his father makes is predictable, so he knows what's coming next.

His father turns slowly towards him. He screws up his nose, contorting his face like a snarling dog about to bite. Then he lashes out, knocking the glass from Ewan's grasp with the back of his hand. The glass goes flying and the pink smoothie ends up on the carpet.

The old man leans in towards him and growls, 'Now lick it up, you cock-sucking faggot.'

Ewan slides sideways to avoid his father and stands up. The old man sways. Ewan weighs over two hundred pounds and it's solid muscle. He could raise one finger and push his father over, but he doesn't. He retrieves the glass, which landed on the dirty shag pile rug and is still intact.

The old man hasn't finished. He jabs his finger in the air. 'Think all this pumping iron makes you a man. You're nothing. I could still give you a thrashing, boy. You think you can just come back here? How you've got the fucking nerve?'

'Someone's got to look after you. That's why I'm here.'

Not strictly true. He came back because it's a condition of his licence. A proper address, an actual paying job, no contact with former associates. These are the boxes that have to be ticked to keep his parole officer off his case. This is how you get them to leave you be and go chasing after some other dipshit who's getting off his tits on weed or whatever and doing stupid shit.

The old man picks up a can from the coffee table, shakes it, puts it to his lips and drains the dregs. He flings it at Ewan; it glances off his shoulder. 'When you went down, that's what killed your mother. After everything else. You finished her off. You boy, you did it.'

Same old, same old.

He's heard it all before. Several zillion times.

He scans the old man; there are tears in his eyes because like most drunks he's full of self-pity. Ewan thinks about his mother. She died when he was fifteen, but he doesn't remember much about her. She always had a fag going, chain-smoked, which was pretty disgusting. He was banged up in a young offenders unit by then. When they came and told him, they said it was cancer.

Ewan tilts his head, cricks his neck. 'I'll get a cloth.'

He returns to the kitchen and searches under the sink for a bucket. His mother had a place for everything and everything in its place. But you'd never guess that now. No bucket.

Feelings? His mother?

No, nothing to speak of, only the vague annoyance that they no longer have a bucket.

He gets a roll of kitchen paper and a dustpan; both are items he's purchased since moving back. When he returns to the sitting room, the old man has slumped on the sofa and is attempting to light a dog end from the ashtray. It ignites briefly and goes out. The old man mumbles a curse and glares at him.

'You got any fags?' he says.

'You know I don't smoke,' says Ewan.

He started weight training seriously when they moved him to adult nick. By then he knew it was the one thing that kept you sane. It was in the prison gym that he met guys like Rusty, an ex-biker serving life; he had everyone's respect, even the screws. He's the one taught Ewan how to be a man. Number one was respecting your own body as the source of your power. Ewan shaved his head, grew a beard like Rusty's, and trained relentlessly. Also, the bigger he got, the more muscle he put on, the safer he was.

Except from the old man.

'Yeah, I've heard all you gym freaks are pansies,' says the old man.

Ewan scoops up the smoothie with a folded square of paper.

'You hearing me, boy? Why don't you answer?'

'Didn't realise it was a question. But I've got one for you, Dad. Why do you never call me by my name? You gave it to me. Maybe you've forgotten it.'

He never uses Ewan's name. Can't bring himself to speak it.

The old man doesn't reply. He gets up and lumbers towards the door. 'Need a slash,' he mumbles.

'Try not to piss on the floor,' says Ewan. 'I just cleaned up in there.'

He can hear the old man in the toilet swearing to himself. Probably crapped his pants again. Wouldn't be the first time. But he can sort himself out.

He sighs and finishes cleaning up the smoothie. The old man is still mumbling to himself in the toilet. So he goes upstairs to get his stuff for work.

As he reaches the narrow upstairs landing, he gets that feeling. Tends to hit him after he gets into it with the old man. It always starts with tension in his shoulders, and then his head goes weird.

Ignore it. It'll pass.

He heads for the box bedroom at the back and shoves open the door. Sure enough, there he is, crashed out.

He boots the leg of the bed. 'C'mon, Jared. Get up!'

His brother moans, turns over and stares up at him. 'Where's my coffee?'

'I'm not your fucking slave. Get up. We're leaving in ten minutes. I don't wanna be late for work.'

'Ooh, mustn't be late,' says Jared in a mocking tone. 'Got to be a good boy now, haven't we?'

'Fuck you! You can walk!' Ewan storms out, slamming the door.

The old man. His brother. They deserve each other. Two peas in a fucking pod. He should never have come back. He knows that.

4

Tuesday. 7.55am

There's a howling darkness, a ravening monster without shape, and it's rushing towards Lexi like a freight train. With a gasp, she wakes up. Her head is pounding, her mouth dry and claggy. Someone is looming over her. She raises her arm defensively as the figure leans in.

'Hey, it's okay, babe.' A soothing voice.

Beth. Holding a mug of coffee.

It all comes flooding back. Renfrew Hall. The blood pumping from that terrible gash in his neck as his life ebbed away. Her terror and her failure to save him.

She's hot and clammy, crashed out in the second bedroom of the rental apartment she's letting Beth use. They drank two bottles of wine, went on to the tequila, got totally wasted.

Stupid!

'Sorry,' she mumbles. 'Bad dream.'

Beth puts the coffee down next to her, then sits on the end of the bed. She's wearing pyjamas covered in penguins and looks about twelve, even though they're both pushing thirty. There's a deceptive innocence about her friend, which, coupled with an irritating amount of energy, makes her seem much younger.

Beth is drumming on the duvet with her index fingers, a compulsive habit. 'You need to chill,' she says. 'You were pretty freaked last night.'

'Was I?'

'You can't let them get to you like this.'

'Like what?'

'You know what I'm saying, babe. Fucking Gemma. You can't let her shaft you.'

Beth means well. She's still the only person Lexi is truly at ease with; surely that's the definition of a best friend. They've known each other since they were little. Met at nursery and have been best buddies ever since. But Beth is also flaky. She never thinks things through. And she certainly doesn't understand the property business.

Lexi struggles to sit up. Her head spins; it's going to be one of those horrible hangovers where you have to drag your addled brain through the day. And that's the last thing she needs.

Serves you right.

She picks up the coffee and sips. Hot and strong, it helps.

'You really think they'll sack you?' says Beth.

'I dunno.'

Gemma will try to, that's for sure.

Gemma is technically her boss, but since the day she arrived at Cavendish Cooper, they've been rivals. Lexi's good at the job; she's worked her way up, so she's had to be. She reads the clients, understands their needs and she makes sales. Unlike Gemma, whose stuck-up manner rubs people up the wrong way. But it's not the only reason Gemma hates her.

There was that awful birthday party at Roger's. Gemma's never got over that.

She looks at Beth.

'Have you got any clothes I can borrow?' she says. To have any chance of dealing with the fallout from this, she has to get to the office, and there's no time to go back to her own place.

'Course. What's mine's yours, babe. You know that.'

Lexi manages a smile. Her friend means this. Beth has a huge heart, no one can deny that. But she floats through life on magic carpet of optimism. She still believes that when the right man comes along, all her problems will be solved.

As if.

The last one turned out to be a high-end coke dealer. He was cheeky and handsome, mixed with the wealthy party crowd who frequent the exclusive West London clubs. Many of them were probably his clients. Beth was on cloud nine, and Lexi tried to be pleased for her. There'd been too many scumbags. But Lexi realised it was all about to go pear-shaped when he told Beth he was going to North Cyprus on an urgent business trip. They arrested him at the airport. Beth was heartbroken. She still is if truth be told. He's also left her pregnant. Pregnant and homeless. Such a disaster could only happen to Beth.

Lexi scans her friend. They know each other so well. Too well, maybe.

'What the hell am I going to do, Beth?'

'No one can blame you. You just walked into something, and you did your best to save the guy.'

For once, Beth could be right, because this was the attitude that the police had taken. The response officers that turned up had been kind. As they swarmed all over the house, one stayed with her asking questions like who was she and why was she there. Did she see anyone else? No. They seemed satisfied with her answers. When the ambulance came, the paramedics wrapped her in a space blanket and told her she was in shock.

Nevertheless, dealing with the police was an unnerving experience. The whole rigmarole of going to the police station. Specialist officers interviewed her and they videoed her statement. It made her feel guilty, which was ridiculous. They needed her fingerprints and forensic samples too, just like a criminal. To eliminate her from the scene, they said. She was an important witness, they said, and detectives would be in touch to talk to her further. It all took so long, and that made her feel worse. By the time she left, she was a wreck, and she still had to drive back to London.

She's done nothing wrong, so why does she feel so guilty?

Say the mantra. You are a good person. You are worthy.

The problem is there's always that niggling thought in her head, clawing at her confidence. Eventually, they'll find out. People will realise who she is. The expensive outfits, the designer labels, will make no difference. They'll see through the mask. She'll never be good enough.

Okay, she's read enough books, watched the videos, she understands the psychology of self-doubt, but that doesn't make it go away. It's always with her, that visceral fear she'll be exposed. One day the life she's built, the career she's built, all her hard work, it won't matter. The house of cards will come tumbling down and she'll lose everything.

She thinks fleetingly of her mother.

Yeah, she'll love that.

'I'll get some paracetamol,' says Beth. 'Finish your coffee.'

Lexi smiles. Beth knows about her demons and her

secrets. She pats Lexi's hand. 'Then get back out there and do what you do . You got this. Don't let the bastards grind you down. Stick it to Gemma, you know you can.' Beth is grinning, those two perfect dimples on either cheek.

They bump fists. Her friend is right.

Never let the bastards grind you down. Better advice than any psychology book.

She smiles. 'Thank you,' she says.

Beth shrugs. 'Hey, for what?'

'For being here, being you. Don't know what I do without you.'

Beth smiles, blows her a kiss and strolls out of the room. Nothing bothers her friend that much, which is enviable. Everything bothers Lexi. She's tried the usual solutions: meditation, yoga, going swimming every morning at six am. At times in her life, the anxiety has paralysed her. After one panic attack years ago, her GP sent her for six sessions of cognitive behavioural therapy. And that helped. Now she can usually see it coming and head it off. Deep breathing. She almost tipped over into a full-blown attack in her car outside Renfrew Hall; it was only the arrival of the cops that stopped it.

She throws back the duvet, swings her legs out, and sits on the side of the bed. Her head is throbbing. How can Beth drink so much and get away with it? Another thing she envies.

Every morning without fail she does her breathing routine. In for three, hold for four, out for five. Two minutes. She manages a couple of rounds of it, but she still wants to puke.

You watched a man die. What d'you expect?

It's not just the booze. Her stomach is queasy with guilt. And she was doing okay. Her life was ticking along pretty well until this. Last year she made more in commission than ever before, and it's all safely stashed in the bank. Money insulates you, it's the only thing that can. She figured that out when she was fourteen, watching her mother struggle after the old man left. Money defines you; it's how the world keeps score. Whether you're marked a success or failure is all about money. Work hard but work smart, that's what she's done ever since. It's the belief that drives her.

She can taste bile rising in the back of her throat and she makes a dash for the en suite. It all comes up, then she sits on the floor next to the toilet, her fingers splayed out across the cold floor tiles. Why did this happen to her?

Bad luck. Bad genes. The usual suspects.

Now her brain is running riot. An unstoppable thought stream. If only she'd known what to do and been quicker off the mark, could she have saved him? She almost turned tail and ran. Surely anyone would? It was such a shock. That's what the paramedic said: she was in shock. But she feels ashamed. A man, a potential client, is dead and she should've done more. They'll pin this on her. They'll accuse her. She knows it.

Stick it to Gemma, you know you can.

Back and forth it goes, the same old quarrel in her head, a ceaseless nattering, like a row you can never escape. She takes a deep breath and counts.

One, two, three, four, five, six, seven, eight, nine, ten. STOP!

She repeats it. Discipline. Self control. These are the only survival strategies that work in the end. If she learned anything from her mother, it's that.

5

Tuesday. 9am

Detective Sergeant Jo Boden arrives at the morning briefing with a large black takeaway coffee in hand. Having a social life in London, not to mention a relationship, is still something she's getting used to, but the fun is certainly outweighing the effort.

She slips into an empty seat at the back of the room next to DC Prisha Chakravorty, who gives her a sly smile. 'Morning.'

'Hey, Prish.'

'You just get off the train from London?'

Boden returns the smile but says nothing. The glow is still with her. Is it that obvious?

'At least you can sleep on the train,' says Chakravorty with a knowing grin.

The fact that Boden is seeing someone is known only to a select few of her colleagues. The ones she is sure can keep their mouths shut. Only Chakravorty is aware of his identity.

The room is filling up; it looks like officers have been drafted in from other units to assist the Major Investigations Team. Word is it's a new murder inquiry. Someone plugs a laptop into the projection system and an enormous Mock Tudor house appears on the screen at the front. Boden gazes at it; the dark vertical timbers against the white walls. It's a replica of the kind of old sixteenth century Elizabethan buildings that still exist at the heart of many English towns and villages, but pumped up to a grandiose scale. It's not a style that Boden admires.

But her contemplation is interrupted, as DCI Rachel Knight steps in front of the screen.

Bloody hell!

So Knight is the Senior Investigating Officer on this one. Boden's heart sinks. She glances at Chakravorty, who shrugs.

'I thought she was on permanent gardening leave,' Boden whispers.

'I dunno. Shortage of experienced SIOs, I guess. Two other murders ongoing.'

Boden has been doing her level best to avoid working with her old boss. And since their last run in, she's succeeded. Knight gave her a lousy write up in her last professional review, questioning her attitude, and that's put pay to her prospects of promotion any time soon. But Boden is beyond caring what the likes of Rachel Knight think about her.

She sips her coffee and folds her arms. It's not a good start.

Knight has a tablet in her hand. She's scrolling through her notes and is decidedly nervous. Looking up, she clears her throat. This kills some of the babble of conversation in the room, but not all of it. Found guilty of gross misconduct and demoted in rank, Knight is far from popular. Attitudes to her range from neutral to she's toxic. According to the gossip mill, she's divorced her husband and cut all ties. He pleaded guilty to money laundering, and because of the assistance he gave to the National Crime Agency, got a lighter sentence. Did Knight have any clue what her ex was up to? Opinions differ.

The DCI raises her chin. 'Right everyone. Can I have your attention please? For those who don't know me, I'm DCI Rachel Knight and I'm the SIO on this inquiry.' She clicks the keyboard of the tablet and another image pops up on the screen. A mugshot of an IC1 male, late thirties, smug expression.

Boden narrows her eyes and peers. No way! Is this who she thinks it is?

Knight continues. 'This is our victim, Craig Jessop.'

Shit!

'Some of you who've worked with me before in Cambridge will know who he is. Started out in a family of villains dealing drugs. But he was much smarter than the average criminal. Moved into property development as a way of laundering cash and worked hard to establish himself as a so-called respectable businessman. His wife helped set up a Food Bank.'

Boden's interest is piqued. This is all beginning to make sense. She imagines Rachel Knight went on bended knee to beg the Chief Constable for this case. It's the road to vindication for her, not to mention revenge, taking down the OCG behind the Jessops. They ruined her career and, arguably, her life. Despite her serious demeanour, the DCI must be gleeful.

Knight's gaze shifts to the back of the room and homes in on Boden. 'Jessop had his throat cut yesterday afternoon at Renfrew Hall. Apparently, he was trying to sell the property either on his own behalf, or for the owners. That's not clear. He was discovered dying on the kitchen floor by the listings agent from a high-end London property agency. He'd arranged to meet her there with a view to them handling the sale. Sergeant Mackie, what have we found out so far about the actual owners?'

Scott Mackie jumps up. He's at the front and turns to face the room. Since his promotion to Sergeant he's taken to squeezing his considerable bulk into a three-piece suit. This has done little to improve his rumpled appearance. Boden glances at Chakravorty, but her face remains inscrutable. If she had a thing for Mackie and vice versa, it never came to anything. Or if it did, they've since fallen out.

'Okay,' says Mackie. 'What we've got on Renfrew Hall is a series of overseas shell companies. The real owners are well-hidden, which would fit with Jessop acting as their front man. But it could be he's laundering proceeds from his own illegal activities. We're doing more digging and liaising with the NCA. Place hasn't been lived in for some time, but it was used as a film set a couple of years back.'

'Thanks, Scott,' says the DCI. 'So, what do we have here? Jessop has certainly upset someone big time. Intelligence reports suggest he's distanced himself from his drug-dealing past. His focus has been on his property business, which has the potential to be more lucrative in the long run. But there's a huge amount of illegal overseas cash sloshing around the UK property market.'

'And your old man'd know about that.' The comment comes from the other side of the room with little effort to be inaudible. The DCI ignores it.

Boden and Chakravorty exchange looks, but inwardly Boden is smiling. This could turn out to be more interesting than your average run-of-the-mill stabbing. And she knows why Knight wants her there. It's payback time for both of them.

6

Tuesday. 9.30 am

Lexi steps out of her cab at the Blandford Street end of Chiltern Street. The dress is dove grey, the most restrained and decorous piece in Beth's wardrobe. Okay, it's too short and too tight, but it'll have to do, as will the borrowed coat. She skips across the damp pavement and buzzes herself into the downstairs lobby. The office is on the first floor, high ceilings, elegant proportions, subject to a recent refurb by an interior designer pal of Gemma's. In Lexi's view, it's turned the place into a bad imitation of an internet start-up; all primary colours, squidgy sofas and table football.

She strides into the office. She's given herself a serious lecture. Act normal and get out in front of this. That's the best strategy in situations of potential conflict. She knows it, but can she do it? Don't hang back, seize the initiative, land the first punch and put your opponent on the back foot. And Gemma Cavendish is not an opponent to underestimate; a weaselly manipulator with a carapace of upper-class charm.

Her father, Roger set the firm up in the early eighties, and it's now one of the top boutique agencies in the London super prime property market. There are the bigger brokerages, with their international offices and hefty overheads, but Cavendish Cooper is nimble and extremely well connected. In the last forty years, they've sold twenty billion pounds worth of property.

That's twenty billion!

Lexi reminds herself of this when she's working a twelve-hour day, and fielding calls from potential buyers who can't quite commit. Until a year ago, the old man himself was still the rainmaker. A huge personality, exuding the confidence of his aristocratic forbearers and Eton education. But he crashed his motorbike, shattered his leg in three places and retired, leaving Gemma to take the reins.

Well, theoretically.

Gemma is a stick-thin blonde and even more of a control freak than Lexi, and she resents the fact her father gave a job to a smart girl who'd bootstrapped her way up, in preference to one of Gemma's Oxford buddies. But Roger Cavendish is always tactical; he knew his over-entitled daughter needed a bit of proper competition, a bit of salt on her tail, to get her moving.

On her first day, when Lexi was introduced to the boss's daughter, Gemma had smiled regally and said, 'Oh, Lexi, that's a lovely name. An old boyfriend of mine had a cocker spaniel called Lexi.'

Things have continued in much the same vein ever since. The incident at Roger's sixtieth birthday party was not Lexi's fault. Gemma was dating this American called Larry; he was third generation loaded, a family as rich as Croesus. Gemma was hearing wedding bells. But having met Lexi at the party, Larry dumped Gemma and started texting Lexi. She told him she wasn't interested—she wasn't, he was awful—but that didn't pacify Gemma. Roger sent her to his villa in St. Lucia for a month to calm down. But when she returned, the battle lines were drawn.

Gemma has taken over her father's glass-walled corner office, and Lexi heads straight for it. Two strong black coffees, four paracetamol and she's buzzing. Gemma is at her desk, but she sees Lexi approaching and immediately busies herself on her computer.

Lexi taps politely but walks straight in. 'Hey, Gemma.'

Gemma does this thing of raising her index finger, as if she's so absorbed in what she's doing, she just needs a minute. It makes Lexi smile. No one could accuse Gemma of not being transparent with her little ticks and psychological tricks.

After about fifteen seconds, she turns her gaze from the screen towards Lexi, and smiles and frowns at the same time. This is her benign headteacher look. 'My God, are you all right?' she says.

'Not really. I know you don't much like me, Gemma. But nearly getting me killed?'

Gemma blinks at her. The expression changes. Now it's a nervous hare caught in the crosshairs.

First punch landed.

Then she laughs, an affected tinkling sound that someone must've told her was ladylike. She stands up. 'For heaven's sake, don't even joke about it, Lexi. It's terrible. I've never heard of such a thing before. And nor has Daddy. He sends you his very best, by the way.'

'That's good of him.'

Shit hits the fan, run to daddy. Par for the course.

Gemma shakes her head and twists her solid gold bangles

nervously. 'The whole thing is dreadful. And so awful for you. I don't know what to say.'

She's on the defensive, which is good. But now Lexi has to dig in and make sure Gemma's got no excuse to try to load the fallout from this on her.

Hands on hips, Lexi positions herself squarely in the middle of the room. 'I told the police everything I know about Mr Jessop, which is basically zilch.' She lets it sound like an accusation.

Gemma blinks rapidly. 'Are they sure it was him?'

'Wallet and phone were found in his pocket.'

'So it wasn't a robbery?'

'I don't know what it was. He's your contact.'

Gemma is flustered, now she's twisting her rings. 'He's a very respectable developer—'

'Was, Gemma.'

'Okay, well, he mentioned the names of several other clients who could vouch for him. Renfrew Hall's a property he'd acquired with a view to updating it and selling it on, but his plans had changed. That's all he told me.'

'His plans have definitely changed now.' Lexi is scowling, but inside she's smiling. Gemma took the easy option; she didn't bother to do a background check, as required by law. They have a company they use for this to verify identity and ensure compliance with Anti Money Laundering legislation. She could've done it online. It would've taken five minutes. But she took him at his word. Relied on his apparent familiarity with their client network. This is on her.

'Didn't you do an online AML check?' Lexi says.

'Oh course I did!' snaps Gemma. But her gaze skitters away.

She's lying.

'Well, that's a relief,' says Lexi. 'Because if they find out we didn't—'

'Do you think the police will want to speak to me, too?' Gemma says peevishly.

'Good chance, I'd say.'

'Obviously, we must help them all we can.'

'Of course.' Lexi pauses before the coup de grâce. 'If I were you, I'd make some calls, Gemma, see if you can find out who the hell this guy really is. Then maybe, depending on what they say, I'd call the lawyers.'

'You think?' She frowns and adds. 'Perhaps I should call Daddy again. See what he thinks.'

Loser.

Lexi shrugs. 'You're the boss.'

Gemma looks frightened. The veil of bullshit she normally operates behind is torn enough to expose her.

'This is just so unprecedented,' she says in a whinny voice. 'We're a highly respected firm. What are people going to say? This business is built on reputation and trust.'

'They'll gossip. But we present a united front, cover our backs, and we manage this. Okay? I'm sure that's what Roger'll tell you. A united front.'

Gemma blinks, tears are forming on her lashes. 'It's just so unfair. I haven't done anything wrong.'

Not much.

'Fuck's sake, Gemma. Neither have I. I'm the one who tried to save his life.'

'Sorry. Awful for you, I know.'

'Yeah. It was awful.'

The two women stare at each other. Gemma looks away first and blows her nose on a tissue. Lexi knows she has the upper hand. For now.

'I've got a busy morning,' she says. 'Call the lawyers.'

She turns and sashays out and across the main office. Teddy Devereux is lounging at his desk. He probably heard all that.

'Morning, Lex,' he says. 'You okay?'

'Like you care,' says Lexi.

'Course I care,' he says, standing up. 'Let me get you a coffee.' He's lean and wiry, his dirty blond hair tied up in a man bun. Many women find him attractive, but Lexi doesn't see it. His face is pointed like a rat. He's there because his father and Roger Cavendish have some ancient tribal connection, and that annoys her. He's also known for poaching other agent's clients, so it's sensible to keep him at a safe distance.

She reaches her own desk. The adrenaline is still pumping. As encounters with Gemma go, this one hasn't turned out too badly. There's a chance she'll get through this unscathed. The firm's reputation will take a hit, but it won't reflect negatively on her. If she keeps harping on how she tried to save him, she could be the hero, not the villain.

She takes out her phone to check her messages. Her eleven thirty is confirmed, which is a relief. But the next text brings her up short.

don't ignore me. I hate being ignored.

What?

She reads it again. Her first thought is that it's her mother. Mum has left a couple of voicemails in the last week saying they need to talk, but Lexi's been putting it off. They don't get on. The resentment is on both sides.

But it's not her mum, not her number. In fact, the number is not in her address book.

Don't ignore me?

WTF?

Teddy arrives with a mug of coffee. 'Everything all right?' he says. 'Only you look a bit—'

'Thanks for the coffee,' she says. 'But I've got to dash.'

Grabbing her bag, she heads for the door and escapes.

7

Tuesday. 9.35 am

Beth is not good at waiting, never has been. She paces the apartment in a fluffy white bathrobe she acquired during an overnight stay at Claridge's. She was technically still with Damian at the time; but one of her girlfriends needed a favour. A very important Saudi client wanted a threesome, and the usual girl she used had let her down at the last minute. It would've been churlish to say no; you never know when you might need a favour yourself.

For instance, if you suddenly find yourself homeless. And if that stuck up cow does sack Lexi, that could become a problem. Not to mention terrible timing.

Beth is too hyped to eat. She made herself a bowl of muesli. It's standing untouched on the kitchen counter next to last night's empty wine bottles.

Could they sack Lex? Surely not.

But she hasn't seen her friend in this kind of state for a very long time.

Lexi is a grafter; she's also smart and tough. When Lexi first got a job in an estate agents, Beth was dismissive. Sales jobs are a nightmare, shit money, relying on commission. Beth has tried it herself a couple of times, cold calling; it was impossible, mega-frustrating, she didn't last. But Lexi stuck with it. She made it work. Top seller in her firm. Beth has never really understood how.

Then Lexi got a job with a concierge firm that dealt exclusively with rich people. The idea was simple: get them whatever stuff they wanted. A private jet, best table at a top restaurant, all that shit. Plus, make them like you and depend on you. Sort of a cross between a servant and a friend. Lexi was brilliant at that too, and she made some top-notch contacts. Then she moved back into property again, but this time an agency that just dealt with the super-rich. It was Lexi's game plan all along. And it all started to make sense to Beth.

She's worked in some fancy clubs, hostessing, and seen the kind of people out there with obscene amounts of money. But getting anywhere near them, let alone into their circle or network, that always felt impossible, until she got a few useful tips from her best mate.

'Appearance and confidence are key.' That's what Lexi taught her. 'It's about messaging, the vibe you put out. I look like you, I dress like you. I'm your people. Part of your tribe.'

Beth had purged her wardrobe of the most trashy items. Focused on a few expensive designer dresses that made her look like a billionaire's daughter. In her teens, she'd spent a bit of time in a shoplifting gang; she still knew the moves and how not to get caught.

Her hair was naturally blonde, which had always been a bonus. But shelling out for an expensive cut, and practicing with the make-up until she could pull off a totally chic but subtle look, more movie star than panda in false eyelashes. Less is more. Nails done regularly too, not too long, never chipped.

She took to hanging out in more upmarket clubs. Dressing right and being stunning got her through the door. Once inside, behaving like she belonged. And the men that hit on her changed. She could be picky, ignoring the ordinary idiots out on the lash, and focusing on wealthy businessmen looking for a woman to take places and show off. She graduated to trophy girlfriend.

Beth had ended up with some good deals; guys who set her up in a rental, took her on fancy holidays. None of them lasted, but she had fun and it was definitely easier than most of the other ways she made a living before.

And it was Lexi's advice that got her there; she'd be the first to acknowledge that. They'd always taken care of each other, more like sisters than friends.

She gazes out of the window and sighs. On her phone, the timer is counting down. Thirty-five seconds to go. The river is rolling by, brown and muddy and full. Okay, Damian was a step backwards. She knew it in her heart. She wasn't stupid, but if school and counsellors and all those people have always treated you as stupid, it's tempting to not disappoint them. Lexi knew it was all a bit of an act; that Beth enjoyed pressing their buttons. Lexi sees her, and that's the kind of friendship that's beyond money. It trumps her connection with any bloke.

The timer bleeps. She hits the button to stop it, goes straight to the kitchen counter, and picks up the plastic wand. It's a digital ovulation kit and it's smiling at her. To be more precise, the smiley face is flashing.

Fuck!

She was hoping that peak fertility wouldn't come for a

couple more days, giving her a chance to see how things panned out for Lexi. He's in London for two weeks on business, so there is flexibility. But now she has to decide. Go ahead or postpone? And it could be months until he's back again.

The girl who told her about the deal and introduced her to the website has had three. Two hundred and fifty grand a piece, plus expenses. The requirements are pretty stringent. The clients want a full and verified medical history, plus genetic screening for certain conditions, and that's impossible to fake. She's seen their private doctor and ticked that box. They also insisted on three months of mandatory drugs tests prior to insemination; that was more of a pain.

And finally they required what they called environmental checks. That meant where you lived. It couldn't be scabby or damp, or likely to affect the pregnancy in any way.

This is why she had to tell Lexi that she was already pregnant. She pretended it was Damian. Just a little fib, because soon she would be pregnant for real. But she needed to convince Lexi to find her a place like this to stay. And the pregnancy helped her swing it.

Not a total fiction. She'll come clean. Lexi will understand.

When the fixer visited the apartment a week ago, she was more than impressed. But Beth was straight. She didn't say she owned the place. She said it belonged to an old school friend who was travelling in South America. A half-lie, then. The birth would be in a private clinic.

He flew in from Hong Kong three days ago. There was no requirement to fuck him. On the contrary, he didn't even want them to meet. But that was probably to keep his wife sweet.

Beth tries to focus her scattered thoughts. Is she panicking unnecessarily? She'd planned to fess up to Lexi when the time was right. Lexi would be likely to point out the obvious: commercial surrogacy is illegal in the UK. Although Beth is sure the police have got better things to do. But after Damian, Beth has resolved to take a break from men, and her friend would almost certainly agree with that.

This is the utilisation of her assets in a completely different way, and she'll be doing good at the same time. Giving a childless couple the family they crave. Looked at in a broader perspective, it's one of the most selfless, not to say altruistic things Beth has ever done. In the end, Lexi will understand that.

Beth looks at her phone. Should she make the call? Once this is done and she gets a positive pregnancy test followed by a scan, it'll trigger the first payment.

A hundred fucking grand! More than a nest egg. Magic money. Freedom money.

And no refunds if she doesn't go to term.

Acting impulsively and regretting it afterwards has always been one of her faults. Things'll work out; they usually do, if you manifest the right attitude and stay optimistic.

She picks up her phone and rings the number.

8

Tuesday. 9.45am

Lexi has learnt the hard way that the antidote to anxiety is realism. Keeping the rational mind in the driving seat is a discipline. It all comes down to self-control. When something unexpected hits, we have a tendency to catastrophize. She certainly does. It's human nature. The survival instinct. Always prepare for the worst.

She walks down Chiltern Street to the nearest coffee shop and she doesn't allow herself to look at her phone until she's been served and found a quiet corner in a booth at the back.

Inhale. Exhale. Stay calm.

She stares down into the swirl of small dark bubbles on the surface of her Americano. There could be any number of explanations for the text she's received.

Taking out her phone, she looks at it again.

Don't ignore me. I hate being ignored.

An unknown number. Someone she knows having a joke? This is the most likely explanation. The events at Renfrew

Hall yesterday were deeply disturbing and have thrown her off kilter. In the backwash of that, anything unusual or out of the ordinary could appear in a sinister light. This is just bad timing.

But is it even sinister? Petulant maybe. Who has she dealt with on a personal or professional level recently who's likely to be petulant if they're feeling ignored? Apart from Mum, and it's not her.

She starts a note on her phone. This could be a long list. She begins with the personal, but the truth is this area of her life is a desert. She abandoned the dating scene some time ago; it was just too depressing. Living alone has never been a problem for her; after the house she grew up in, and her parents' fights, it's a blessed relief.

Having her own place was always the dream. Buy. Trade up. That's her strategy. Her present place is a one bedroom in a former local authority deck-access block in Stoke Newington. The building has attracted aspirational twenty-somethings like herself. Hanging baskets abound in the summer. The neighbours are friendly without being intrusive, and it's well lit at night.

It's surrounded by the right sort of shops, an artisan bakery, some good delis, and an independent coffee roaster. There's a community vibe, and a well-kept park nearby where parents take their kids to play, old people stroll, and there's a 5K parkrun on Sundays. It's a good neighbourhood. A place to belong.

But what if this is a neighbour? Someone who knows her, but not that well.

There's a creepy guy, middle-aged and desperate, who lives alone on the floor below. He always looks at her as if he's creating a mental image to add to his porn library. She's never rude if he speaks, but she always avoids him if she can. And you never know, people have funny reactions.

I hate being ignored?

Is he called Dennis? She taps the name into her phone and writes *stalker?* next to it.

A less obvious neighbour? This is turning into a guessing game.

She loves London; it's her city, her adopted home. She grew up outside the capital, on a rundown housing estate in a depressing new town. A post war project to create idyllic homes outside the urban sprawl, it had turned into its own version of a concrete jungle. A bleak, dead end place, she couldn't wait to escape. But it was only thirty miles from London with a fast train service. As teenagers, Lexi and Beth had become adept at fare dodging; they headed for the capital every weekend.

However, the city has its ugly side, and Lexi is well aware of that. The thing that's never mentioned in any of her firm's glossy catalogues is that like any large metropolis, it's full of hidden dangers, because predators like anonymity and places they can hide in plain sight.

So who's the neighbour you wouldn't suspect? Because, to be frank, poor old Dennis probably hasn't got the balls.

She scans through all the front doors in her building in her mind's eye. Such a cool place. There's not much turnover of residents, but she doesn't know everyone. The two gay guys next door are friendly and funny, and helpful with DIY problems, like sorting out a dripping tap. There's a young couple with a baby on the other side, more reserved, she hears the occasional row, as they struggle with the ups and downs of new parenthood.

Most of her other neighbours are no more than nodding

acquaintances. An elderly couple, several flat shares, various singles. No one stands out as an obvious weirdo.

Could this be some vengeful ex she's forgotten about? The last person she dated, if you can call it that, was a guy she met at a Christmas drinks party of an old college friend. It was one of those rather awkward neither-of-us-wants-to-be-alone-at-Christmas hook-ups. His name was Mateo, he was Spanish, a bit shy, a junior doctor. They had a week of energetic sex with copious amounts of booze between Christmas and New Year, then they both went back to work. A few texts. They finally met for a drink. He was between shifts, looked exhausted, and told her he'd just applied for a job in New Zealand. That was ten months ago.

Lexi finishes her coffee. She looks around her. In a certain light, on a wet, grey morning, anyone can look suspicious. A boy clutching a backpack, shivering, dark hair, middle-eastern appearance, nervous eyes that meet her gaze then scoot away. Is he a jihadist about to set off a bomb? You live in a city like London nowadays, you're going to have that passing thought from time to time.

Stop it! Pull yourself together.

This is frustrating and pointless. She can't let a random text throw her off her game. The Renfrew Hall incident was both shocking and appalling.

Incident? Well, what do you call it?

This is how the police describe a major car crash. Even a huge multi-vehicle pile-up is still an incident. Makes it sound more benign than it is. But this isn't a car crash, it's murder. She doesn't want to even think about that aspect. She watched a man die, had his blood on her hands, and she's still reeling from it, which is why she's freaking out about a stupid text.

She glances at her phone. She has an eleven-thirty in

Knightsbridge and she can't afford to be late. Not for Arif Yildiz.

He's the most important contact on her client list; a developer who specialises in high-end refurbs in the most expensive parts of London. He's currently got three mews house he's ripping apart to create a spacious urban home about two minutes from Harrods. This is the top end of the market. Five thousand square feet of absolute luxury. If Lexi can win this listing for her firm, then she'll be untouchable. Gemma won't be able to sack her; more likely she'll be begging her to stay.

It's a brisk walk to Marble Arch tube. She considers a cab, but looking at the state of the traffic, that's risky. Baker Street is gridlocked. It's two changes to get to Knightsbridge, but her phone puts the journey time on foot at twenty-eight minutes. A safer bet. With her trainers on, heels in her bag, Lexi strides out. She still has a nagging headache, but she's dealt with Gemma. Her day is improving.

The physical exertion is calming. She gets most of her exercise from walking. For a while, at school, she was into athletics. She was a sprinter and quite fast. But it came to nothing. Her mother regarded her teenage ambitions as a stupid waste of time. After the old man took off, her mother worked two jobs, and she was a moaner. Everything was always wrong or too expensive. Lexi left home as soon as possible.

The mews are tucked away, narrow, still partly cobbled, a quiet and unexpected haven from the nearby bustle. Yildiz has a good eye and deep pockets; he's renown for snapping up the best property on the market, usually before it even comes to market. He has several projects on the go at once. At Cavendish Cooper, they have a nickname for him: the Big Fish. Landing him and one of his top-drawer listings means a substantial commission, both for the firm and the individual agent. But he's slippery and likes to play rival brokerages off against each other. Rumour has it he recently made a girl from Sotheby's cry.

Lexi reaches the entrance to the mews with ten minutes to spare. She ducks into a coffee shop across the street, ignores the scowling barista and slips into the disabled loo. She swaps her trainers for heels, tidies her hair and touches up her make-up.

At eleven thirty on the dot, she rings the doorbell. The outside is still shrouded in scaffolding and plastic sheeting, but the door is plain grey, discreet, with a small camera and button keypad set into the wall.

The Big Fish opens the door in person. He's large, portly, with iron grey hair slicked back from a domed forehead. He peers out at her through square, thick-framed glasses, concealing cold reptilian eyes.

He tilts his head and smiles. 'Hey, right on time.'

The accent is hard to pin down. English with dialect. That's how Gemma describes it, usually with a sneer. Her class and race snobbery is ingrained, but she's good at covering it up when dealing with the likes of Yildiz. The reality is most of their clients are from abroad; these are either resident non-doms, who flit back and forth between the UK and their home country, or rich immigrants whose wealth qualifies them for a Tier one visa. And Lexi knows this is one reason Roger Cavendish hired her. Her tawny skin and dark hair could be Mediterranean, or Arab, or Asian and points east. It's all about the messaging; she looks like one of them. It's her trump card.

She meets his gaze. 'Punctuality is basic courtesy in business, Mr Yildiz.'

He beckons her to enter. 'We can certainly agree on that.

Call me Ari. Sounds like a Cockney barrow boy, I know.' He chuckles at his own joke.

She steps into the hallway. Highly polished marble floor, vaulted ceiling. It's the first time they've met, but he still leans forward and they brush cheeks, left then right. A professional air kiss. They hardly touch. All very proper and above board. He smells of something spicy and expensive.

He's wearing brogues, but she still slips off her shoes and pretends to ignore the fact he's watching her; judging, assessing. There's nothing salacious in his gaze. At least she hopes there isn't. It's business, and one question hangs in the air. And Lexi knows it's the same question for both of them.

Are you going to give me what I want?

She lets her eye travel up to the chandelier hanging above them. A brief memory of another chandelier flashes into her mind, but she overrides it. This one is modern, a mass of hanging teardrops and far more expensive.

'Wow!' she says. 'You'd never guess you could get such a grand hallway in a mews. That's clever.'

He accepts the compliment with an inclination of the head. 'The whole interior has been rebuilt around a steel frame. The Georgian facade is all that's left of the original mews.'

'Brilliant!'

He nods in agreement. He thinks he's brilliant too. 'Shall we?'

They head for the glass staircase, which goes both up and down. He pauses, turns and frowns. 'Renfrew Hall. What a shitshow, eh?'

Lexi stares at him. He's watching her like a smug toad.

How the hell does he know about that?

She tries not to panic and decides not to lie. What would be the point?

'It was…truly awful,' she says, with a shudder. The reaction is real; no need to fake it.

'I'm sure,' he says. His hands are folded in front of him, head tilted with a quizzical look of concern. He's waiting for her to say more. The silence is awkward. His gaze is heavy and penetrating. It's a delicate moment; she can't risk offending him.

'I… did my best for him,' she says.

Subject closed. Move on.

He nods sympathetically. 'So it was your firm. I'd heard rumours, but nothing concrete about the brokerage involved. And you personally? You were the agent. That's terrible, Lexi.' With a sad smile, he shakes his head.

A sucker punch, straight to the gut.

Bastard! A simple trick. You fell for it.

She feels pathetic. How did she not see that coming? He set her up.

His eyelids flick open and shut like a lazy lizard, that's just swallowed its insect prey. 'Let's start with the kitchen, shall we?' he says.

Lexi feels like a complete fool.

9

Tuesday. 11.30am

As they plough through the puddles on the long drive approaching the house, Boden gazes out of the window. Chakravorty is behind the wheel, and they haven't spoken much. The fields are green and waterlogged from the continual rain. But the sky is brightening, a watery winter sun struggling to break through in a lull between the showers.

'What d'you think then?' says Chakravorty.

'About what?' says Boden. She knows she's being obtuse, but so was the DCI in the conversation they had after the briefing.

Knight had called them to the front. She'd looked Boden in the eye, and what she said sounded sincere. 'Jo, I know we've had our differences…'

Somewhat.

'But there's an opportunity here for us to put the past behind us and move on. I'm sure we both want that.'

Boden had the advantage in height, and made the most of it, towering over Knight, as she replied, 'Absolutely, boss.'

'I will be relying on your experience on this one, you know that,' the DCI added.

No mention of the dodgy attitude.

Knight glanced at Chakravorty. 'And I'm aware the two of you make an effective team.'

To Boden's ear it was condescending, plus there was no guarantee she'll listen to Boden's opinion any more than she has in the past. Rachel Knight is the kind of person who thinks she's both right and righteous; she doesn't take advice. It seems unlikely that has changed.

You do your job. And that's all you can do.

Boden is trying to put this into practice in her life. Now that she has a life again. Her thoughts drift to Cal, and that makes her smile inwardly. The unexpectedness of it all. The excitement. It's early days and she remains wary, but seeing him, and she's not ready yet to call it anything more than that, is transforming her life.

The sharp pointed gables of the house in the picture emerge from behind windblown trees at the end of the drive. The recent storms have stripped most of their remaining leaves. The house itself is stark and brooding, despite the activity at the front. Various police and forensic vehicles are parked up, people are coming and going.

'Remember that movie?' says Chakravorty.

'Can you be more specific?' says Boden.

'I'm rubbish at titles. I saw it last Christmas. My mum loves historical stuff. It was about this poor girl, and she discovers she's got rich relations and she's been left this amazing house, but it's haunted. I'm sure this was the house.'

'Looks haunted. What happened in the end?'

'Can't remember. My dad fell asleep and was snoring. So I went and helped my aunties in the kitchen.'

Boden chuckles. 'You do Christmas and Diwali?'

'Yeah. My oldest brother's wife is white. They have three kids, so they want both. So we do both.'

'Sounds ideal.'

'Not really. It's mayhem in our house from November to January.'

Boden thinks of her own fractured family. Her mum alone in London, her dad and his second family in Norfolk, and her spending her Christmases travelling between the two.

This year? Just you and Cal?

They pull up at the front of the house next to an enormous fountain. The surrounding pool is full to overflowing and choked with fallen leaves, although it looks as if it's been turned off for some time.

Boden glances at it. 'Unless they've found the murder weapon yet, someone'll have the job of draining that,' she says.

As they get out of the car, Mackie comes bouncing out of the house, wreathed in smiles. Since his promotion, he's become insufferable.

'Hey, girls,' he says. 'We could do with some help with the door to door. Y'know, if anyone saw or heard anything.'

Chakravorty gives him a baleful look.

'Really,' says Boden. 'I think I'll look at the scene first.'

Mackie chuckles. 'No need. It is Jessop, and he's definitely dead. Throat slashed. Expertly done, if you ask me. It's got to be a professional hit.'

'In your vast experience of murder investigations, DS Mackie.'

'Oh c'mon, Jo, don't be snotty.'

'Then don't try to boss me.'

He holds up his palms in surrender. 'Sorry, just trying to save time. I know the DCI is keen to crack on with this. Of course, the other theory is it could be the ghost. You seen the movie?' He gives her a mischievous grin.

Boden can't help smiling. Despite his promotion, he's still Mackie, his brash energy and enthusiasm attractive and annoying in equal parts.

'Right,' he says. 'Boss wants me to go and talk to Jessop's wife. She's had the knock, but we need to follow up and get her talking if we can.'

'Good luck with that,' says Boden. She means it; Kate Jessop will stonewall him.

Mackie sticks out his chest, shooting a tentative smile at Chakravorty, who looks away.

'Well, y'know,' he says. 'I'd best get on it. Case to solve.'

Mackie strides off towards his car.

Chakravorty sighs. 'Could he be any more of a dick? Like we need him to explain a d to d?'

What happened between these two?

'He'll calm down once he's fallen on his face a couple of times,' says Boden.

She shows her ID to the crime scene officer at the door. He logs her and Chakravorty's details. They get suited and booted, and they go in, following the designated route to the kitchen.

The body is still being photographed and videoed in situ. Boden knows Chrissie, the crime scene manager, and gives her a friendly nod. Then she lets her eye travel around the room. It's large. She counts four entrances and exits, and has an unused, musty smell, in addition to the metallic tang of blood. No one's done any cooking in it lately, nor has it been cleaned. Boden runs her gloved finger through a film of dust on the worktop.

She turns to Chakravorty. 'Why kill him here?'

'Opportunity,' the DC replies. 'Big old creepy house. Killer followed him. Easy place for an ambush.'

'Yes, but he was here to meet someone, wasn't he?'

Chakravorty checks her tablet. 'Yeah, a property agent, Lexi Harper. Appointment was for four o'clock. She was late because of the weather. She found him dying. Tried to help.'

Boden turns to the Chrissie. 'Any sign of the murder weapon?'

The CSM shakes her head. 'I did a preliminary assessment of the house with DS Mackie when we arrived. But there are twenty-seven rooms. The rest of it looks unused. Nothing obvious. We'll start a detailed forensic search as soon as we get some reinforcements. But I've been told the SIO wants us to focus on the kitchen.'

Boden nods and smiles. This is typical of Rachel Knight. She'll drive the team for a fast result.

The kitchen is vast, bigger than most restaurants. Built for a bevy of servants, but the appliances and fittings are old and in need of updating. Boden wonders about Jessop and this place. Why was he here, and what was his plan? Is it a vehicle to launder cash? But if so who did he upset in this process?

'Why a knife and not a gun?' says Boden. 'Shoot someone at a distance, less of a problem with forensics.'

'Not a professional hit?' says Chakravorty.

'Or they cut his throat to make a point?' says Boden. 'But what point? And why here?'

'Perhaps Mackie'll find out from Jessop's wife?'

'I doubt that, Prish. Craig Jessop was still quite an old-school villain. He knew how to protect his family. And the best protection is ignorance. The wife was his respectable facade. Ask no questions, turn a blind eye. Whatever she thinks or suspects about his death, she's unlikely to share it with us.'

'Where do we start then?'

'This place. Someone must've been looking after it. A caretaker or someone like that. Why here? We figure that out, we may get to the motive, and, with luck, that'll lead to a suspect.' She smiles. 'Unless of course, it was the ghost.'

10

Tuesday. 11.33am

Lexi follows Big Fish down the winding glass stairway to the basement. This gives her a chance to compose herself. It's easy to be angry, because the bastard wrong-footed her, but that isn't going to play here. And anyway, she can turn it around and use it to her advantage. Course she can.

Inhale. Exhale. Reset.

Men like Yildiz want you to know who's in charge, who wields the power. And that's what he's doing here, putting down a marker. He doesn't give a shit about what happened at Renfrew Hall. Why would he? He's just using it. News of the murder is all over the net and hard to miss, so it's not like he's even taking a particular interest.

It's a classic move on his part, but for her, it's the data she needs. Selling someone is a bit like a game of poker; you watch for the tells. Read them. Use them.

Yildiz pauses at the bottom of the stairs and waits for her to catch up with him. She takes her time.

'You okay?' he says.

Lexi tilts her head and gives him a look.

Not too coy. He's not stupid.

'I'll be honest, Ari,' she says. 'I was nervous about meeting you today. I wanted to be on my A game, and I'm not. Yesterday, a man bled to death in front of me, and I felt powerless. I'm just an ordinary girl, trying her best to do the job. I work ten-hour days, I always go the extra mile for my clients. But stuff like that, honestly, I was out of my depth.'

He frowns and nods sympathetically. 'Tough call for anyone. We can do this another day, if you like.'

'Oh, no. I wouldn't dream of it. Business always comes first. I'll be fine.' Girly, breathless. She gazes up at him. She's quite tall, but stoops and hunches her shoulders to reduce her height. It gives him the advantage. He's standing squarely in front of her, barrel-chested, flabby-jowled.

He nods some more. He seems to like what she's doing: deferring to his power, playing the damsel in distress? Behind the cynical, Alpha male exterior, is Ari a damsel man?

His eyes soften, crinkling at the edges as he smiles.

Course he is.

'Tell you what,' he says. 'Let's have a coffee.' He pulls a small metal hip flask from his pocket and holds it up. 'I carry this for emergencies.'

She gives him what she hopes is a winsome smile.

'Thank you so much for being so understanding.'

'Maybe you're still in shock. Who wouldn't be? And I appreciate you keeping our appointment, in the circumstances.'

Who were you going to pass it over to? Teddy? No way.

She sighs and gives a demure shrug. 'Stuff happens. You have to buckle down and move on, don't you?'

He nods, scanning her. Still the iron front, but his manner is subtly different.

Okay, so report me to the feminist police. But what woman hasn't played this game?

She follows him through into the kitchen. It's in a newly excavated sub-basement at the back of the property, granite and steel and gleaming, with large skylights; it has everything that a professional chef might need. Ari opens a tall floor to ceiling cupboard door to reveal a La Cimbali coffee machine, alongside various other high-tech appliances.

Lexi claps her hands. 'Oh, that's so neat. Everything tucked away.'

He nods and chuckles. 'Bean to cup,' he says. 'Press a button, does it all. Perfect every time.'

Sounds like some advert.

He produces white, bone china mugs from another cupboard, slots one in place, and presses the button.

Lexi just smiles serenely.

Yeah, idiot proof.

Once she's perched on a bar stool, a cup of coffee in her hand, with a nip of Napoleon brandy added from his flask, she says casually, 'A couple of days ago, I spoke with a contact of mine in Dubai. She's married to a cousin of the Emir.'

This is the pitch she's planned. Now they've connected over her ordeal, she hopes he's receptive to it.

'Oh,' he says. His face remains inscrutable.

'She's been key in facilitating a number of sales for us.'

Well, one sale. A second one fell through.

'The family trust her because she has impeccable taste. She's a real design buff. I think she'd love this place.'

Ari's listening, his hooded lids flicking up and down again. 'And you can get her here?' he says.

Pigs might fly.

'If I can give her a video tour first, with your permission, of course, I think she might consider making the trip.'

'Sounds promising.'

Lexi sips her coffee and waits. Hopefully, the hook is in.

Ari arranges his bulk on another of the bar stools. Then he inhales and says, 'I like you, Lexi. You're a smart girl. Some guys don't like that. That's not me. I think we can do business. You've been honest with me, so I'll be honest with you. I see an opportunity here. We should explore that.'

'Absolutely. I can call her and—'

He raises a peremptory index finger. 'I'm talking about Renfrew Hall.'

WTF?

'Not sure I quite…'

He cranes round and looks right at her. 'I'm a great fan of the Arts and Crafts movement. So perfectly English. A terrific brand. And this is a great example, I hear.'

'Well, yes. I didn't know you were interested in country houses.'

'Why wouldn't I be?'

'They can require a lot of work, and so the profit margins wouldn't be the same as with this place.'

'Surely that depends on the acquisition price. You've got a murder and a police investigation.' He shakes his head. 'Messy. Very messy. So I reckon the owners might be amenable to an offer.'

'What sort of offer?'

'I'm sure, if you put your mind to it, you can persuade them into a considerable reduction. That would impress me.'

As Lexi absorbs this, it dawns on her that this has been the Big Fish's agenda all along. Somehow he knew. But how?

She cups her mug nervously. 'What are we talking about here?'

'I'm guessing on the open market you might have valued the property at eight or nine mil, give or take, because the basic elements are there, but it needs a total refurb, which, as we both know, costs. To make this viable for me, I'm going to say three, max. In the circumstances, that should be doable.'

Lexi looks at him. He wants her to get him Renfrew Hall at a knockdown price.

She raises her eyebrows. 'A third of the value? That's not a reduction. It's a fire sale.'

He beams. 'Yes. But value is always subjective. In this business, you have to grasp the opportunities that come your way, don't you?'

He laces his fingers and rests them on the counter in front of him. 'I have faith in you, Lexi. If you can broker a deal for me on Renfrew Hall, then you'll be top of my list for this place, too.'

He makes it sound simple. A straightforward property deal; nothing out of the ordinary.

Lexi's head is in a spin. Arif Yildiz plays hardball; she already knew that. Her skin is prickling. He's outmanoeuvred her, again.

All she wants is to walk away from Renfrew Hall and never have to think about the place again.

But how can she?

11

Tuesday. 11.40am

Ewan has a four-by-four up on the hydraulic lift. He's doing the final checks, making sure each item on the list has been done. He peels off the latex gloves. A sense of completion, the feeling of a job properly done, this is always calming for him. He likes to be busy; it keeps him focused. Less time to think.

The dealership is next to a brand new retail park on the edge of Luton; it's a prime location, close to the airport and near an M&S Food Hall. As the boss likes to point out, this is where the people with money go, the people who buy brand new cars.

The garage and body shop are housed in a cavernous warehouse at the back of the dealership. Ewan walks out and across the yard to the main building that houses the showroom.

He goes into the back office and places his tablet on the counter. The boss, Trey, looks up from his desk in the corner.

'All good,' says Ewan. 'No problems. Ready to roll.'

Trey chuckles and lounges back in his leather desk chair.

'C'mon, man. You know what you gotta do. Don't try to duck it.'

Ewan sighs.

Trey inherited the business from his grandfather, but he's changed and expanded it beyond recognition. He's turned a small repair shop full of grease and oil into a slick dealership selling high-end, mainly electric vehicles. Clients get a premium service when they buy from Trey Robinson, so when they're ready to trade up, they come back.

And part of Trey's customer service package is that the mechanic, or rather technician, who fixes your vehicle makes you a personal video explaining and showing you what they've done.

Ewan meets the boss's eye. He hates it.

'Don't be camera shy,' says Trey. 'Lady that owns this, once she sees what a pretty boy you are, she won't be able to wait for her next service.' Ewan doubts that.

No one can deny that Trey's success is built on understanding his customers.

Ewan goes to the locker room and changes into clean overalls. Navy blue boiler suit with loads of pockets. The company launders them; the policy is this is a high-tech operation, customers don't want to see the dirt. But it still annoys Ewan that he's required to prance around like a fag for some old cow with a fancy car.

He admires Trey, his determination coupled with an open-hearted personality. Plenty of people would've looked for a reason not to hire Ewan, but Trey had given him a shot.

At the interview, Trey looked him up and down, and said, 'If you're a man who's got something to prove about who you are now, not who you were when you were a crazy kid, then this is the place to do it. We all need a second chance.'

They shook hands on it, man to man, no bullshit, and Ewan had a job. It helped that Trey's grandfather and Ewan's grandfather were acquainted, although both gentlemen are long dead. Ewan and Trey attended the same primary school, so Trey probably remembered what had happened. Most people did.

New overalls on, Ewan heads outside to the front of the dealership, where the latest models are lined up. Trey likes the opening shot to display the glossy showroom. It's drizzling a bit, but Ewan stands under the awning, holds up his phone in front of him, paints on a smile and presses record.

'Hi, I'm Ewan, and I'm going to take you on a quick tour to show you what we've been doing to your vehicle.'

As he clicks the phone off, he notices one of the sales girls watching him through the huge plate-glass window.

She's super cute, and she knows it. Her name is Felicia; he's seen her name tag, which sits just above her left breast, like an invitation. Means you have to stare at her tits to find out who she is. But it strikes him she's the kind of girl who likes that, the kind of girl who likes to tease. She wears a tight skirt and a smart blouse that dips down at the front, and you can always hear her coming because she clips around the showroom in these shiny black kitten heels.

Kittens are playful. But mind the claws.

Spending your teenage years and most of your early twenties locked up in an all male prison doesn't do much for your sex life. Ewan did stuff with other boys inside. It's what everyone did. But that was then, and despite what the old man thinks, he's not that way inclined. He knows this, because when he gets too close to Felicia, he gets a hard on. And she loves that. She really does. You can see it in her eyes. Feels like they're laughing at you all the time. But she's tiny, not even as high as his shoulder. He could just scoop her up in his arms and chuck her over his shoulder. He looks back through the window, stares right at her. And he will. When he's ready, he'll have her. It's what she wants. He'll fuck her brains out and send Rusty a postcard.

One day. Not yet.

First, he needs to focus on the task in hand. Get this stupid video done. Keep the customer happy, which keeps the boss happy. And then there's the other thing. When he was inside, he made himself a promise. That's his priority for now.

He looks at his phone again and muses. Is it time for another text yet?

No, he'll wait. No rush. Let the bitch wonder.

12

Tuesday. 12.15pm

The gatehouse at the entrance to Renfrew Hall is built in the mock Tudor style of the main house, but it's a baby version. The same features on a much smaller scale. Boden can't find a doorbell, so she raps on the solid oak door.

When the first responders arrived the previous afternoon, the caretaker came to see what was going on, gave his name, but disappeared before officers at the scene could question him.

Chakravorty consults the tablet in her hand. 'Mason Green,' she says. 'Drives a beat up old Land Rover.'

She points to the vehicle parked at the side of the house, olive coloured with a torn canvas hood.

Boden knocks again.

The door opens a crack. Boden looks down and a large brown teddy bear sticks his nose out, and behind the bear two giggling eyes.

'Hello, Mr Teddy,' says Boden. 'Is anyone at home?'

'He's called Simba because he's very fierce,' says a small voice.

'Like a lion?' says Boden.

'Yes!' the child replies gleefully.

Chakravorty gives her a sidelong glance. 'You saw that movie, then.'

Boden grins. 'Took my mum to the musical in London.'

The door opens a bit more to reveal a girl of about four clutching the teddy to her chest. The child is barefoot, an unruly mop of dark, curly hair, and a pair of skimpy pyjamas.

At midday?

Boden and Chakravorty exchange looks.

Boden squats to the child's level. 'Hello, I'm Jo,' she says. 'And I'm very pleased to meet you, Simba.' She takes the bear's paw and shakes it. 'Where's Daddy?'

The door opens wider and a man in a T-shirt and boxers appears behind the child. He's rubbing his sleep-tousled hair and smells of alcohol. It looks as if he's just woken up.

Boden stands up and produces her warrant card. 'Mason Green?' she says. 'I'm DS Boden and this is DC Chakravorty.'

He clutches the doorjamb to steady himself and screws his eyes up at the light. The hangover from hell is Boden's guess. He beckons. 'Right, yeah, thought you'd be round.'

Boden and Chakravorty follow him into the house. The little girl scampers ahead of them into the sitting room. She climbs onto the sofa and nestles in the corner under a snuggly blanket.

The place is freezing. There's a wood-burning stove set into a larger stone fireplace. The door to it is open, but it's full of cold ash which has spilled out onto the hearth.

He gestures at it dismissively. 'Run out of logs.'

There's no sign of anyone else, and the place is messy.

Plates caked with last night's food. Several beer cans and an empty whiskey bottle on a cluttered coffee table. An armchair with a pillow and a blanket on it.

He catches Boden's eye, and there's a hint of embarrassment. 'We sleep down here. Bloody freezing upstairs.'

Boden studies him. A shaggy beard, but he's young. Mid twenties?

'Just you and, I'm assuming, your daughter, Mr Green?'

'Lily,' he says. 'Just us.' He rubs his face to wake himself up. Then he adds, 'My girlfriend left.'

'That's tough,' says Boden. 'And you're the caretaker for Renfrew Hall?'

'Sort of.'

'Sort of?'

'They let me live here rent free if I keep an eye on things. Renting costs an arm and a leg. It's impossible, so I stay here for Lily.'

'They don't pay you?' says Chakravorty.

'Well, yeah. Sort of. It's complicated.'

'Complicated how?' says Boden.

Mason Green stretches his neck one way and then the other, wincing each time.

Boden gives him an appraising look.

Someone gets murdered, he gets wasted?

'That's quite a hangover you've got there, Mason,' she says.

He shoots her a guilty glance and huffs. 'What? A bloke can't have a couple of drinks now?'

Boden smiles. 'Tell us about your complicated relationship with the owners of this place?'

He sighs. 'Sorry. You're right. Had a few too many. Last thing I need is for this to go pear-shaped too.'

Boden waits for him to say more.

He folds his arms defensively. Or perhaps he's just cold. 'Okay, well, my dad worked here for the old lady for twenty-five years. He was the head gardener. Used to be staff, loads of people worked here when I was growing up. Lady Orme died five years ago and her son sold the place.'

'Do you know who he sold to?' says Boden.

Green shakes his head. 'Some foreign company. I can't remember the name. Lawyer came to see me, offered me a regular wage to stay on. Got that for about three years. They had contractors come in to look after the grounds, and cleaners for the house. They made a film here, y'know. I was an extra. Played the gamekeeper.' He smiles wistfully. 'It was fun. Got paid for that too.'

'Then what happened?' says Boden.

'Sold again. Money stopped. I didn't know what was going on. Then Mr Jessop turned up.'

'The new owner?'

'Yeah, I assume. He said he was planning to do the place up. It's Grade II listed, so they have to get all the permissions. He offered me cash in hand, once a month, to caretake. But the place was shut up. Not much to do. He got rid of the cleaners and the gardening firm.'

'So you were working for Mr Jessop and saw him once a month?' says Boden.

Green nods. 'Until last summer.' He grimaces. 'Is it him that was killed? It is, isn't it?'

'We haven't formerly identified the victim yet,' says Boden. 'When did you last see Mr Jessop?'

Green shrugs and shifts from foot to foot. 'I dunno. Late August. He used to pay me seven hundred a month. But I hadn't seen him, so I called him. He came over and gave me a couple of grand.'

'In cash?' says Boden.

'It's not illegal, is it?'

'I'm not the tax man, Mason. We're just trying to work out what's happened here.'

'I haven't seen him for two or three months. I rang again, left a message, but he didn't get back to me. We—me and my girlfriend—didn't know what to do. She got fed up. She's always hated being stuck out here. And with no money coming in. She left. About a month ago.' He shakes his head bitterly. 'I mean, what kind of mother walks out on her little girl? She always was a selfish cow.'

He plonks down in the armchair and puts his face in his hands. Lily, still clutching Simba, climbs off the sofa and puts her arms round him.

Boden glances at Chakravorty. The DC is tapping notes into her tablet.

'Okay, Mason,' says Boden. 'Where were you yesterday afternoon?'

'Here,' he says. 'Y'know, looking after Lily. Pouring with rain. I do a bit of work on a local farm. They let me take Lily with me. But it was too wet.'

'You were here. So, tell us what you saw.'

'It was dark. We were watching telly. I saw these flashing blue lights go past the window.'

'Nothing before that? Other vehicles coming or going?'

He shakes his head, lifts his daughter onto his knee and cuddles her.

'And what did you do?'

'I went up to the Hall to check it out. Told the cop my name. But I couldn't stay, because I had Lily in the Land Rover with me and it was cold.'

Boden nods and waits. Mason Green buries his face in Simba's fur as he clutches his child. He says nothing.

Boden walks over to the window; it looks out onto the

drive, just inside the main gate. The gate is in two parts, around ten feet high, elaborate wrought iron, currently standing open, with a police car parked on the other side of it, blocking the entrance.

'Is the gate usually open or shut, Mason?' says Boden.

'Shut,' he mumbles.

'Was it shut yesterday?'

'Yeah, I think so.'

'Did my colleagues have to stop to open it?'

'I'm not sure.'

'Would it normally be locked?'

'No. The farmer I sometimes work for uses a couple of fields for their cattle. Maybe it was open. I can't remember.'

'And you didn't notice any vehicles coming through the gates earlier in the afternoon?'

'No…I…listen, I don't know what happened. And I didn't see anyone except the cops.' His gaze slides away.

There's the lie. He knows something.

Boden faces him. 'Let's see if we're clear about this. You and Lily were watching television. You see flashing blue lights, police vehicles heading for the Hall. You go up there in your Land Rover and take Lily. You come back here, and you get drunk?'

He shoots her a surly look. 'I didn't just do that. We came back. I made beans on toast for our tea. Later on, when Lily had gone to sleep, I had a couple of drinks.' Tears well in his eyes. 'Y'know, none of this is bloody easy. I'm on my own, with a kid. And no bloody money. I drink to cope. Is that what you want me to say? Is that a crime?'

'We're only trying to establish the facts. So, thanks for your help?'

He exhales. 'Yeah, I know. Sorry.'

Boden and Chakravorty head for the front door. As they

step outside, Boden turns and says, 'By the way, Mason. Who told you someone had been killed?'

He shrugs. 'I overheard the paramedic talking to this woman. A stabbing, they said. She was really upset; they were wrapping her in a silver blanket.'

'Did you speak to her?'

'No.'

'Know who she is? Why she was there?'

'No idea.'

'Okay, Mason,' says Boden. 'Thanks for your help.'

Boden and Chakravorty head for their car.

'Reactive,' says Chakravorty. 'What do you think?'

'He's desperate. Probably worried about losing his home. But he knows more than he's letting on, and he's lying about not seeing anyone,' says Boden. 'Question is why?'

'If Jessop had an appointment to meet a property agent,' says Chakravorty, 'wouldn't he stop and mention it?'

'Yeah, you'd have thought so, wouldn't you,' says Boden.

13

Tuesday. 12.30pm

Lexi takes an Uber back to the office. A pervasive headache, courtesy of last night's alcohol binge, has her temples in a vice. The paracetamol she took first thing has worn off. Lounging back against the cheap faux leather upholstery, she wriggles her backside. Beth's dress is way too tight; it's cutting into her midriff. Her stomach is bloated. Stress. Booze. Both. They always used to wear each other's clothes when they were younger, so perhaps she's put on weight. But she hasn't got time to go home and change.

Yildiz has made his position clear. After the chat in the kitchen, he gave her the briefest tour of the mews development. He seemed impatient and kept checking the enormous Rolex Oyster on his wrist. She did her best to engage him, oohing and aahing over all the luxury fittings. He wasn't interested. He checked his phone a couple of times and made no apologies. She was relieved when he ushered her out of the door.

As she rides in the back of a cab, gazing out at the belching, crawling London traffic, it feels like she's caught in a rattrap. Whoever Mr Jessop was, the actual owner of Renfrew Hall, or a front man for the real owners, he probably wasn't a good person. Good people don't get their throats cut. But Yildiz wants her to broker a deal. In effect, he's given her an ultimatum. If she hopes to get a look in with the mews development, she must deliver a deal on Renfrew Hall first.

She knows what she should do: refuse and walk away.

What's stopping you?

The question nags at her. The UK property market is full of shady individuals with criminal connections intent on laundering cash, usually from illegal sources abroad. From sanctioned Russian oligarchs to South American drug cartels, they all want to stash their wealth in a perceived safe haven like Britain. Any respectable property firm has to be vigilant about who they're dealing with, carrying out due diligence checks and staying within the law. But the money laundering legislation has loopholes, and the big bucks involved present a huge temptation. Bending the rules a bit, or avoiding digging too deeply, these are all common practices. At times, keeping on the right side of the law is a high-wire act in itself.

The drive back to the office is only a couple of miles, but part of the carriageway on Piccadilly is flooded, which has brought traffic to a standstill. Blocked drains from the endless rain? A couple of buses plough through, creating a minor tsunami.

The cab driver slaps his steering wheel and curses under his breath. But Lexi is grateful for the delay; it gives her some thinking time. She considers calling Gemma and decides against it. This is like a game of chess; she needs to plan several moves ahead.

If Gemma has dithered and done nothing yet, that will be

one conversation. But if the lawyers are already involved, and their advice has been sought, it becomes more tricky. Lexi isn't sure which she'd prefer. Maybe the latter; that would let her off the hook.

She's not bent, nor does she want to be. It's taken years of hard work and playing it straight to get into this position with a first-rate firm. Why would she throw that away? Reputation is everything. There are plenty of crooks in the property business. If in doubt, steer clear.

But Arif Yildiz's proposal has thrown her. A man of his stature doesn't achieve the success and respect he has, selling to tech billionaires, minor royals and movie stars, the great and the good, if he's in any way dodgy. Or perhaps it's a test, one of his notorious games to see if he can push her buttons? He likes to catch people out; she's heard about that. But what if he's just seen an opportunity, and he's going for it? Where's the illegality in that?

Lexi is at a loss. How can she be sure? Doubt makes you weak. You need a belligerent, almost narcissistic confidence to compete with these people. She doesn't have it. Not yet. She can bluff her way through plenty of situations, but is she out of her depth?

Anxiety is mushrooming inside her brain, overwhelming her thoughts. This happens. It's an old pattern, going back to childhood and her fear of the dark and creatures lurking under the bed. It takes effort not to panic. That's the important thing. She must not panic.

Hooking Yildiz was the strategy for guaranteeing her position at Cavendish Cooper. Once he was onboard as her client, she'd be set up, one of the firm's big earners. Untouchable.

Do not panic!

When she was little, Lexi used to bite her nails, chew

them down to the quick. Disgusting habit, her mother said and slapped her for it. There was a lot of slapping back then. It still took her years to break it. Underneath her acrylics, her real nails are short and stubby.

Her little finger has found its way to her mouth, and she's gnawing the skin at the side.

Stop!

Easier said than done. She clasps her hands together to prevent them straying.

If she loses her nerve, she's sunk.

Front it out. You can do this.

She thinks about what Yildiz is asking: broker a deal. That's all. If at any point she doesn't like the look of who she's dealing with, she can walk away. There's room for manoeuvre here. If she just tells him no, then what?

No risk, no reward.

For the rest of the journey, she gives herself a strict talking-to. In these situations, it's easy to become your own worst enemy. Dial down the emotion, detach and play this move by move.

By the time she walks into the office, she's back in control of herself, at least.

Gemma is at her desk looking frazzled; she doesn't appear to have moved since Lexi left.

Lexi strolls over to Gemma's assistant, Pia, a ditzy Sloane with the concentration span of a gnat.

'Hey, Pia,' says Lexi. 'What's going on?'

'She's been trying to get in touch with Roger,' says Pia, with a vacant smile.

'And?'

'He's not answering. It's his pilates. I think.'

Lexi takes a deep breath and walks into the boss's office. Gemma looks up at her like a cornered rabbit.

Shit! She's more scared than you.

Gemma gives her a brittle smile. 'Teddy says you were seeing Big Fish this morning.'

Bloody Teddy's been snooping again.

Lexi folds her arms. 'I was.'

'How'd it go?'

The next few moments could determine whether Lexi becomes one of the top property agents in London.

'Well,' she says. 'It was very interesting.'

Make her wait.

She gets out her phone and checks it. This is Yildiz's trick. Give the impression she has more important things going on.

'And?'

Lexi continues to stare at her phone. 'He could be a potential buyer for Renfrew Hall.'

Gemma blinks a couple of times. 'What d'you mean?'

'He wants Renfrew Hall.'

'As a refurb?'

'I assume. Says he's a fan of Arts and Crafts.'

'Oh.'

Gemma is staring into space like a glum little elf, twisting her boney, bejewelled fingers in front of her. She appears to have lost the plot.

Lexi shrugs. 'Well, if we're still in a position to get the listing. Do you think we are?'

'But…surely…you said call the lawyers.'?

'Yeah, I know.' Lexi sighs. 'I watched poor Mr Jessop die. I've been in shock. But I've been thinking. We shouldn't be hasty.'

'Hasty?'

'We've done nothing wrong. The police are looking into this. They'll find out what happened. Probably nothing to do with Renfrew Hall. You did the necessary checks. If Mr Jessop was just a front man, then the owners will probably still want to sell. Or if he was the beneficial owner, then his family. Have you got contact details for them?'

'Only a number for him.'

'Email address?'

Gemma shakes her head.

Lexi raises her eyebrows.

'The thing is,' says Gemma. 'When I asked you to go and meet him yesterday afternoon, I sort of assumed you'd do the AML check.'

'What? You told me this morning you did it.'

Gemma gives her a bland smile. 'Did I? This whole thing has been so upsetting. And I've been so busy. I was confused.'

The bitch!

Lexi can't trust herself to speak. Does Gemma think she can lie her way out of this? Undoubtedly, she does. And it's as predictable as it is transparent.

But that doesn't solve the Yildiz problem. Lexi sighs. This leaves her with no option.

She'll have to take this to Roger.

14

Tuesday. 1.15pm

Beth arrives at the hotel in Park Lane. She's dressed down: jeans, suede boots, a casual jacket and a funky scarf. Her persona for the afternoon is the student daughter of a wealthy family. The security in these places is fierce. They're always on the lookout for faces that don't fit. She's been ejected from enough posh hotels in her time to know.

She approaches the concierge desk with a swagger, adopts an American drawl—she's not bad at accents—and addresses the hard-faced cow who's sizing her up.

'Hey,' she says. 'Chelsea Lau. My aunt's expecting me.'

The woman checks the screen in front of her, gives her a chilly smile, and says. 'Certainly, Ms Lau. The Empress Suite, which is on the tenth floor. The lifts are over there to your left.'

'Thank you.' Beth wanders through the opulent foyer, checking her phone. She gets a few glances. But no one can

81

be sure; she's as likely to be part of the global elite as not. The security guard's eyes flick over her and move on.

As the lift door closes on her, she smiles to herself. Running the gauntlet always gives her a buzz.

The Empress Suite is at the end of a long, plushly carpeted corridor. Beth smiles as she passes the maid, pushing her loaded cleaning cart. The girl is about her age, but hollow-cheeked and tired. Long shifts and minimum wages, she wonders how some people survive.

The door to the suite is opened by her supposed aunt, AKA the fixer who visited her at the flat. Beth has only met the woman once, and she does indeed have an aunt vibe about her. Middle-aged, a bland face with rimless glasses, expensive but anonymous clothes; she exudes respectability without being in any way memorable. Beth wonders if she is actually a nurse, as she claims.

The aunt invites her into the spacious entrance foyer, which leads through an archway to a sitting room with an overstuffed sofa and two wingback chairs. As they enter, a door to the left clicks shut. So he doesn't want to meet the woman who's about to bear his child. Or perhaps he's just gone to jack off.

The information she's received about the couple who are about to become her clients is sketchy. He's Chinese, she's English, which is why they want a Caucasian surrogate, preferably a blonde. They both work in tech, a catch-all term to Beth, and obviously they're loaded.

Beth had a secret fantasy that she'd get a pop star or someone famous. How cool would it be to know you're the real mother of Kim Kardashian's baby? Maybe next time.

But Aunty is speaking and she needs to pay attention.

'…and I will perform the insemination. Then you should remain lying on the bed for fifteen minutes. Okay?'

Beth nods. She has her headphones, so she can listen to music on her phone.

'Shall we?' Aunty opens the door on the right, which leads to the suite's main bedroom. The picture windows look out over Hyde Park, where the last clinging leaves are ready to shed. The sky is colourless and cold. But inside the bedroom is all creams, warm yellows and gold. Two elegant nightstands flank the king-sized bed, each with reading lamps and fresh flower arrangements.

Beth flings herself on the bed. She could live in a hotel suite.

Aunty picks up a large fluffy white bath sheet.

'Spread this on the bed, use the bathroom and get yourself ready. I'll be right back.'

She disappears.

Beth kicks off her boots. She wishes she could spend the entire afternoon here, not just the allotted fifteen minutes. She'd order room service and champagne; this is what she used to do with Damian. Why can't the Chinese guy do that? A seduction followed by a proper shag. Didn't she read on the net that if the woman climaxes, she's more likely to conceive? Surely that would be the sensible approach? And his wife need never know.

Stop it. This is business.

She wanders through to the spa-like marble bathroom. A deep soaking tub, glass-enclosed, multi jet shower, double vanity with backlit mirrors. She sits on the toilet and pees.

A weird thought slips into her head. What if the baby she's going to have was Damian's? But having a kid without a ring on your finger is plain stupid. Her own mother proved that. And there's the sleepless nights and the shitty nappies. Who needs it? She'll be happy to hand the sprog over and collect her money.

She returns to the bedroom, spreads the towel on the bed, removes her jeans and knickers, and waits. Checking her phone, she scrolls a bit, watches a couple of vids.

After about ten minutes, Aunty reappears. Now she's wearing nurses scrubs and vinyl gloves.

'It'll be a few minutes,' she says.

'Listen,' says Beth. 'Wouldn't it be easier if we just did it?'

Aunty gives her a shocked look. 'Absolutely not.'

'I'm just trying to increase the chances.'

'I'll be using a speculum and performing an IUI, an intra uterine insemination procedure, which places the sperm directly into the uterus. This is how it's done in the clinic and delivers a much higher success rate, which is what our clients expect.'

'Okay,' says Beth. 'Will it hurt?'

'Not at all,' says Aunty.

She's fucking lying.

Beth can tell by the expression on her face. She's had gynae stuff before, when they come at you with a speculum. And it always hurts.

Think of the money.

Beth has had many unpleasant experiences in her life, and this is how she's got through them, by thinking about the money.

15

Tuesday. 1.30pm

The pilates studio is in Porchester Road, near Royal Oak underground station; Lexi gets the address from Pia. Disturbing Roger during a personal training session is not ideal, but since Gemma is being both duplicitous and useless, it seems to Lexi she has little choice.

She spends a damp, packed tube journey preparing her pitch. Roger is retired. He doesn't involve himself in the business, except when he does. Lexi's first task is to persuade him that this is one of those occasions.

The studio is in a converted industrial space down a cobbled alley. But once inside, it exudes health and harmony. Beautiful and not so beautiful people, but all in designer sports gear. You can tell the trainers, they're the beautiful ones. The roof is full of skylights, the colour scheme is tints of grey and violet, the background music is gentle and bluesy. The girl on the desk proves helpful. She buys Lexi's tale of an urgent business message.

Has she never heard of texts?

And Lexi is directed to the mezzanine floor, where Roger is on a mat in the weight training area lifting kettlebells. He looks remarkably fit for his age, tall and loose-limbed, with a good head of salt and pepper grey hair. As she approaches, he pauses and smiles.

No surprise. He's expecting you. Gemma called. Of course she did.

She smiles back.

He puts down the weights and shakes his head sorrowfully. 'My dear girl, are you all right?' His voice is deep and mellifluous, like a toff in a historical TV drama. She's always found it comforting.

'I've been better.'

'In all my years, I've never heard of such a thing. I was just telling Kwame…'

The trainer stands beside him, arms folded, feet apart, with muscles like carved mahogany. He shakes his head too.

Lexi knows they're both being polite. She could get annoyed, she could get tearful if she thinks about what happened. So far, she's had two kinds of responses: voyeuristic curiosity and total indifference.

'Just give us five minutes,' says Roger. 'And we'll be done. Kwame here has saved my life. I never miss a session. He has such skill, both with the pilates and the weight training. I'm only walking around on two feet because of him. After the accident…' he sighs.

'Yeah,' says Lexi. 'Of course. Finish up. I'm happy to wait.'

For an instant, her gaze meets Kwame's and there's a flash of affinity; like her, he understands the food chain and his place in it. They're both used to waiting.

She retreats to the small health food bar on the ground floor. And waits.

Forty-five minutes later, Roger appears, kit bag slung over his shoulder.

'Sorry,' he says with a pained expression. 'Kwame insists I finish up with a sauna. This poor old body of mine is such a wreck.'

'It's not a problem,' says Lexi.

'Did you get yourself a homemade yogurt smoothie? They are to die for.'

Lexi got herself an overpriced cappuccino, which, in her opinion, should have contained more than one shot.

'Let's walk,' says Roger. 'I always walk home, keep the circulation going after a session.'

Lexi nods. You can't rush a thoroughbred racehorse. Only when it's been allowed to circle and refuse a couple of times, will it enter the starting gate.

They set off towards Westbourne Park Road. Roger lives at the Notting Hill end. He's been in the area since his hippie, post-student days, and waxes lyrical about how he couldn't live anywhere else.

'Such a sense of community. And of course, the carnival. You know, when I first came here, I lived in a squat. My father was appalled.' He chuckles. 'But it's changed a bit since then.'

Somewhat.

Two divorces may have dented Roger's property portfolio, but his current home, a three-story, stucco-fronted Victorian townhouse, is still worth nearly as much as Renfrew Hall, in Lexi's estimation. She's visited a couple of times, social events connected with the firm, but she's never been there with him alone.

He unlatches the spiked iron gate and holds it open for

her. She walks up the half-dozen stone steps to the front door, wondering if this could turn awkward.

Roger is too smart to be sleazy. Nevertheless, he has a reputation as a womaniser. His last wife was younger than Gemma, and his silver fox charms coupled with wealth mean he's never short of girlfriends half his age.

He unlocks the front door and taps the key code into the alarm.

'Welcome,' he says.

Lexi doesn't want to over-interpret the roguish look in his eye. However, she's definitely getting a vibe. But he strolls ahead of her down the hall towards the kitchen, dumping his bag en route.

He pours two glasses of water from the filter on the tap and places them on the kitchen island.

'So,' he says. 'Yildiz wants Renfrew Hall.'

Lexi feels a rush of relief. He knows this is serious. Strictly business then.

'He wants Renfrew Hall at a knockdown price. Strikes me, this is an opportunistic move on his part.'

'You could say that.' Roger sips his water. 'And what do you think?'

'I'm not sure.'

'My daughter is shitting bricks because it appears we didn't do due diligence on this fellow Jessop. She seems to have no real clue who he is. Or rather was.'

Lexi shrugs. Interesting that Gemma hasn't tried the lie out on her father yet. Perhaps because she knows he wouldn't believe it. She lets the remark hang in the air.

Roger inhales and exhales. 'Well, it is what it is. Can't blame Yildiz for sniffing out an opportunity. Don't much like the man, but he's damned good at what he does.'

Lexi waits. Should she tell him that Yildiz is dangling the mews development, the serious money, as bait.

Keep that to yourself for now.

Sipping his water, Roger strolls round the kitchen. Its clean lines and polished concrete worktops appeal to Lexi. It's the kind of place she'd have, will have. One day.

He puts his glass down with a snap. 'Reputation is everything. You know that. We don't do business with criminals.'

'Absolutely not.'

He meets her gaze. 'But…there's no harm putting out a few feelers?'

Feelers?

He puts his hands on his hips. 'If we can establish who the seller is now, then we can decide. Proceed with caution. I think that's the ticket.'

Lexi considers this. Gemma should know who the sellers are. She didn't do her job properly, so now Lexi has to pick up the pieces. And do it discreetly, which won't be easy. And Gemma will continue to try to shift any blame onto her.

Roger smiles at her. He seems to read her mind.

'If anyone can make this work, Lexi, you can. And that won't go unnoticed. I can promise you that.'

16

Wednesday. 6.30am

Ewan is up before dawn. He's worked two weekends in a row, so the boss has given him the day off. Trey's a fair bloke, bit soft in some ways, but nobody's perfect.

As it gets light, the brothers are on the road and heading for London. Jared bitched a bit, but truth is he loves the bike as much as Ewan does.

It's a Triumph Trident. Ewan got it secondhand and it needed a bit of work, but he knew a bargain when he saw it. He stripped it down, practically rebuilt it. Now it goes like a dream.

When he was inside, getting a proper bike, a real man's bike, was his fantasy. He plastered his cell with pictures of super bikes from magazines. Of course, Rusty was a biker, a real one percenter, who rode with the Angels back in the day and had the tats to prove it.

'Once you're out, you take a ride for me, boy.' That's what he told Ewan. 'Loved that old hog as much as my own life. Only time I was truly free.'

Ewan toyed with getting a Harley, but if he's honest, he prefers his Triumph. Harley's are fine for the States, and long rides through wide open country. But the Triumph is a more English bike, and cruising into the city, snaking through the morning rush hour, with his brother riding pillion, makes him high as a kite. They're on a mission. Like urban warriors. Like crusaders. This is how it's meant to be.

It wasn't difficult to get an address. North London, an old block of flats that's been tarted up. Easy enough to find.

By eight o'clock, Ewan is parked up across the street. He leans on the bike, sipping his coffee and biting into a bacon roll. He's body is zinging with energy, fuelling up and preparing for action, like a soldier.

'What do you reckon?' says Jared.

Ewan wipes his mouth. 'According to intel, this is where the bitch lives.'

'What do we do next?'

'We wait.'

'I need a slash.'

Ewan huffs. 'For Crissake, Jared, could you be any more of an old woman?' He points to the brick wall behind them. 'Be a man. You need to piss, take a piss.'

'What? Like in the street?'

'Why not?'

'What if someone sees?'

'Go round the fucking corner. Find a wall to hide behind, if you're so bothered.'

Jared disappears. Ewan stares at the flats. A bloke with a big old Alsatian dog comes out of a door on the ground floor. He gives Ewan a chary look.

Ewan smiles. 'All right, mate?'

The dog tugs on its leash. It can smell the bacon roll and tows its master towards Ewan.

Ewan ignores the man and addresses the animal. 'Yeah, I know what you're after. You want my breakfast, don't you?'

The dog lips its lips.

'He's a bit of a greedy sod,' mumbles the man.

Ewan devours the rest of the roll, then lets the dog lick his fingers.

'You got some balls,' says the man. 'Most people are scared of him.'

Ewan rubs the dog's ears. 'Nah, he's all right, aren't you, boy? What's his name?'

'Buster.'

'I meet a lot of dogs in my line,' says Ewan. 'Deliveries.'

'Expect you would.' The man reins in the dog; he's anxious to be off.

'Perhaps you can help me. Got a delivery here for a lady in your block.' He unzips his pocket and pulls out a slip of paper. 'Number six. Lexi Harper. You know which door that is?'

The man points. 'Yeah, up there. First floor at the end.'

'Know her, do you?'

The man shrugs. 'As a neighbour.' He gives Ewan a mistrustful look. 'I need to get on.'

Ewan grins. 'Cheers mate. Have a good day.'

The bloke scuttles off.

Tosser.

Ewan wonders if he should get a dog. Expensive though. He checks the time on his phone. Eventually, she'll leave for work. They just have to wait.

Jared comes wandering round the corner zipping his flies.

'Where the fuck have you been?' says Ewan.

'I couldn't find anywhere private. Ended up in someone's

yard. Then I saw this women gawping at me out of the window.'

Ewan laughs. 'I bet you made her day.'

'It was embarrassing.'

'Don't be a wuss. Put your helmet on. We're going to park up round the corner, wait until she comes out.'

'Have you got the knife?'

'Course I've got the knife.' Ewan pats the pocket of his leather jacket.

'You gonna do her?'

'Depends. I've been thinking about that.'

'Depends on what?'

'I think maybe that's too quick. I got a better idea. We follow her.'

'Why?'

'Are you dense, or what? We follow her and take pictures. Stalk her. Everywhere she goes.'

'What if she takes the tube? Can't follow her then.'

'Doesn't matter. We get as many pictures as we can and send them to her.'

'You mean like to scare her? So she knows we're stalking her.'

'Yeah, scare her. Phase one of the campaign. Frighten the bitch. I wanna freak her out. Then she'll know we mean business.'

17

Wednesday. 9am

After a good night's sleep in her own bed, Lexi is feeling more confident and in control of the situation. It's a damp morning, a leaden sky, but the rain is holding off, so she takes the bus part of the way to work and walks the rest. There is every chance that she can broker the deal that Yildiz wants, and do it without breaking any laws. Whatever happened to Jessop, she did what she could for him. She was an innocent bystander, and now she has to move on.

She walks into the office with a spring in her step, but as soon as she turns into the reception area, she sees them. The tall one, M&S trouser suit, is reading the mission statement on the wall. The smaller Asian woman is scrolling on her phone.

Why the hell are they early?

She glances at Pia, who's at the reception desk dithering over her keyboard.

'Have you offered them coffee?' Lexi whispers.

Pia gives her a look of blank incomprehension. 'Do you…I mean, I thought…Gemma never said what to…'

'Just do it,' says Lexi.

But before she can escape, the tall one has turned round and is looking straight at her.

Lexi can't help feeling flustered. There's something in that gaze. Steady. Penetrating. Or is it about knowing who they are?

You've done nothing wrong. Chill.

She steps forward. 'Morning, I'm Lexi Harper…I..um believe you're here to…'

The woman pulls out a wallet with a badge. 'Yes,' she says with a smile. 'I'm Detective Sergeant Boden. My colleague, DC Chakravorty. I'm afraid we're a bit early. You can never tell if the train'll be cancelled, so we got an earlier one.'

'That's really not a problem. If I'd've known…but anyway…can we get you a coffee?'

'We're fine.'

Why doesn't she stop staring!

Lexi is mildly panicked. She was expecting the murder team detectives to be male and older. Balding and paunchy, obvious authority figures. But two girls, one not much older than her, the other younger? It feels like a trick.

'I'll see if Gemma's…she's my boss…'

'No rush,' says DS Boden equably.

Lexi scurries through the main workspace towards Gemma's corner office. But the door stands open and it's empty.

Bloody typical.

Gemma is not the best timekeeper. She regards it as a prerogative of her position to swan in, coffee in hand, after everyone else. But she knew the police were coming first thing this morning. They have an appointment. This looks like a deliberate avoidance tactic to Lexi.

Lexi goes to her own desk, plonks down her backpack, removes her trainers and slips on her heels. She needs to calm down.

Breathe. In for three, hold for four, out for five.

She does two minutes and it helps. This doesn't have to be bad. She hasn't done anything wrong. In fact, if she can set up some kind of rapport with this girl, it may work to her advantage.

Shoulders back, chin up, she heads back to the reception area. Now the cops are both scrolling on their phones. The DS is smiling to herself, probably texting her boyfriend.

'Sorry to keep you waiting,' says Lexi. 'My boss, that's Gemma Cavendish, has been held up. The traffic's awful this morning. But let's go into the conference room. I'm sure she'll be here soon. You sure you don't want coffee?'

The cop is watching her. She tilts her head, grins, and seems to relent. 'Okay, black. Thank you. Prish?'

The Asian girl looks up. 'Green tea?'

Lexi glances at Pia, who is frozen like a nervous sheep. What the hell has she got to worry about?

'Pia? Could you?'

'Yeah, sure, absolutely,' says Pia, jumping to her feet.

The two cops follow Lexi to the conference room. It's large and impressive, which is the idea. The long table seats twenty. Lexi positions herself at one end and invites the cops to join her. But the DS wanders over to the window and looks out.

'This is a lovely part of town,' she says.

What? Now they make conversation?

'The property business is about location. I'm sure you've heard that,' says Lexi, trying not to sound patronising.

'Yeah, but you're not a regular estate agent, are you?' says the cop.

'No. We deal exclusively in the super prime market.'

'Rich people?'

'Very rich people,' says Lexi with an apologetic smile.

'So, how do clients come to you? Mr Jessop, for example?'

She's straight in. No messing. No prisoners. Lexi is taken aback. She was hoping they were going to sit down and she'd recount the events at Renfrew Hall, the stuff she's already told them, and Gemma would explain about Jessop; that was the plan. But she's facing them alone and Gemma has landed her in it again.

Fortunately, Pia arrives with a tray of drinks. The business of unloading it on the table, asking who wants sugar, gives Lexi a moment to recover her composure.

She picks up her mug of coffee.

You've got this.

Being abandoned by Gemma may seem like a problem, but reconfigured and seen in another light, it could be an opportunity. The trick is to see it as such, and Lexi has a talent for this. She's proved it on a number of occasions. As she sips her coffee, an idea is forming in her mind.

Could it work? Do you dare?

The adrenaline is pumping, but she keeps her tone calm and matter-of-fact.

'Mr Jessop,' she says. 'I'd never met him before, because really it was like an interview. He was interviewing me, us, our firm to decide if he was going to give us the listing. And, with a property of this value, it would be standard practice to talk to several brokerages.'

The DS nods.

As Lexi speaks, her confidence grows. 'But we are one of

the leading smaller boutique firms in the field. And our repu-tation speaks for itself. I'm sure Mr Jessop would've known us by repute. That's probably why he picked us.'

'You're saying he just picked you, and you wouldn't make any inquiries about him prior to taking such a meeting?'

'Well, that depends. I understand from Gemma that we have clients who know him, and may well have recom-mended us to him. From our point of view, it's sensible to see the property first, assess whether it fits our client profile, then we inquire into the seller's bona fides. Frankly, we're a busy firm and that's less work.'

The Asian girl looks up from her tablet. 'Aren't there Anti-Money Laundering checks required by law?'

'Yes, basic online stuff. And we have a firm that provides that service for us.'

Not your problem if Gemma didn't do it. And is now lying.

They're both staring at her, which is unnerving.

Boden smiles. 'When did he get in touch with you?' she says.

'Well, Gemma can confirm the details. But I think she spoke to him four days ago.'

'Three days between the call and the appointment. Is that normal?'

'There was a weekend in between. That might've been the reason. Gemma will know.'

The cops exchange a surreptitious glance, which is even more intimidating. But perhaps it's just technique.

'Look,' she says. 'Until we know we've got the job, we don't do a full profile. That costs money. Once lawyers and bankers become involved, it costs a lot of money. When I went to Renfrew Hall...' The scene in the kitchen flashes through her brain, the blood creeping across the stone floor. Her hand flies to her mouth. This isn't planned. 'Sorry.'

'Take your time,' says the cop.

Lexi swallows. 'It was very preliminary. Mr Jessop was just a prospect from our point of view.'

'Depends on the house?'

'Yes.'

The cops exchange another glance.

'Okay,' says the DS. 'Now we've looked at the video interview that you did on Monday evening, but I'm afraid I'm going to ask you to run through it all again, make sure there's nothing that's been left out. Can you manage that?'

'Of course,' says Lexi.

That was easy enough.

She hesitates. If she's going to do it, now's the opportunity. The DS seems friendly enough; she's a girl like Lexi, just trying to do her job.

'Actually,' says Lexi. 'There was one thing I forgot to mention to your colleagues. I was so upset. In shock, I guess.'

'That's understandable,' says the DS. 'You have had a very difficult experience.'

Lexi takes a deep breath. 'I tried to help him. I really did.' The tears well in her eyes. She has no need to fake it. 'This awful…well, gash in his neck, and so much blood. I used my scarf to try to stop the bleeding. And for a couple of minutes, it did slow it down.'

The cop's face is blank, impossible to read.

'And he was trying to talk to me. Does he have a wife, or a partner? He was pretty incoherent, but he seemed to want me to tell her something, give her a message.'

You've done it. It's out there.

'What sort of message?' says the DS.

'Well, I think he wanted me to tell her he loved her. The

whole thing was appalling. I didn't realise until afterwards that these were his dying words.'

The DS doesn't speak. A knot of anxiety tightens in Lexi's stomach. She has to make this convincing.

'What were his dying words?' says the other cop.

'They were hard to understand, but I think he was just saying tell her I love her. Something like that. Does he have a wife?'

'Yes,' says the DS.

Course he does.

'Well…could you tell her this? It may comfort her.'

The DS nods. Lexi hesitates.

'Or maybe even, if you think it's okay, I'll tell her myself. What she must be going through, it's the least I can do. I did… sort of promise him.'

The DS is scrutinising her. Judging her.

Lexi smiles and adds, 'Obviously, I don't want to intrude. Only if it would be a help to her, poor woman.'

The DS smiles back. 'Obviously. I'll have to ask my boss.'

Lexi takes a deep breath.

You've just blatantly lied to a cop. Are you mad?

18

Wednesday, 10.30am

Boden and Chakravorty thread their way through the side streets of Mayfair down towards Oxford Street. Boden watches the young DC; her eyes dart about, taking in the expensive shopfronts and the loitering tourists. This is the London of money, luxury and fun, and she's enjoying the buzz.

She turns to Boden. 'You know your way round the back streets really well, don't you? Do you miss being in the Met?'

'Some aspects; others, not so much.'

'I'm guessing they treated you badly?'

Boden chuckles. Chakravorty is sharp and curious, as good with people as she is with data, a combination that Boden suspects will take her far.

'That was then, Prish,' she says. 'I don't dwell on the past.'

When DCI Knight told Boden she'd be taking the trip to London to interview the witness, she was secretly elated. If this is a gesture from the boss to get her onside, she'll take it. She texted Cal straight away. As part of the Met's Protection Command, the job takes him all over the country, and sometimes the world, and their relationship is circumscribed by this and the fact she works in Cambridge.

But he texted back. *Minding a royal who's visiting a hospital. Could probably get away for an hour.*

They fixed a rendezvous at their favourite coffee shop in Soho.

As they walk, Boden mentions it to Chakravorty and asks if she wants to tag along.

'You sure? I don't want to be a third wheel. I can hang out at King's Cross and wait for you.'

'Prish, don't be daft. We're not teenagers.'

Chakravorty catches her eye with an amused glance. She gets the implication. Since Cal Foley came back into her life she feels like a love-sick adolescent. But is it that obvious?

She shakes her head ruefully. 'Whatever.'

They head down Manchester Street. It's overcast and threatening drizzle, but Boden has always enjoyed walking round London, particularly the more elegant parts of town. And now that she's seeing Cal, it does make her long to return. But she knows she needs to put such yearning away. It does her no good. Makes her dissatisfied.

Take each day as it comes.

The job of interviewing the witness and reviewing her video statement took a little over an hour. Lexi Harper had a shocking experience, no question of that, and seems to have dealt with it well, which would've taken some nerve. The main purpose of the interview was to tease out anything else she saw or heard that could give a clue as to the perpetrator, and also to find out more about the ownership of Renfrew Hall. But there was nothing on either count. She didn't see any other vehicles. She heard a door bang, possibly a back door, which she'd already mentioned. She freely admitted the house spooked her, and she got out as soon as she could. Boden left a card, but it seemed unlikely they'd need to follow up.

They reach the front of the Wallace Collection, which faces a quiet, tree-filled square. Finally, away from the noise of the traffic, Boden phones the boss.

'You don't think they know who Jessop is, then?' says Knight.

'No,' says Boden. 'It seems likely he picked them, and they wouldn't check him out in any depth until they'd seen the property. That's what they're saying, although sounds like a bit of arse-covering.'

'They might've suspected he was dodgy, but ignored it?'

'Possibly. Depends how thorough their AML checks were. But they may have only realised since he's been murdered.'

'Tell me about Lexi Harper.'

'About thirty. Mixed race, tall and chic, quite a head turner. Immaculately turned out; the make-up, the hair, the nails, the high heels. Serious businesswoman look, not flashy, but the jacket she was wearing would cost me a month's salary. She came over as tense, upset by her experience, but confident and professional.'

'Okay. Did she add anything useful to her statement? And did you talk to the woman that runs the firm?'

'Harper didn't see or hear anything useful, but she was a bit fixated on passing on Jessop's dying words to his wife. Her boss, Gemma Cavendish, didn't show.'

'What were his dying words?'

'Bit vague. Basically, that he loved her. This could be

Harper's guilt coming out. She failed to save him, and she's feeling bad about that.'

'Odd, isn't it? He thinks of his wife,' says Knight.

What's odd about that?

Boden reflects, not for the first time, on the cold and detached nature of the DCI. Very few psychopaths are villains or killers; they're CEOs or other law-abiding citizens, operating under the radar, but with a lack of empathy and a degree of ruthlessness which helps them get ahead. And she does wonder about Rachel Knight.

'Well, boss, she's offering to speak to Kate Jessop and pass on the message in person.'

'Interesting. And it could be useful for us. She stonewalled Mackie. Her position is she knows nothing about her husband's business.'

'We expected that.'

'Doesn't mean we stop pushing. Means we push harder.' Knight's tone is terse; she's under pressure.

Boden is irritated. This is typical of the DCI. Nothing is ever enough for her.

'You think we can use a meeting with the witness to crack her open? Isn't that a bit unfair on the witness, boss?'

Also, it won't work.

'Well, it's her idea. Tell her we'll ask Mrs Jessop.'

Knight ends the call in her usual abrupt fashion. Boden pockets her phone.

Chakravorty smiles at her. 'Is she hassling for us to get back?'

Boden sighs. 'No, she didn't say anything specific.'

There's a resentment bubbling up inside Boden, and it's hard to pinpoint why. But every interaction with the DCI has this effect on her. It's the boss's attitude and her thinly disguised narcissism. Everything is about her. Boden has the sense that she and her colleagues are just being used. Knight doesn't respect them. She regards them as tools to further her own agenda.

'Good,' says Chakravorty. 'It'll be nice to meet Cal again. So where are we going?'

'Soho.'

Forget Knight. Enjoy the break.

The day is brightening between the showers. They've got half an hour, so they've got time to walk along Oxford Street and check out a few shops.

Boden smiles to herself. It's been a long time since the prospect of snatching a coffee with a man in the middle of the working day has got her this excited. What does it mean?

Don't overthink it.

She smiles at Chakravorty. 'Maybe we'll get lunch too. I think we deserve it.'

19

Wednesday. 10.45am

Lexi slides from side to side in front of her standing desk; there's a soothing rhythm to the motion and it has a calming effect. She's trawling the net for any mention she can find of a property developer called Jessop. The name that pops up repeatedly is an East Anglian based businessman called Craig Jessop. And it's not good. A couple of exposés suggesting criminal connections in his past. If this is him, there's no way he'd pass a proper AML check.

It took less than twenty-four hours for the murder at Renfrew Hall to hit the online news feeds, but the victim remains 'unidentified', although there's plenty of speculation. As yet, little has surfaced in the mainstream media. Then suddenly an item jumps to the top of breaking news: a second victim discovered at Renfrew Hall.

Shit!

What the hell did she walk into? Two murders! She

freezes. It shakes her. How close did she get to becoming a victim herself?

Probably closer than you think.

She goes to refill her coffee cup. As she's pressing the buttons on the machine, Gemma strolls in and passes her. With a toss of her sharply-cut blonde bangs, she avoids Lexi's gaze and heads towards her office. The attitude. The arrogance. A switch in Lexi's brain flips and rage surges through her whole body. The egotism of the bitch; her laziness and stupidity landed Lexi in this mess. Then she lied and tried to pin it on Lexi, and left her to deal with the police.

Putting her cup down with a snap, Lexi steams across the room in the direction of the boss's office. She's about halfway when her phone buzzes. She glances at the screen. Boden? That's the cop.

She hesitates. Gemma is hanging up her Balenciaga coat and folding her silk scarf; she's not going anywhere.

Lexi answers the phone. 'Sergeant? I've just seen the news, a second victim at Renfrew Hall.'

'Yes, we have discovered a second body.' The cop is so matter-of-fact, which makes it worse.

Lexi retreats towards her own corner. She'd rather not be overheard.

'I can't help thinking…' she says. 'Well, y'know…I guess I'm luckier than I think, aren't I? That could've been me.'

The cop doesn't answer. There's a moment's silence. Then Boden says, 'The reason I'm calling is to let you know I've spoken to DCI Knight, she's the SIO on this case…'

DCI, SIO, what's she on about?

'…and we will speak to Mrs Jessop and find out if she wants to talk to you, unless you've changed your mind.'

Lexi is taken aback; she wasn't expecting them to agree.

As soon as the police left the office, she was regretting her ploy. It was crazy and impulsive, not her usual behaviour.

You can't back out now.

'Oh, well yes, that's to say no. I haven't changed my mind. I'm still prepared to do it.'

'Okay.'

'When…er.. I expect you don't know…'

'No. We'll have to get back to you.'

'Thank you.'

Lexi hangs up. Why the hell is she saying thank you? This is turning into a nightmare. How on earth is she going to pitch this poor woman? Your husband died saying he loved you, and by the way, can we still have the sale? It was ridiculous. More than that, it was obscene. In their business, the ethical line could sometimes waver, but that definitely crossed it.

She notices Gemma peering at her like a nervous hamster through the glass wall of her office.

Bloody Gemma!

She strides towards the corner office and stops in the doorway.

'Did you forget the police were coming this morning? Detectives from the murder team.'

Gemma tosses her head, but there's a hint of embarrassment in the pink of her cheeks.

'I discussed the matter with Roger,' she says. When she's trying to sound professional, she uses her father's first name. 'He felt it would be better if I left it to you.'

She's lying. Again.

'Really? This guy was your contact.'

'It was felt that…'

'Gemma, I'm not going to carry the can for your mistake. I've looked up Jessop on the net. Took me five minutes to find out that he's dodgy. There's no way you did an AML check. And now you think you can lie and say you assumed I'd do it. That's just bullshit.'

Gemma's chin goes up. The eyes snap.

'I think, Lexi, you need to be very careful how you speak to me and what you appear to be accusing me of. I am your employer. Also, you're the one who went to Renfrew Hall to meet this client. We only have your account of what actually happened there.' Her boney hand is shaking, but her gaze has sharpened. The hamster has morphed into a rat.

It's a stand-off. Lexi looks the other woman up and down.

Classic Gemma.

Paint her into a corner, she attacks.

She sighs. If, for once, Gemma would just say I was busy, I fucked up, sorry, that would make all the difference. But she won't. And, if Lexi challenges her too directly, Roger will back his daughter. Yet he still looks to Lexi to make the deal work, still plays them off against each other. Whichever way you slice it and dice it, she's being used.

The only way she'll change that dynamic and her status in the firm, is if she gets Yildiz the deal he wants on Renfrew Hall and he gives her the mews development in Knightsbridge, too. Roger won't be able to ignore that. Then she'll be the one hanging up her coat in the swish corner office.

'Now,' says Gemma imperiously. 'Unless there's anything else, I have a very full diary this morning.'

Lexi turns on her heel and walks across the room back to her desk. She catches Teddy smirking at her as he chats on the phone. A couple of the other agents are at their work stations, plus the admin assistants, but they all have their heads down, eyes averted, pretending to be hard at it. You could cut the atmosphere with a knife.

Plonking down in her chair, Lexi pulls out her phone for

something to do and to avoid the smug, rivalrous gazes of her co-workers.

The mistake was to lose her temper. But the emotional rollercoaster of the last couple of days has wrecked her usual composure. Her thoughts are spinning at a mile a minute.

The second victim could've been you. You could've been killed!

She needs to calm down.

On autopilot, she scrolls through her notifications; some dipshit has sent her a stream of photos. Probably trying to sell her something she doesn't want. She clicks on one at random. A video. Of a bus? It's pulling away from a stop, on what looks like Euston Road? Then the camera zooms in, and she sees herself standing on the pavement.

WTF?

This is her this morning, getting off the number 73 bus at the British Library on Euston Road. She got off the bus there and walked the rest of the way to work. And someone videoed it? She clicks on the other photos, some still shots, some videos.

And they're all of her, on her way to work.

20

Wednesday. 11.15am

Beth is in bed, eye mask on, blinds shut; she's had a rough night. The insemination left her sore, and it took ages. There seemed to be problems at every stage of the process. He had an important business call, or that's what the go-between said, so they waited half an hour for him to produce the semen. Then the insertion of the speculum made Beth bleed. Had this woman ever been a nurse?

But it was done, and Beth is praying it's worked. The idea of doing the same again next month does not appeal. She celebrated it being over by going for drinks with a couple of girlfriends. Nothing rowdy, just a few cocktails in a bar.

But they had a deal on espresso martinis, and one thing led to another. She can't remember how she got home. But according to her Uber account, she took a cab.

She pulls up her eye mask and peers at the time on her phone. Ordinarily, she has a good head for booze, but perhaps the martinis didn't mix with the Xanax she took before going to the hotel to meet her surrogacy client. The result is a bilious headache and a parched mouth. Her mascara has turned sticky and is gumming up her eyelashes. She hates that.

She flings back the duvet, climbs out of bed and heads for the en suite bathroom. Peeing is uncomfortable, but she's had worse after a forceful shag. She gulps down handfuls of water from the cold tap, then grabs some cotton pads and a cleanser to remove her eye make-up. The cleanser is expensive and soothing on her lids, bought on the credit card Damian gave her until it got blocked.

Don't think about him, not today.

What she needs is juice and carbs. She grabs her bathrobe, the one nicked from Claridges, from the back of the door, and heads for the kitchen.

She finds a full carton of orange juice in the fridge, cracks it open and drinks. Cold and super sweet and slips down with ease. She knows what Lexi would say: use a glass. Lexi's finicky about stuff like that. Living with her would be an actual nightmare. Times she's been forced to crash on her mate's sofa have always produced conflict. It's doubtful if Lexi could live with anyone; she has to micromanage every detail of her personal space. Her home is her sanctuary. Everything in her flat is neat and colour coordinated, and not a speck of dust.

Having consumed half the orange juice, Beth searches the cupboards for cereal. There's a bag of muesli, part of her recent drive to be healthy. She tips some into a bowl, but she's out of milk, so she douses it in the rest of the orange juice. Once she's got this down her, plus a couple of paraceta-mol, the day will look better.

She gets a spoon from the drawer and carries the bowl through to the living area where she plonks down on the sofa.

London is spread out before her in mid-morning bustle, although with the triple glazing she can't hear any of it. She loves this place. On the fifteenth floor it's like living in a bubble up in the clouds. She can see gaggles of tourists congregating outside Tate Modern. The river flows past down below, turgid and brown. Then something catches her eye, something tiny and dark, maybe an oil drum, bobbing along on the current.

A shiver runs up her spine. She's not one for dwelling on the past. What matters is today, having fun today, because what the fuck else is there?

The phone buzzes in the pocket of her robe. Balancing the bowl on her knee, she pulls it out.

Lexi.

'Hey babe,' she says. A vague sense of unease creeps into her head. She has to tell her friend about the surrogacy deal; the longer she puts it off, the worse it will be.

'Sounds like you're eating,' says Lexi.

'Breakfast.'

'Oh, late night then.' She can hear the tone of disapproval, but ignores it.

She puts the bowl of cereal aside. 'Lex, I got something I need to tell you about. Well, explain to you.'

'That sounds ominous. I'm guessing this is about Damian.'

'No…well, not really…well, yeah, it's sort of about him.'

'Beth, if he goes down, which he probably will, the charges he's facing, that's ten years in jail. You want to put your life on hold until you're forty?'

'Well, actually, he told me he'd get out sooner, because…'

'Babe, listen to yourself. Five years? Ten years? What the fuck?' She's coming over angry and sour, which strikes Beth as odd. Okay, she's right about Damian, and she knows it. But she doesn't usually bang on about it.

Even through the fug of her hangover, Beth can sense that something is way off kilter with her friend. And after this shitshow at Renfrew Hall, is that any surprise?

'Lex,' she says. 'What's going on?'

From the background noise, Lexi must be outside and walking.

'Just popping out to stretch my legs and get some coffee. Gemma's being a pain this morning.'

'So what's new?'

Beth waits. She can hear an inhalation of breath down the line.

'Okay, well,' says Lexi. 'This weird thing happened.'

Now we're getting to it.

'What sort of weird thing?'

'Someone's sending me messages. And photos.'

'You mean like dick pics? I'm always getting them. Best to ignore them.'

'No, the photos are of me this morning, on my way to work. And a video of me getting off the bus.'

'That is weird. Like they're following you?'

'Yeah, and there're loads of them. It's creepy.'

'Babe, you've got a stalker.'

'I figured that much. But what the hell do I do? I'm walking down the street now. I tell you, I thought twice about even leaving the office. What if they're following me now?' Her voice goes up in pitch, undercut with panic. 'I don't understand. What do they want?'

'They want to frighten you. That's what they get off on, these blokes. It's about power.'

'Well, they've succeeded. I'm spooked. And I'm on a

busy street in broad daylight. I keep looking around. It could be anybody.'

'You want me to come and meet you?'

'No, I've got a business lunch. I just had to talk to someone about it, or I'll go crazy.'

'Mate of mine got stalked by her ex. She went to the police and everything. They were useless.'

'You think this is someone I know?'

'Probably.'

'But who?'

Beth ponders this question. Unless Lexi's been having secret hookups that she knows nothing about, there's hardly anyone to choose from.

'The doctor?' she says.

'Went to New Zealand,' says Lexi. 'And I'm pretty sure I didn't do anything to upset him.'

'What about a client, or someone at work? Like someone you've beaten to a deal.'

'That's possible. I hadn't thought of that.'

'You're always telling me what a cutthroat business it is.'

'Could be that. Someone pissed off over a deal.'

'The thing is, Lex, don't let them get under your skin. It's a game. They only win if they freak you out. I mean, what are they gonna do?'

'You're right. This is some arsehole broker, I bet you.' Her voice is firmer, more Lexi. The wobble has gone. 'Thank you. What did you want to talk to me about?'

'It'll keep. Tell you when I see you.'

'Love you lots,' says Lexi. This is their usual sign off, but today she means it, which makes Beth smile.

'Yeah, me too,' she says. 'Call me later.'

She hangs up, picks up the cereal bowl. But it's turned to

mush, doesn't look appealing. She wanders back into the bedroom, takes off the bathrobe, and crawls back into bed.

21

Wednesday. 1.30pm

The restaurant is in Kensington; it has three Michelin stars and no prices on the menu. Lexi's conversation with Beth has helped get her back on track. She suspects Teddy Devereux could be her stalker. They started at Cavendish Cooper at about the same time. But her sales figures speak for themselves, and as she pulled ahead of him, she's sensed his resentment on a number of occasions. But, as Beth said, he only wins if she lets it freak her out.

Head held high, she breezes through the gilded double doors as if she belongs. The maitre d' escorts her to Yildiz's table. He's already there and stands up to greet her.

'I'm so glad you could join me,' he says.

Lexi received a call from his personal assistant at eleven, so pretty last minute. Maybe someone else cried off.

'Thank you for inviting me,' she replies, as the maitre d' pulls out the chair for her to sit.

'This is just a little local place I use. But my wife will

scold me if I don't stick to fish and salad.' He pats his paunch as he sits back down.

Lexi smiles. The fact he's mentioning his wife is good. He's making the point upfront that this is strictly business. Since she's been a property agent, Lexi has had plenty of lunches with businessmen angling for something extra on the side. It's ranged from flirting to a Kuwaiti billionaire who offered her a hundred grand a month to be his live-in mistress. Rumours abound about Yildiz's hardheaded business methods, but he's not known to be a sleaze.

Frankly, she's relieved. After the morning she's had, she doesn't need any more nasty surprises.

But what does he want?

He's relaxed, all charm and politeness, but something in his gaze doesn't quite match.

The maitre d' turns towards her. 'A drink for madam?'

'Just some mineral water, thank you.'

'Oh, but you'll have a glass of wine with your food, won't you?' Yildiz says with a chuckle. 'I grew up on the shores of the Mediterranean. Food and wine should never be taken separately. It's sacrilege.'

Lexi inclines her head. 'I don't want to be a stuffy Brit.'

He grins. 'You could never be that.' He glances at the maitre d'. 'Tell the sommelier to find me a nice lemony Sancerre.' He turns to her. 'You like Sancerre?'

She nods.

The man dips his head and retires. A female server fills their water glasses.

'Let's choose,' says Yildiz. 'Then we can talk.'

The menu isn't long, but each dish is precisely described. She picks halibut, he opts for goujons of monkfish. The ritual of ordering gives her time to consider why she's here. In her last encounter with Yildiz he was brisk to say the least. He has a reputation for being mercurial, but today he's playing the perfect host.

Be careful.

The sommelier brings the wine, and once Yildiz has approved it and it's poured, he swirls the straw-coloured liquid in his glass and says, 'These are very strange times, Lexi. Are you a student of history?'

Bizarre opening question.

'I did it at school.'

'I started in this business building holiday villas in Cyprus. When I first came to this country, men like Roger Cavendish would not give me the time of day. That's the British upper classes for you. Don't get me wrong, I bear no grudges, and in fact, I admire Roger. He had vision and built a good business on it. But his daughter is a charmless harpy. She's mediocre, and without her family connections, she would be nowhere. Nothing.'

If he thinks he can trick her into bad-mouthing her boss, he can think again.

She sips her wine and says nothing.

'But the wheel of history turns, Lexi, and now it favours people like us. We demand our place at the top table, and we make that demand with our ability, our talent, and our hard work. My impression, when I first met you, is that you and I are cut from the same cloth.'

'I'll take that as a compliment,' says Lexi.

'It's sincerely meant. I have a reputation for being difficult. Unpredictable.' He shrugs and grins. 'But let me tell you a secret: it's a carefully cultivated front. Keeps people at bay. Keeps them guessing. But my business model is simple: a top quality product.'

'Your developments are certainly known for their opulence and attention to detail.'

He bows his head. 'Thank you. I never skimp, because I know that our sort of clients expect the best. I give it to them. There's no trick to it. I'm a very simple man. I have been married to the same woman for over thirty years. We were childhood sweethearts. We have grown up together. We have four lovely children, and I told each one of them, I will pay for your education, but that is it. I won't bankroll you. You stand on your own two feet. And they have.'

He pulls out his phone and shows her a family photo. The wife is elegant and poised. There are three smart young men in their twenties and a beautiful daughter. It looks like a picture taken for a glossy magazine. In the background, a couple of palm trees and a blue Mediterranean sky. Idyllic. It's hard not to be envious.

'You have a lovely family,' says Lexi.

Yildiz looks at the photo himself and smiles with pride.

'In many ways, you remind me of my daughter,' he says. 'She is the eldest, keeps the boys in order. She went to Harvard Business School, and now she works for a hedge fund.'

And?

Lexi feels a prick of impatience. Why's he telling her all this? Opening up, and the flattering comparison with his daughter? What's it about?

He's peering at her over his wine glass. What's he expecting? Some personal confidence in return? She feels the pressure to say something; she doesn't want to be rude. Not to a potential client who's buying her a Michelin starred lunch.

'My parents are divorced,' she says. 'I haven't seen my father for years.' Not strictly true. They weren't married. He went to work one day and never came back.

He frowns with sympathy. 'That is truly sad,' he says. 'Family is everything to me. It's what I work for.'

She doesn't reply. And she certainly doesn't want his pity.

Fortunately, two servers arrive carrying plates covered with steel cloches. The plates are placed and unveiled. But as the maitre d' describes each dish, Lexi's thoughts skitter away.

Her father. That bastard is in her head now. Last she heard, he'd scuttled back up north to Manchester, living with some woman who already had a couple of kids. He's always been a user. And a liar. She understands her mother's bitterness, but it doesn't make it any easier to stomach, which is why she rarely goes home.

She stares at the perfect arrangement of the items on her plate. Order appeals to her, because growing up there was no order. The old man with his fags and his beer slumped in front of the telly, watching the football. Her mother always angry, shouting at him, shouting at Lexi.

Yildiz picks up his knife and fork. 'It's not where you start,' he says. 'It's where you finish. What matters is whether you've got what it takes.'

Lexi doesn't reply; she doesn't trust herself. He's pressing all her buttons and that doesn't help.

What it takes? Such a cliché. She's been standing on her own two feet since she left home at sixteen. She worked her way through college and still came out with thousands in student debt. She knows more than most what it takes.

Slicing into the halibut she takes a bite; it's delicious. She savours it, then she meets his gaze and smiles.

'I know what you're saying, Ari. And I think I know the question in the back of your mind. Can I get you the deal you want on Renfrew Hall? And the answer is, I'm working on it.'

He smiles. 'Cut to the chase. I like that.'

'I'm hoping to talk to Mr Jessop's widow. And I'm

hoping that, despite her grief, she's still amenable to moving forward.'

'I think if anyone can do this, you can.'

She tilts her head. 'Good. Because I think that too.'

He chuckles. 'I like you, Lexi. I knew we'd get on. And I don't say that about many people in this business.'

He raises his glass.

She raises hers. 'Thank you.'

22

Wednesday. 6pm

Lexi takes a cab home and has it drop her as near to the entrance to her block as the driver can get. The area is well lit, but she's taking no chances. This could be Teddy playing games, but what if it isn't? If her stalker is out there, he'll be freezing his arse off in the cold and damp of a November night. She'll soon be safe and warm behind her own front door.

Her lunch with Yildiz was surprisingly enjoyable. She brought up the subject of Renfrew Hall, and once that was dealt with, they chatted with ease. He entertained her with tales about Cyprus and his early experiences in the property business; he was both charming and funny. He allowed her to see beyond the facade of his spiky reputation, and it was hard not to be flattered.

When she got back to the office, Gemma was lurking.

'That was a rather long lunch break.'

Lexi savoured the moment, much as she'd savoured the halibut.

'I had lunch with Arif Yildiz.' Then she mentioned the restaurant and had the pleasure of watching Gemma's jaw drop. Gemma slunk away to her office.

The rest of the afternoon was uneventful, ploughing through emails and other admin tasks.

As she walks from the cab to the entrance to her block, she gets out her keys and holds them with the metal blade of the door key protruding between her fingers. It's habit, one she acquired when she lived in less salubrious places.

Inside the building, it's fine. Clean, well-lit communal areas and walkways. She takes the stairs to the first floor. Approaching her flat, she can hear music coming from next door. Her neighbour, Sam, is in his kitchen cooking; she gives him a wave as she passes his window.

She unlocks her door, flicks on the lights and picks up the mail from the mat. Mostly advertising rubbish, but on the top is a folded sheet of lined paper torn from a notebook. Dumping her backpack, she opens it and reads: '*herd U need a Housemate to keep U company*'

She stares at it. The handwriting is small and awkward, like a child's. And the first word is misspelt, missing the a.

It makes no sense. Someone looking for a room to rent? In London, rents are exorbitant and people go to desperate lengths to find somewhere. But this is a one-bedroom flat and she has no wish, and no need to share it.

She takes her coat off and hangs it up in the hallway. Her trainers are next. She's about to carry them through to the bedroom with her backpack, when her gaze snags on the cushion that peeps up above the back of the sofa in the sitting room.

The cushion is scarlet, a contrast with the dove grey sofa. And it moves.

Lexi freezes in her tracks. Did she imagine this?

The open door to the sitting room is in front of her, and the back of the sofa faces her. The kitchen is to her left, the bedroom to her right.

Someone's here!

But how? There's no way they could get in. When she first moved in, she had a new deadlock fitted on the front door. The windows all have locks. The only other person with a key is Beth. It must be her. She's fallen asleep on the sofa. And yet…something feels odd.

Don't be so paranoid.

'Beth?' she says with as much firmness as she can muster. 'Beth, wake up.'

No reply.

'Beth, for Chrissake! You're freaking me out.'

As she walks down the hall towards the sitting room, the red cushion twitches again, only slightly, but it does move.

She flicks on the main light. No Beth.

But something moves on the sofa. It's orange, with dark blotchy scales and a sinuous, fluid motion.

A snake? A fucking snake!

She can't believe her eyes. The creature is coiled in the corner of the sofa and is burrowing under the cushion.

Panic floods through her. She opens her mouth and screams. A raw and reflexive howl of fear. She turns on her heel, rushes down the hall to the front door and wrenches it open. As she steps outside, her next-door neighbour comes out of his front door.

'Lexi? Are you all right?'

She can't breathe. She's sobbing and gasping with terror. 'There's…a fucking…snake on my sofa…'

'Shit!' He hurries towards her.

Her heart is racing and her head spins. An unbelievable pain tears through her chest, and as her legs turn to jelly, she collapses into his arms.

23

Wednesday. 7pm

Beth trots up the stairs in Lexi's block. She received a call from Sam, her friend's next-door neighbour. Lexi has had a panic attack. The story became garbled after that, and she wasn't listening. She was already halfway out of the door. But it concerned a snake. A snake in Lexi's flat. How?

As she hurries along the walkway leading to the flat, a beefy, bald-headed bloke comes out of Lexi's front door and he has an orange snake, about five feet long, draped round his shoulders. He's cradling its head in his left hand and crooning to it. Beth stops in her tracks.

Shut up!

There's an Alsatian dog sitting patiently beside the door. Dog and snake eyeball each other. The snake's forked tongue flicks briefly from its mouth. The dog raises its muzzle and sniffs. A second bloke emerges from Lexi's flat. He pats the dog.

'Good boy. He won't hurt you.'

Lexi appears in the doorway of the next door flat; she has a blanket wrapped round her shoulders. Beth rushes forward to meet her. They hug.

'My god, babe. You okay?'

Lexi nods. She does not look okay.

Sam and his husband, Ben, come out of the flat behind Lexi.

'Well,' says Sam to the one with the snake. 'What d'you reckon?'

'It's a corn snake, not fully grown. He won't do you any harm.'

'Not venomous, then?' says Lexi.

'No. They're very docile. He probably thought the sofa was a nice, snuggly place to have a kip. They feel the cold.'

'But how did he get into the flat?' says Sam. 'And where did he come from?'

'He could come through a fairly narrow gap, crack in the floorboards or the skirting.'

Beth thinks about her mate's flat. There are no cracks. She had the whole place redecorated last summer. It's pristine.

'What about the letterbox?' says Lexi.

The second bloke, the one with the dog, bends down and flips open the letterbox at the base of Lexi's front door.

'You got a three or four-inch gap,' he says.

The other man strokes the snake's head. 'Yeah, he'd get through there, wouldn't you, buddy? But someone would've had to open it for him.'

Sam turns to Lexi. 'If someone put him through the letter-box, we should maybe call the police?'

Lexi doesn't reply. She glances at Beth.

The stalker?

Lexi has that sharp little crease she gets between her

brows, as if she's in pain, and it means her anxiety's ramping up. She could tip over the edge again. Beth has to step in.

'You'll be lucky,' she says. 'A burglar kicks your door in, and you phone them. All you'll get is a crime number to claim on the insurance. No one actually comes.'

This is Beth's instinctual reaction. Don't call the cops unless you have to. They get involved, it'll get messy. And Lexi's had enough stress in the last couple of days, with the interviews and the forensics. Does she need big boots tramping through her flat?

Lexi nods. 'She's got a point. And I don't think I could take the hassle.'

Sam shrugs. 'I know what you mean,' he says. 'We are talking about the Met here. They're overstretched.'

Lexi relaxes a bit, but it's marginal.

'Okay,' says Beth. 'It's not poisonous. But where would you get a snake like this?'

'Oh, loads of places,' says the snake nut. 'Lots of pet shops keep them, because they're the perfect snake for beginners. Not expensive. Easy to handle. Do you wanna hold him?'

Beth takes a step back. 'No, you're all right,' she says.

But Lexi puts out her hand. 'Can I?' she says. She reaches out and touches the snake's head. 'He's beautiful.' She lets the snake nut wrap the creature around her.

That's Lexi. Bigger balls than any bloke.

'It was the shock of it,' says Lexi. 'Coming home and finding him. Thanks for coming out like this.'

The snake nut smiles and shrugs. He glances at the bloke with the dog. 'When my brother called me, I said I was happy to help. Snakes get misunderstood. No need to be scared of most of them.'

Yeah, tell that to the stalker. Cause that's exactly what the bastard intended.

'Would you like to keep him?' says Lexi.

The snake nut beams like a kid. 'You sure?' he says.

Course she's sure!

Lexi hands the snake over.

She smiles at the guy with the Alsatian. 'Thanks, Tony. I really appreciate your help. Both of you.'

'I don't know if this is relevant,' says Tony, 'but this morning, first thing, I was taking the dog out, and there was this geezer looking for you, asking which was your flat. Said he had a delivery. I thought it was pretty suss. He didn't look like a delivery driver to me.'

'What did he look like?' says Lexi.

'Youngish, early twenties. Dark hair. Beard. Good set of leathers. Fancy bike. I think it was a Triumph. Quite cocky. I didn't like his manner.'

Beth glances at her friend. She's still, almost frozen. She nods.

'Well, thanks again,' she says.

Tony, his brother, the snake and the dog troop off in a line and disappear down the stairs. Lexi turns to Sam and Ben and thanks them too.

'You want us to give the flat the once over?' says Sam.

'Would you?' The relief in Lexi's voice is palpable.

Lexi, Beth, Sam and Ben spend the next quarter of an hour going through every room, searching every cupboard, nook and cranny. There's nothing. Not even dust under the bed. Very Lexi.

Ben seals the letterbox from the inside with tape.

Beth watches her friend; she's holding it together, just.

Once the place has the all clear and the boy's leave, Beth turns to her and says, 'You okay?'

Lexi shakes her head. 'I had a full-blown panic attack. Blacked out. Felt as if I was going to die. That hasn't happened for years.'

Beth goes into the kitchen and pulls a bottle of wine out of the fridge. She gets glasses from the cupboard and pours two hefty measures.

Lexi is in the sitting room peering at the sofa. 'You think I should get this cleaned?'

Beth comes through and hands her the wine. 'Looked like a pretty clean snake to me. Do they shit?'

Lexi exhales. 'I'm getting an industrial cleaning firm in. And a mailbox on the wall outside.'

Beth sips her wine. 'I've just gotta say, babe, what the fuck are we dealing with here? I mean, a snake?'

Lexi picks up a sheet of paper from the coffee table and hands it to Beth to read.

Blue ink, the writing is tiny. *'herd U need a Housemate to keep U company'*

'Weird. Someone's got it in for you, big time.'

'But who? I thought it might be Teddy from the office.'

'Does he fit the description?'

Lexi shakes her head. 'Older. No beard.'

Beth shrugs. 'Guy in his early twenties? How old's the average broker?'

'Older than that.'

'Maybe someone put him up to it, but...'

Suddenly, from nowhere, a sequence of random thoughts tumble through Beth's brain. It happens sometimes. Stuff connects. Waking up with a hangover, the juice, the muesli, the oil drum far below bobbing along in the river. The river.

She stares at her friend. 'What about Ewan? He's the right age.' He's also Lexi's cousin.

Lexi stares back. 'Ewan's in jail.'

'Last you heard.'

This is all making sense, a terrible sense.

'What if they let him out? He was only fourteen. Kids serve less time. Lex, you need to call your mum and ask her.'

Lexi takes a huge swallow of wine. 'I'm not calling my mum.'

'You have to. Or I will.'

'It's not Ewan. That was all a long time ago.'

'Yes, but—'

'It's not Ewan.' She's emphatic, too emphatic.

Is she thinking this too?

Beth holds out her hand. 'Give me your phone. I'll do it.'

Lexi glares at her. 'That's going to seem peculiar, isn't it?'

'Who cares? Babe, we need to know, even if it's just to discount it.'

Lexi sighs. 'Actually, she's left me a load of messages.'

'Your mum?'

Lexi nods.

This is no co-incidence. She never calls. Lexi doesn't get on with her mum. To be fair, no one does.

'I'll get more wine. You call her.'

Beth goes to the kitchen and refills their glasses. Glancing through the door, she watches Lexi pacing in the sitting room, phone to her ear. It's ringing.

'Hey, Mum. Yeah, I know you've been calling. I have been meaning …. yeah, but it's work, Mum…okay, but—'

Then her tone changes. 'What? When? How d'you know?' Lexi has stopped pacing, and she's got a face like a bulldog chewing a wasp. She exhales. She clicks the phone onto speaker.

Her mother's voice is whinny. To Beth, it always sounds like she's telling you off.

'...I went round to your uncle's. He's a wreck with the drinking and everything. But he told me, Ewan was released on licence a month ago. He's staying there.'

Oh, shit.

'Have you seen him?' says Lexi. 'What does he look like now?'

'How the hell should I know?' says her mother. 'He's got a job in Luton and he's got a motorbike, but I really do think, Lexi, that the least you could do is—'

Lexi clicks the phone off and tosses it on the sofa. Her hand flies to her mouth and her face crumples. She sinks down onto the sofa and sobs.

Least she's forgotten about the snake.

Beth reaches out and hugs her tight. 'Sssh. It'll be okay. We're in this together. Like always.'

'What does he want?'

'It's not your fault, Lex. Never was. You have to hang on to that.'

24

Wednesday. 8.30pm

The cab driver helps unload the two suitcases outside the high-rise tower near the Tate Modern. Lexi is struggling with her backpack and a hessian bag of all the food she emptied from the fridge. Beth and the cab driver wheel the cases towards the main doors.

Lexi thanks him; she'll add in a decent tip.

The electronic doors slide open and the concierge comes out from behind his desk to help them.

This is the kind of place several million buys you. It buys you help. And security. A private, luxurious bubble, with a gym and spa on site. This is what Lexi wants.

One day this'll be for real.

Lexi is still in a spin. She couldn't stay in her own flat. Not tonight. Not until…

Until when?

It's just temporary. A precaution.

The owner of the apartment, the one Beth's using, is

Chinese; he has a portfolio of twenty apartments in the block, including the penthouse, occupied by his daughter, who's studying in London. Lexi has arranged a six month rental of the apartment with a client from Dubai. But he doesn't fly in for at least another week, and, fortunately, the final paperwork isn't signed. She'll have to invent an excuse and find him somewhere else. Give herself some breathing space.

She, Beth and their luggage pile into the lift. They didn't speak much during the journey over here. Lexi announced she was moving in with her friend, and Beth agreed it was the best plan. But what choice does she have? Lexi senses she's not one hundred percent behind the arrangement.

As soon as Beth unlocks the front door, Lexi can see why. Shoes abandoned on the mat. Glancing into the main bedroom, an unmade bed, and in the kitchen, a litter of unwashed dishes and mugs.

Beth gives her a sheepish look. Lexi tows one of her cases into the guest bedroom, heaves it up on to the bed and unpacks. Beth hovers in the doorway.

'Sorry,' she says. 'I know it's a bit untidy. But I wanted to get over to yours as quick as I could.'

Lexi is too wrung out to be angry. Holding the snake and making her peace with the creature took her last ounce of resilience. But she had to do it, otherwise how will she ever be at ease in her own home again? She refuses to be robbed of that. 'Have you got any tea?' she says.

'Yeah,' says Beth enthusiastically. 'Or more wine?'

'I don't need to drink any more.'

She needs to get her head straight. Now the shock has subsided, she needs to think.

Could this be Ewan?

She doesn't want to think about him. It's been a struggle,

but she's done her best to shut all that away. She had to in order to survive.

Her cousin got sucked into the gang culture when he was just a kid. He ran wild and no one could stop him. She remembers her Auntie Mari's despair. He was fourteen when he was involved in the stabbing of another boy in the park. His fingerprints were on the knife and he was convicted of murder.

Lexi can still see him in court; the void behind his eyes. No emotion, just hate.

Mari died a year later. Lexi remembers her aunt; gentle and kind. She was the only one in the family who never gave Lexi a hard time.

Once her case is unpacked and everything put away, Lexi returns to the main room. Beth is in the kitchen area. She's cleaned up, made tea in a teapot and is arranging cheese and biscuits and some fruit on two plates.

In terms of her mate, this represents a big effort. Beth is trying to take care of her.

'You need to eat something,' she says.

'Thanks,' says Lexi. 'And thanks for coming over so quickly.'

Beth brushes this off. 'You're always there for me.'

Lexi perches on the bar stool at the kitchen counter. As she picks up a grape from the plate, she realises she is hungry. The last thing she ate was lunch in a fancy restaurant, but that feels like aeons ago now, and the excitement of connecting with Yildiz has been blotted out.

Beth pours the tea into delicate bone china tea cups. She must have found them in a cupboard somewhere. A concierge firm has furnished and equipped this whole place to cater for the tastes of the global super rich, so of course it has floral patterned tea cups.

Lexi picks up her cup and sips. Somehow the refinement added by the cup makes the tea taste better.

Beth is frowning. 'There's something I need to explain to you,' she says.

Lexi sighs. 'Don't worry. I'll get a cleaning firm in here too when you leave. It's no big deal.'

'It's not that.' She takes a breath and is nervous, which doesn't bode well. Lexi's heart sinks.

'It's about me being pregnant. I wasn't when I told you that. But it was only a teensy white lie, because now I probably am. And when I told you, I knew I would be.'

What the...?

Beth can be obtuse at times, and that's usually a sign that she's got involved in something she shouldn't. Her moral compass is erratic to say the least.

Lexi exhales. 'Do I want to hear this?'

'I don't want you to think I'm lying to you.'

'Except you appear to be telling me you have. Just tell me, Beth, because I don't have the energy for this.'

Beth folds her hands as if she's trying to keep her body under control, but she can't stop fidgeting. Since they were kids, she's never been able to keep still, and stress makes it worse.

'Okay,' she says. 'I'm doing this surrogacy deal for a couple in Hong Kong. The money will set me up, and y'know, it's a good thing to do.'

Lexi stares at her. This is outlandish even by Beth's standards.

'What? You're not pregnant by Damian. You're having a baby as a surrogate?'

'Yeah.'

'Commercial surrogacy is illegal in this country.'

'Well, yeah, theoretically.'

'It's the law. I don't think there's anything theoretical about it.'

'But who's going to know? It's all arranged. A private clinic and everything. I thought you'd be pleased, babe, because it's me standing on my own two feet and not relying on some bloke.'

Lexi scans her friend. The hopeless naivety mixed with streetwise guile.

'Are you sure you can do this?' she says.

'What do you mean?' says Beth.

'I mean can you be pregnant for nine months, give birth to a baby and then just give that child away?'

'Why not?'

'The emotional impact, for starters. It could tear you apart.'

Beth isn't listening. 'It's two hundred and fifty grand. So four kids is a million quid. I'll be set for life.'

'You're planning to have four?' says Lexi.

'I dunno yet. Maybe.'

Lexi considers explaining to her friend the myriad ways in which this could go wrong, not to mention the emotional trauma it might entail, but she doesn't have the strength. It'll have to keep for another day. The more pressing problem is Ewan.

She shrugs. 'I don't know what to say.'

'I'm really sorry I lied to you. It wasn't intentional.'

It was, but not according to Beth's logic.

Lexi drinks her tea. Forgiving Beth depends on understanding Beth. Lexi's childhood was far from easy, but compared to her friend's, it was a breeze. Beth's mother was an addict who remained half a step ahead of social services, which kept her daughter out of care and available to fetch and carry her mother's drugs. Then there were Beth's looks; a little blonde angel preyed upon by most of the men who passed through her chaotic home and her mother's bed. For most of their primary school years, Beth only ate a proper meal when she came to Lexi's house.

'That child follows you like a stray dog.' That's what Lexi's mother said. But she still laid an extra place at the table for Beth. It was one of the few good things Lexi remembers her mother doing.

Lexi gazes across the Caesarstone quartz worktop at her friend. She runs her fingertip across the silky smooth pebble coloured surface. She loves the lush attention to detail, the sheer extravagance of it. This is what she wants, this is what she craves. Order. Impeccable design. A place that will remind her every single day that she's made it, she's escaped and she's never going back. The life of resentment her mother's lived will not be her life, and she's reached a safe harbour. Wealth gives you that; serious money. It's the only thing that can.

But her career, her plans, her ambitions are all spiralling out of her control. A client gets murdered right in front of her.

Now this.

'I've been thinking,' she says. 'What you said about Ewan. Maybe you're right. What if this is him?'

Beth tips her head to one side, as if shaking off an unpleasant notion. 'He's probably crazy enough,' she says. 'He was a crazy kid.'

Lexi nods. The thought, the suspicion, has been eating away at her throughout the taxi journey. 'Yeah,' she says. 'Crazy enough to stalk me and send me pictures to frighten me, crazy enough to shove a snake through my letterbox. But what if it's worse than that?'

'Worse how?'

'The text I got. It said: don't ignore me. I hate being ignored. But how had I ignored him?'

'Had he tried to contact you?'

'No. I think it implies he's already done something, something I shouldn't ignore.'

'Like what?'

Lexi doesn't want to say it. It's too horrible to contemplate, but it makes sense. After all, Ewan is a convicted killer.

'What if he cut a man's throat, leaving him for me to find?'

'Shit! This thing with your client.'

'Yeah, the client I went to meet at Renfrew Hall.'

'But how did he know where you were going?'

'What if he didn't? But he was following me. The weather was terrible. Tony, my neighbour, said the guy had a motorbike. Mum said Ewan has a motorbike. In the rain, I wouldn't have noticed that.'

'He knows where you live, probably where you work too.'

'It's opportunistic. He follows me to Renfrew Hall. I'm obviously meeting someone. He gets inside through another door, moments ahead of me, and slits my client's throat. Because it'd only just happened, Beth, seconds before I got there.'

'That's just evil.'

'He's a killer. The kid he stabbed when he was fourteen, he knifed in the neck. He knew exactly what he was doing. The boy bled out at the scene.'

'Are you gonna tell the police?'

Are you?

Lexi exhales. This is what she should do. She should phone the detective who came to see her.

But that's like admitting it's your fault.

The thought grates on her. Gemma would feel vindicated, her view of Lexi confirmed. She'd be crowing. She'd have the perfect excuse to get rid of Lexi.

Lexi sighs. 'Tell them what? I can't prove any of it, can I? All I'd be doing is admitting this is my fault. It happened because of me. And that's my career gone. Everything I've worked for. What firm's going to employ a broker who got her client murdered?'

25

Thursday. 10.30am

Boden sits at her desk, texting on her phone. The morning briefing has just finished, the specific difficulties of the case are emerging and the frustration in the team is mounting. The DCI is giving everyone grief.

They've discovered a second body in an overgrown spinney some distance from the house. It's yet to be identified, but it makes sense that a man like Craig Jessop wouldn't have gone there alone; he'd have taken some security.

Two brutal murders, an isolated house in the middle of nowhere, accessed by country lanes with no traffic cameras. The property has some outdated security cameras of its own, but they were disconnected at the relevant time. The digital forensics unit has found nothing useful. This is making any comings and goings difficult to track. All the vehicles entering and exiting the wider area have to be checked, which takes time, and they need more analysts with the skills to do this.

Boden made the point about the caretaker again and was told he was on a list to be re-interviewed. But the boss doesn't seem to view this as a priority. At that point in the briefing, Boden tuned out.

Her thumbs glide across the screen.

Really sad it was so short. Miss you x

She and Chakravorty had made it to the coffee shop in Soho, only to discover that Cal Foley needed to leave five minutes later.

He texts back. *That's the royals for you. She decides to take her kid for ice cream, so we have to jump x*

Picking up her coffee, Boden takes a sip. The disappointment of only seeing him briefly travelled home with her and, when she woke up this morning, it was still there, like a lead balloon. She feels flat and more than a little tetchy. Just taking things as they come is fine in theory, but the reality is it's freighted with letdowns like this which are making her miserable.

And so is work, currently.

The idea of asking Kate Jessop if she wants to meet the witness has turned into something more coercive in the DCI's mind. To Boden, this is wrong. Doesn't matter who the Jessops are; Kate is still a woman whose husband has been murdered. Also, it's impractical. She may have agreed to talk to Lexi Harper, but where does that get them? The boss seems to be expecting them to put pressure on Lexi Harper to ask questions, using her as some kind of proxy. Boden feels lumbered, and belligerent about the whole thing.

She and Chakravorty will be escorting Harper to meet Kate Jessop. Boden has arranged to collect the witness from Cambridge station.

Boden's gaze travels across the room to where Chakravorty is leaning over the shoulder of one of the analyst.

They're discussing something on the screen. The young DC talks with her hands when she's excited, waving them around. She's full of enthusiasm for the job, and Boden envies that, because it seems to be something she's lost.

She can't work out if this is just because of Knight; a bad boss can taint everything. Or is it about Cal and always wanting to be somewhere else?

Pull yourself together.

She needs to focus on the case and what she should be doing. But she's lost her enthusiasm, mainly because this is Knight's show and taking the initiative and following a lead of your own is not welcome.

Getting up, she wanders over to the coffee machine for a refill. Perhaps it's simple. She's restless and dissatisfied because it's time to make some changes. It's time to go. But go where?

She should be a DI by now. She has the experience, and she thinks she's demonstrated the ability. But it isn't how the system works. She's stuck in the logjam of the lower ranks. Knight's last review hasn't helped either.

And if she moved back to London, could she move in with Cal? Are they even ready for that? Probably not. What they have is fun, but what if she's more into him than he is to her? That thought scares her. She's made herself vulnerable before and the results were disastrous.

She could go and live with her mother in Greenwich. But that could only be a short-term solution. They'd drive each other nuts.

As she watches the coffee trickle into her mug, she notices someone at her elbow, speaking.

It's Chakravorty.

'Sorry,' Boden says. 'I was miles away.'

'You okay?'

'I'm fine.'

The universal lie.

'We think we've got an ID on the second body. Liam Cox. Remember him? He's one of Jessop's guys.'

'Oh yeah,' says Boden. 'Good work.'

And she paints on a smile.

26

Thursday. 11.15am

Ewan has just finished an oil change when he gets called into the office by Trey.

The day off, the mission, went pretty well. Just him and Jared. When the two brothers work together like that, he feels relaxed, far more relaxed than the rest of the time.

Trey has a big, old-fashioned wooden desk, solid oak, and he loves to swivel around behind it on this stupid leather chair, like he was some top executive. Ewan knows he'd hate it. Stuck behind a desk all day. And it's given Trey a paunch.

Trey steeples his fingers. 'So, big man,' he says. 'Good day off?'

Why's he asking? None of his business.

Ewan shrugs. 'Took my bike out.'

Trey nods, inhales and scratches his head. He seems more distant than usual. 'Got a bit of a problem here, Ewan. But I'm hoping we can sort it out.'

Some customer must've complained. The other

mechanics get this quite often, but it hasn't happened to Ewan.

'Okay,' says Ewan.

'You know Felicia, works in the showroom?'

The dumb bitch who keeps wiggling her arse at him?

He nods.

'She's made a complaint about you.'

Ewan can't help smiling.

What's the complaint? That you haven't fucked her yet?'

Trey is frowning. 'Why are you grinning? This is serious, man. She says you're always staring at her, you make inappropriate noises when you pass her in the corridor, and you deliberately rubbed up against her last week and…well, she thinks you had a hard on.'

Ewan huffs. 'C'mon, bro. The stupid cow is making stuff up.'

Trey shakes his head. He seems pissed off. 'I'm not your bro, Ewan. I'm your boss. And I don't see what motive she'd have for making something like this up.'

'Surely it's obvious.'

'Not to me.'

'Ever since I got here, she's made it clear what she wants.'

Trey has this fancy silver pen and he's tapping it on the desk. 'How do you mean?' he says.

What? You gotta spell it out for the idiot?

'It's obvious. She wants me to give her one. And she's pissed that I haven't.'

Trey stands up, rests his fists on the desk and leans forward, that little belly of his hanging down over his belt. 'Are you serious?' he says. 'I can't believe you're saying this.'

'It's the truth.' He just about stops himself from saying bro.

Trey puts his hands on his hips. He's a good thirty pounds overweight. He needs to get down the gym.

'Okay, look,' he says. 'I know you've been inside, and that's a very macho environment. But it's no excuse. You can't talk about women like that nowadays. It's not cool.'

'Why not?'

Boss or no boss, time to tell him some home truths.

Ewan folds his arms, stands tall. This fool needs to know who he's dealing with here.

'Prison's not so bad,' he says. 'I learned inside how to be a man. And especially how not to get pussy-whipped. I mean, let's get real here. You've got all these girls on sales so that when guys come in to buy a car, they can flash their tits, and flutter their eyelashes and make the sale.'

Trey seems perplexed. He shakes his head. 'Man, you are completely deluded. More than fifty per cent of my customers are women, and many of them like to buy from another woman. I don't know who's been feeding you all this misogynistic bullshit.'

Ewan stares at him. He feels calm, although Trey looks quite riled.

'Well,' says Ewan. 'That's your opinion.'

'It's not just an opinion, Ewan. It's about values, our values as a business, and the crap you're talking is plain wrong. Felicia may have been friendly to you initially. We're a friendly team. And we have a bit of banter, but there's a very clear line. And Felicia's not interested in you. Not in the slightest. She's getting married next month.'

He's taking her side.

Ewan can feel that prickle in his head and the itch in his fingers. You think you can rely on a guy, that he's a mate, a bro. Then, for no good reason, he shafts you. If Ewan had a blade, he knows what he'd do.

Trey is huffing and pacing. He's a big bloke, but out of shape; Ewan could take him, no problem.

Trey shakes his head. 'I'm disappointed in you, Ewan. Really disappointed.'

Cuts both ways.

'And you give me no choice. I'm going to have to let you go.'

Seriously?

'What? Because of that bitch?'

'You are way out of line, man.'

Something in Ewan's head ignites. It's like an explosion, and the energy needs to come out.

He grabs the front of the huge desk with his two hands and heaves it up and over towards Trey. The laptop, a full cup of coffee, a phone, a stack of papers, the posh pen, it all goes flying.

Trey jumps back like a scalded cat.

'What the fuck!' he shouts.

The desk lands on its side with an almighty crash, knocking over the fancy leather chair, and leaving Trey trapped in the corner.

It's quite amusing.

Trey is steaming. He bunches his fist, but he's powerless. Defeated. 'You have got a fucking screw loose!' he shrieks. 'And they are gonna put you back inside. I'm calling the police.'

Ewan raises his middle finger and offers it to Trey. He doesn't speak. Doesn't need to. He's made his point.

Turning on his heel, he strolls out.

27

Thursday. 2.15pm

It's not ideal. The police called Lexi out of the blue saying Mrs Jessop has agreed to meet her. She thought about backing out, but where would that get her? It wouldn't get her the deal.

As she steps off the train, she wonders if it will be the two girls she met before. She hopes not. That will make it more difficult not to speak about Ewan. But here they are, waiting for her. Her heart sinks.

You should tell them.

They escort her to a plain-looking hatchback; she's relieved it's not a squad car. Who wants to be seen, even in Cambridge, being driven away by the police?

On the train, Lexi dozed; she couldn't help it. She was awake most of the night, a bundle of nerves and indecision. Then in the early morning she had a nightmare, the one about the river. A child screaming. She woke enervated and drifting in a mental fog. Then she had to rush around, rescheduling appointments and placating clients. Her laptop decided to play up and, as she struggled to sort that out, Beth was wittering on about some plan she'd come up with in the night. Beth's plans usually involve financial scams and invariably go wrong, so they're best ignored.

She sits in the back seat of the police car and wonders what the hell she's going to say to Mrs Jessop.

What can you say to someone whose husband has been brutally murdered?

It seemed like a good idea when she came up with it. Now, she just feels sick.

The two police officers are quiet, oppressively so.

'Is it far?' she says, really just to break the silence.

'Another half an hour,' says the DS. 'It's out of town.'

Lexi racks her brains for the girl's name. But it's gone. She thinks about Arif Yildiz and Renfrew Hall. She told him she could do this.

Don't lose your nerve, not now.

She knows the technique. When you're overwhelmed with problems, break it all down. Separate them out. Focus on the priority. This afternoon it's making contact with Jessop's wife. Whatever Ewan thinks he's up to, she's fairly sure he hasn't followed her to Cambridge. She sat in first class, in a corner seat, and she could see right down the carriage. She wondered what he looks like now. Would she even recognise him?

The buildings thin out, they turn off the main road and they're in a country lane. Hedgerows, flat, grey-green water-logged fields, flocks of birds rising up from the flooded land. They pass a farm, and Lexi gets curious. This is not the place you'd expect a supposed HNWI like Mr Jessop to live. It's agribusiness; vast fields of cash crops, not much livestock, rural without being in any way picturesque.

A sudden break in the hedge reveals a large single-storey property with a low-pitched roof set well back from the road with a white picket fence and a long wrap around veranda. It's incongruous in this landscape. As they pull up at the high, steel barred gates, a bedraggled horse gazes at them over the fence and tosses its head. It seems the late Mr Jessop built himself a picture perfect American style ranch house with white wooden siding in the middle of the flat East Anglian countryside.

Lexi can't help doing the calculation. It's habit. Despite the terrible location, with stables, land and an assortment of outbuildings, she would value it at a couple of million; it would depend on how much land.

The DS presses the intercom on the gate and says her name.

DS Boden, now she remembers!

The gate slides back, and as they drive in, the front door opens. A woman with a teenage girl clutching her arm appears in the doorway.

'I forgot to mention,' says Boden. 'There are two teenage daughters.'

Kids too. It gets worse.

Lexi and her two escorts get out of the car. Boden leads the way up the steps onto the veranda.

'Good afternoon, Mrs Jessop,' she says.

The woman gives the cop a supercilious scowl. Her fair hair is pinned up in a French pleat, the eyes are puffy, but flinty grey and unrelenting. There's something quite formidable about her. But grief does funny things to people. The girl is thin and clingy, but she has her mother's eyes.

Mrs Jessop turns her gaze to Lexi, but it doesn't soften.

'You'd better come in,' she says. 'But those two can wait in the car.'

This dismissal of the police is as surprising as it is arrogant. But they don't seem that bothered. DS Boden shrugs.

Mrs Jessop leads the way inside and makes a point of slamming the door behind her. Lexi finds herself in an airy modern space with smooth timber flooring the colour of honey. Light filters down from a series of Velux windows in the vaulted ceiling. The overall effect is stunning.

With the detectives banished, Mrs Jessop relaxes. She's wearing leggings and an old T-shirt, but she has a gym-honed body. Dressed up, she'd be every inch the trophy wife. She turns to Lexi.

'Sorry, I can't remember your name.'

'Lexi. Lexi Harper.'

'Kate Jessop.' She squeezes the girl, who's still tucked under her mother's arm. 'This is Imogen, my youngest daughter.'

Lexi smiles at the kid, who looks totally forlorn.

'Well, the first thing I want to say—'

'Yeah,' says Kate sharply. 'Let's go in the kitchen.' She takes the girl by the shoulders. 'Find your sister. I think she's watching something in the den.'

The girl looks reluctant.

'It'll be okay,' says Kate, squeezing her hand.

The kid turns and wanders away through an open archway that leads into what looks like a sitting room.

Kate Jessop, brows puckered, watches her go. She turns to Lexi. 'Since…it happened, she doesn't want to let me out of her sight.'

The grief is there, tightly controlled but raw, just below the surface. This was a happy family; now it's broken.

A cascade of guilt floods through Lexi.

This is all your fault!

'Understandable,' she says.

'Yeah,' says Kate. Then she jerks her head as if to erase a thought. 'Do you like gin?'

'Um…yeah.'

Lexi follows her into the kitchen, predictably large, high tech with gleaming steel cabinets and marble surfaces.

'You have a lovely home,' says Lexi.

Pathetic sales patter.

Kate doesn't reply. She reaches into a cupboard and brings out a bottle of expensive looking artisan gin. 'I had a lovely home,' she says. 'Now I've got a house I'm going to have to sell.'

She pours two hefty slugs into highball glasses and gets a bottle of tonic from the fridge.

The tonic fizzes as she unscrews it. 'I love that sound,' she says. Her chin trembles, but she holds it together. 'Craig worked long hours, but when he got home, it'd be G and T, feet up and chill. This was our ritual, catch up on the day, connect. You married?'

'No, I'm single.'

Those flinty eyes slide away for a second and off into the distance across the flat farmland stretching away outside the large picture window.

Oh shit, you should not be here.

As Kate pours the tonic into the gin, Lexi notices the tremor in her hand. Kate smiles to herself. 'Don't drown it. That's what he'd say.'

She adds ice from a tray in the freezer, then they take their drinks over to the long refectory style table. Lexi counts twelve chairs. Kate invites her to sit at one end.

'Well,' she says. 'You wanted to tell me something?'

Lexi feels a rush of panic. This is so wrong. She realises that now.

'I'm not sure where to start…'

Kate's chin goes up, but there are tears welling in her eyes.

'The police said you were there when…'

'Yeah. I tried to…do what I could to help, but there was a lot of blood.'

An involuntary shudder goes through Kate Jessop.

This is awful. You're making her pain worse.

But Lexi ploughs on. What choice does she have? 'It was hard to make out what he said. But I think he was talking about you…and your daughters…he wanted you to know how much he loved you. And I promised him I'd come and tell you.'

Kate's head dips down. She grips the glass until her knuckles are white. Her whole body convulses with silent sobs.

'I'm so sorry,' says Lexi.

She doesn't realise how sorry, poor woman.

Neither of them speaks for several moments. Lexi waits. She sips the gin; it helps. Her eye strays out of the window. There are three more horses in a field at the back. There's money here, but Kate just said she'd have to sell. Lexi wonders if this is a matter of emotional or financial necessity? Could be either.

Kate raises her head. She's classy, dignified in the way she holds herself, but did she grow up accustomed to all this? Hard to say? Her dislike of the police is blatant, which is not quite the attitude Lexi would've expected, and suggests some of the stuff written about her husband online could be true.

She reaches across the table and brushes Lexi's hand with her fingers. 'Thank you for coming,' she says. 'And for trying to…well, you know. It can't have been pleasant for you.'

Is that it? Meeting over.

Lexi sighs. 'Well, I hope it brings you some comfort.'

If you're going to do it, it has to be now.

Lexi opens her bag and pulls out a business card. 'I hope this isn't inappropriate or offensive to you, but your husband was our client. If I can do anything in the future, with regard to Renfrew Hall…or whatever, I'd be only too pleased to help you. Just call me.'

Kate Jessop's eyes harden.

Oh shit. That didn't go down too well.

Then she says, 'Did the police ask you to question me about Renfrew Hall?'

'Oh my god, no.' The surprise is genuine, and that seems to have an effect.

Kate is scrutinising her. 'I thought that's why they brought you, to get information.'

Why wouldn't she want to give the police information?

You know why.

'They said nothing to me. And it was my idea to come here.'

'Your idea?'

'Yes.'

There's an awkward silence. Kate is intently scanning her, and it's not a comfortable sensation.

'Sorry,' says Kate, tossing her head. 'I am grateful to you for coming.'

Read the client. Answer the question they're not asking. That's what Roger taught you.

'We deal in the super prime property market,' says Lexi. 'We have some extremely high-profile clients, many from overseas, and confidentiality is an absolute priority with us.' She hesitates. 'It may be why your husband chose us.'

Kate nods. She glances at the card.

'Thanks again for coming,' she says briskly, and she stands up.

Lexi stands up too. 'Please accept my sincere condolences,' she says.

She follows Kate out of the kitchen and towards the front door.

The property business is tough, and she's pulled a few strokes in her career that she's not proud of, but nothing like this. This is a new low and she feels deeply ashamed. This is not who she is.

28

Thursday. 3.15pm

Beth joins the slow stream of people being funnelled through a labyrinth of corridors and checkpoints towards the security scanners. First there's a walk-through metal detector archway, where she's instructed to empty her pockets and place her bag in the tray. This is a bit like the airport, so it's not so bad. Then there's the full body scanner, which looks like something out of a sci-fi movie. Belmarsh is a high-security jail, that's why it has all this stuff.

She moves up for her turn and is directed to step inside the circular chamber. An eerie beam rotates around her, tracing over the contours of her body. This is the intrusive bit; they can see everything, probably including what you had for lunch. She watches the blank face of the guard above his screen as he scans her image for any hidden contraband.

Once she emerges the other side and collects her bag, a stoney-faced woman in blue vinyl gloves pats her down. The place smells of body odour and disinfectant; it's revolting. But she's doing this for Lexi. It's the only way.

It took her about half an hour on the phone, being passed from pillar to post, to blag a visit at short notice. She finally got to speak to a woman officer who was sympathetic and agreed to allow it on compassionate grounds.

Damian is on remand awaiting trial, and such prisoners are granted more access to visitors, including their lawyers and family. A pregnant girlfriend ticks that box.

Beth makes it through to the visitors' pen. A harsh overhead light illuminates a row of cubicles divided by thick reinforced glass. On the other side are the prisoners, seated and waiting. She checks her number. Seventeen. As she walks along the row, it's a bit like the viewing area of an aquarium except the specimens are human.

She gets to her allotted cubicle and there he is. His face lights up with joy at the sight of her and her heart melts. She can't help it. He's so gorgeous!

This is such a bad idea.

He grabs the telephone receiver on the side of the cubicle and puts it to his ear. She sits down and picks up her handset.

'I'm so glad you came,' he says. 'I thought we were done.'

'Well,' says Beth. 'Don't know what they told you?'

'Just said you were coming. Only told me about an hour ago. I was over the moon, because I've been talking to my lawyers, and they're pretty hopeful this can all be sorted out.'

'You mean without a trial?'

'Maybe.'

Beth doesn't know much about the law. Okay, she's aware Damian was selling drugs. But how is that such a big deal that they keep you in jail? Why couldn't he get bail?

'Exactly,' Lexi had said to her. 'Think about this Beth.'

And Beth had thought about it. She and Lexi had discussed it, too.

Damian has a brother. She's met him a couple of times. He's older and Beth got the impression he ran things. Damian once admitted that he was scared of his brother. Said he'd done some bad shit. But that wasn't Damian; she knew it in her heart. All the times she's gazed into his eyes. Okay, he's a bit bent, but not a wicked man, not really. She's encountered some psychos in her life. She can tell the difference.

Lexi's opinion is that Damian's brother is a gangster, which is lucky, because that's what they need.

Beth looks at Damian through the glass. He's still got a bit of a swagger. Even in grey prisoner sweats, he's still such a cool dude, and the sight of him still gives her a fluttery feeling in her tummy. It could be love. She's never been that sure what love is. She knows about sex, desire, pleasure, but love?

'I'm here because there's something I need to tell you,' she says. 'I'm pregnant.'

It's another twelve days before she can take an actual test, but she's pretty sure it'll be positive. That so-called nurse used a speculum to make sure the sperm went right up inside her, so why wouldn't she be? It hurt enough.

'Babe!' says Damian, clenching his fist in a victory salute. 'Wow! I mean, wow! That's made my day.'

And she's glad. Being locked up must be depressing.

Explaining to him why the baby looks half-Chinese is a task for another day. She's got time to figure something out.

'How far gone are you?' he says.

Beth is not stupid. She's done her calculations. It's been three weeks since he was arrested. The last time they slept together was a few days before that.

'I wasn't sure,' she says. 'Did a test last week.'

'I can't believe we're going to be parents. And I am going to get out of this place, I promise you.' He's so excited. It's really touching. He'd be such a great dad, too.

'The reason I didn't come before,' she says, 'is I've had a few problems.'

'What sort of problems?'

'I needed somewhere to stay, and Lexi arranged for me to house-sit a place for her. A fancy apartment in that new block near Tate Modern. Just a temporary thing.'

For some reason, Damian is not that keen on Lexi. Beth wonders if he's jealous because she and Lexi are so close.

'If I'd known, I could've found you somewhere,' he says.

The flat they'd been sharing was ransacked by the police. The floorboards were ripped up, the bedding and furniture slashed. They even took Beth's laptop. He didn't mention that. It's a sore point.

'I know,' she says. 'And I know you and Lexi don't always see eye to eye.'

'I got no problem with her. She's the one got a problem with me.'

'I've known her forever, and she looks out for me. And you are in here.'

He shrugs. 'Can't argue with that.'

He is so good-looking, it's unfair. If he was bald or had bad breath, or treated her badly, this would be far easier. She finds herself drifting off into a fantasy about what might have been if she was having his baby and he wasn't in jail.

Concentrate.

'Okay, babe,' she says. 'Here's the thing. And this is a bit complicated. Lexi's got a cousin, bit younger than us. We used to hang out as kids. And he's after us.'

'What d'you mean after you? What does he want?'

'That's a good question. It's all just bad family stuff, going way back. Anyway, he's been following Lexi.'

'Like stalking her?'

'Yeah, and she went to meet a client at this huge fancy million pound estate out in Hertfordshire. He got there before her and slit the guy's throat.'

Damian's eyes widen. 'Are you serious? Who is this guy?'

'He's been inside. Just got out. He's on licence. Went down at fourteen for stabbing another kid. I'm telling you babe, he is batshit crazy.'

'Why doesn't she just tell the cops what happened?'

'She's got no proof. We know it's him, but you know what the cops are like.'

'Certainly do,' he says with some bitterness.

'And there's also a problem in terms of her job. If her bosses find out this has happened because of her, they'll sack her. It's all totally unfair. She doesn't deserve this.'

She waits. He's got that little puckered bit between his eyebrows that he does when he's thinking. She wishes she could reach out and touch him. It's such a physical yearning.

'I think,' he says, 'for the time being, you need to steer clear of her. I know she's your friend but...'

'He's after me, too. I should've said that. Sending texts, threatening. He knows if he hurts me, he hurts Lexi. He put a snake through her letterbox.'

'What? A live snake? Was it poisonous?'

'Probably.'

Damian sighs. 'Okay, I'm going to have a word with... y'know.' He gives her a direct look and nods. 'The important thing is, I don't want you to worry. You need to take care of yourself and our baby. You'll get a call.'

She smiles. 'Thank you,' she says. 'I'm really missing you, y'know. All I want is to snuggle up.'

And it's the truth.

She can see the tears in his amazing green eyes. He brushes his nose with his hand. He's too choked to speak.

They sit quietly for a few moments.

Then, for the rest of the visit, they talk about babies and baby names. He wants Albie for a boy after his granddad, and Ivy for a girl. She's okay with Albie, but prefers Willow for a girl. It's lovely imagining their child and the family they'll have. Okay, it's a fantasy, but a nice one.

Belmarsh is a bit of a trek out into south east London. To get back to the apartment, Beth takes a bus, then the Jubilee Line from North Greenwich. The journey is over an hour. As she walks from Southwark station back towards her temporary home, it starts to rain. She shelters under a shop awning and her phone rings.

'That Beth?' says a male voice.

'Yep.'

'You got a name for me?'

It's the only way out. Best all round.

'Ewan Burns.'

'Address?'

'Think he's staying at his dad's. In Luton. Number twenty-four, Portland Way.'

The phone goes dead. No sign off. Beth stares at the screen for a moment. Unknown Caller on her calls list. She deletes it.

She smiles to herself. Done and dusted. Lexi will be relieved.

It's pouring now. Noticing a coffee shop a few doors along, she scampers down the road towards it. She plans to

buy herself a large hot chocolate with cream and marshmallows. She deserves it.

29

Thursday. 4.30pm

The cops drop Lexi back at the station. She heads straight for the nearest shop and grabs two cans of ready mixed gin and tonic from the fridge. Her encounter with Kate Jessop has thrown her into a downward spiral of regret and remorse. More alcohol seems like the only solution.

The drive back into town in the police car was silent and uncomfortable. DS Boden asked her how it went. She replied, 'Horrible.' They left her alone after that. Any possibility of discussing her cousin flew out of the window. She could hardly trust herself to speak. Did they realise what a manipulative piece of shit she is?

When she got out of the car, DS Boden said, 'I'm really sorry, Lexi. For what it's worth, I don't think we should have put you through that.'

This made it ten times worse. If only they knew.

'I offered,' said Lexi. 'Thanks for the ride.' And she scuttled away like a rat.

Her train is cancelled and the next one delayed. By the time she boards, there are no seats in first class. It's packed, although she finds a seat opposite an elderly couple who watch her consume her second G and T as if she's an alcoholic. But she's beyond caring.

When she gets to King's Cross, it's peak rush hour and the queue at the taxi rank winds halfway round the building. She opts for the tube. Three large drinks on an empty stomach and she's tipsy. The shoving and buffeting she suffers as she navigates her way to the platform and onto a packed underground train bounces off her.

As she hangs to the rail, her eyes dart from face to face, wondering if her cousin is here concealed in the tightly packed mass of passengers. Is this where it happens? A knife slipped between the ribs? It would be so easy.

The second body at Renfrew Hall could've been you.

But she survives the tube journey and arrives back at the apartment, wet and frazzled.

Beth is waiting for her with a bottle of champagne on ice and two crystal flutes.

Removing her raincoat and dumping her umbrella in the kitchen sink, Lexi gives her friend a quizzical look. 'What's this in aid of?'

'We're celebrating.'

She frowns. 'Celebrating what?'

'I've solved the problem of Ewan.'

Lexi stares at her, as her fuddled brain grapples with this statement.

'What?' she says.

'He's not going to bother you anymore.'

'How do you know?'

Beth's gaze slips off to one side and she scrunches up her

nose. This is what she does when she's been up to no good, doesn't want to lie, but can't tell the truth.

'Babe, it's best you don't ask too many questions,' she says.

Lexi has a plummeting sensation. She knows instantly; they're headed for the abyss.

WTF has she done now!

'Beth,' she says, in an ominous tone, 'tell me you haven't done something really stupid.'

'Why do you immediately jump to that conclusion?' says her friend with a pout. 'That is so not fair, Lex. I've been all the bloody way to Belmarsh for you this afternoon. Plus, I've lied to a guy that I actually quite like.'

'You've been to see Damian?'

'Yes.'

'You told me, you promised me you were done with him.'

Beth is getting antsy and annoyed. She shovels her fingers through her hair. 'Yeah, and that was the truth. But there was no other way to sort this out. Ewan is crazy and fucking dangerous. He could kill you, babe. What the hell was I supposed to do? You said you couldn't go to the police.'

Lexi stares at her. She has a splitting headache, and an eerie feeling that if this situation was bad before, it just got a hundred times worse.

'I didn't,' she says, with as much calmness as she can muster. 'I haven't decided yet.'

Too late now.

'Whatever,' says Beth with a flounce of her blonde mane.

She doesn't think she's done anything wrong. Beth may come over as an angelic cherub, too beautiful to be bad. The reality is she's also a toxic pixie.

Lexi plonks down on a stool, leans her elbows on the kitchen counter, and puts her face in her hands.

'So you don't want any champagne?' says Beth in a petulant voice.

Lexi raises her head. 'What I want is for you to tell me exactly what you've done.'

Beth exhales, more a huff. 'Look,' she says. 'It'll work. That's all you need to know. Ewan will be gone.'

'Gone where?'

'He'll be dealt with.'

'Dealt with? What are we talking about here?'

'I don't know. I told Damian he was threatening me. He said, well he implied, someone would sort it out.'

Lexi could throttle her.

'How?'

Beth is squirming now, but there's no way Lexi is letting her off the hook.

She's not so innocent. She knows what she's arranged.

'How Beth?'

Tears are forming in those cornflower blue eyes, but Lexi is too furious to care.

'I did this for you,' Beth wails.

'What are they going to do? Beat him up? Kill him?'

'I don't know.'

'Didn't you think to ask?'

'I…Damian said he didn't want me to worry.'

Lexi shakes her head. 'Let me get this clear. You'd dumped him. But now you rock up and tell him what? How come he's so eager to leap to your defence?'

Beth gazes at her, eyes full of tears. 'I just told him I was pregnant.'

Lexi picks up Beth's phone and flings it across the counter at her. 'Call him. Call him now and tell him to stop this.'

'I can't.'

Lexi grabs the phone. 'Okay, then I will.'

'Lexi don't! You'll get him in trouble. And anyway, he'll just have spoken to his brother. Y'know, it gets passed down the line. Once the wheels are in motion…'

Lexi can't remember when she was last this angry. If ever.

She folds her arms. She's jittery with adrenaline and the remnants of the booze, but her thoughts are sharp with rage.

'The wheels are in motion? By this you mean you've arranged to have someone maim or kill my cousin. On my behalf. And presumably you've given them his name and where to find him.?'

Beth's gaze skitters to the floor.

She has!

Inside, Lexi is incandescent, but her voice is icy. 'You're part of a conspiracy to commit murder. And you've implicated me in it. Is this what you're telling me?'

'I did it to protect you. You've seen what Ewan can do. He's a killer. I'm sorry if you think I've overstepped—'

'Overstepped?'

Inside Lexi, the last shred of control snaps. The words explode from her, laced with venom. 'You're a liar and a criminal, Beth. I don't know why I'm surprised. It's what you've always been, isn't it? But I've ignored it. Let you play me. So the fucking joke's on me now, isn't it?'

Beth is sobbing. 'We've always looked out for each other. I was only trying to—'

Lexi holds up her hand. 'No, Beth! Just no. I won't be part of this. We're done.'

'You don't mean that.'

They stand facing each other. Lexi can feel her heart thumping.

'I do. Pack your stuff. Get out. Now.'

'Where will I go?'

'I don't know. And I don't care. And don't tell me you're pregnant. That's just another one of your scams. You come near me again, I'll go straight to the police with all of this. They'll arrest you.'

You should do that anyway.

Beth sinks to her knees, crying like a child.

A frustrated toddler, more like.

Lexi stares at her. 'Oh, spare me the melodrama. I know all your tricks. I'm going to take a shower. When I come out, if you're still here, I'll call the police.'

30

Thursday. 7pm.

Beth rocks back on her heels as the bedroom door slams shut behind Lexi. Some bad shit has happened in her life. People have said vile and malicious things to her; water off a duck's back.

But this is Lexi! The cruelty of her friend's words cut like a knife. Is that what she really thinks? Why would she turn on Beth like this? It makes no sense.

You did this for her!

Why doesn't she see that?

Beth stands up; her limbs feel like lead. She wipes her face with the back of her hand. She's quivering all over. They should be drinking champagne, not this. It's a nightmare. Lexi can rant, but Beth's never seen this sort of anger from her before. Icy cold, like she doesn't care.

She wanders into the main bedroom. Does Lexi really expect her to pack up and go? No, she'll calm down in the shower. She'll change her mind. They'll sort it out. They always do.

She's giddy, and not in a good way. A little worm of doubt is wriggling through her brain.

She's never been mad like this.

Beth picks up her underwear from the floor and tosses it on the bed. She can't stop her hand from shaking. It was like a barrage, a tornado of hatred. From her best friend!

She sits down on the bed. She needs to calm herself.

To be honest, Lexi is being a complete bitch about this. Okay, she's stressed, but that's because of Ewan. So all the more reason she should be thanking Beth for finding a solution. And she isn't. Quite the opposite. She's dumping all her anger on Beth, which is completely unfair. And the things she said…

But brooding is no good. The more you think sometimes, the worse things get. She pulls her suitcase out of the cupboard, but her head won't stop. It just keeps churning it all over.

What has Beth done to deserve this?

Fuck all!

She's a loyal friend. Rock solid. They don't always see eye to eye, but that's what matters. That's at the heart of everything, knowing who you can trust, knowing who's always got your back.

Beth wipes away another tear.

You've always been there for her. Always.

Lexi can get snotty about legal niceties, but she's never called Beth a criminal before. She knows full well Beth has only ever ripped off the kind of nasty bastards who thoroughly deserved it, or people who were so loaded they didn't care. She's shoplifted, which is technically a crime, but only from big stores, and they just write it off. No one is actually harmed.

Lexi may think she's got no conscience, but that's not fair, either. She considered carefully the implications of going to Damian for help. Shit, it took some planning! Of course, she thought about it.

And she's tried not to dwell on what Damian's brother, Marcus, might do to Ewan. But he's not going to murder him! They'll just beat him up a bit. The point is she had to make a choice, and the choice was to protect her friend. Ewan is a cold-blooded killer; he cuts people's throats. And Lexi did definitely say she couldn't go to the cops because she'd lose her job.

Beth is getting wound up, and it's because of the injustice of Lexi's behaviour. It's getting to her. Hauling an armful of clothes from the wardrobe, she dumps them in the suitcase. She tops it off with the contents of the drawers. She barges into the en suite and sweeps the toiletries and makeup into a large plastic bag, adds them to the suitcase and bangs it shut.

She's agitated now, and nearly forgets her shoes. Re-opening the case, she tosses them in.

As she wheels the suitcase down the hall, she can hear the shower in Lexi's en suite bathroom. Part of her wants to storm in and give her friend a piece of her mind. But that won't help. Lexi is stubborn and has a slick argument for everything. And she always thinks she's right. But not this time. She needs to learn that she can't treat Beth like this and expect her to take it. There will be consequences.

Beth positions her case by the front door, takes her coat off the rack and puts it on top of the case, then she goes back down the hall and opens the door to Lexi's bedroom. Inside, Lexi's clothes are arranged in an anally neat pile on the bed, with her bag next to them. The door to the en suite is ajar, tiny billows of steam are escaping into the room.

Tiptoeing forward, Beth crosses to the bed, picks up the bag, extracts Lexi's wallet and sorts through her credit cards. She returns the personal cards to the wallet and selects the business credit card. Lexi doesn't use it that much, so that should give her a couple of days' grace before anyone twigs it's been lifted. Anyway, it's the firm's money, Gemma's money, not her friend's.

She pockets the card and creeps out. The shower goes off, but she's already halfway down the hall.

Opening the front door, she wheels her case out, slips her coat on, and heads for the lift.

What will Lexi think when she finds Beth has gone? Maybe it'll bring her to her senses, and she'll realise what a total cow she's been.

As the lift arrives, Beth remembers that she's left the champagne in the kitchen. A bottle of Veuve, not cheap rubbish. Oh well.

Riding down in the lift, she scrolls on her phone. There's a Travelodge near the Shard listing rooms for £75; that'll do for now. With a contactless limit of a hundred on the business card in her pocket, that won't be a problem.

She's feeling defiant. Lexi has to learn that she can't treat her best friend like this.

31

Thursday. 9.30pm

The smell of pepperoni and melted cheese fills the small living room. Ewan and Jared are sprawled on the threadbare sofa, pizza box between them, cold beers on the table, eyes fixed on the TV. They're watching one of the Mission Impossible movies; Ewan loves them, mostly because of all the motorcycle stunts.

On screen, Tom Cruise launches his bike off the roof of a building and lands on the building next door in an impossible stunt.

Bussin'!

'Can you do that?' says Jared with a mischievous grin.

Ewan looks at him. 'One day,' he says. 'It'll be me up there doing movie stunts, then the smile'll be on the other side of your stupid face.'

Jared laughs and punches the air. 'You go for it, bro!'

Ewan raises his can of beer. 'I will.'

Suddenly he gets this rush of warmth. Just hanging with

his brother always does the trick. It helps him get back on his game and brush off the crap. And today was crap.

Getting sacked doesn't bother him; he'll get another job. What's nettled him is Trey's attitude. The whole thing is total bollocks. Ewan feels let down; he thought Trey was one of the good guys. Why would he take the side of some stupid bitch? It just goes to show you never know who you can trust.

But he has his brother.

He holds up his fist. 'Love you, man.'

Jared bumps it with his. 'Faggot,' he says with a chuckle.

There's a burst of gunfire on screen. Ear splitting, which is why Ewan doesn't hear the hammering on the front door.

Bang bang bang. He hears it this time.

He huffs. Here we go. This has happened a couple of times since he's been home; the cops get called because the old man has been found passed out drunk. They bring him home, so it becomes Ewan's problem. He's not happy. Why can't they stick him a cell to sober up?

Putting down his beer can, Ewan pauses the movie with the handset and heads for the front door.

'He pukes everywhere, you can clear it up this time,' he says over his shoulder to Jared, who gives him the finger.

The front door shudders with another thump.

'Yeah, all right. I'm coming,' mutters Ewan.

He opens the door, but it's not the boys in blue. Two blokes, black hoodies. Ewan has spent enough time inside to know who and what they are.

The one at the front, larger and older, eyeballs him.

'Ewan?' he says.

'Depends who's asking.'

'Just want a quick chat. Can we come in?'

Ewan answers by slamming the door in their faces. He

scoots back to the kitchen, wrenches open a drawer and pulls out a sharp little boning knife. He waits.

They take two goes to boot the door in. It collapses inwards, hinges broken, lock twisted and gouging half the wood from the doorjamb. It always was a crappy door. Ewan's been meaning to get it fixed.

The big one appears in the hallway, baseball bat in hand. He's built like a heavyweight boxer, grey hair slicked right back, large eagle tattoo on his neck. The kind of old school bruiser who thinks he's still invincible.

He sighs. 'That's not very friendly,' he says. 'We just want a word.'

Ewan steps out of the kitchen. 'Who sent you? Trey? 'Cause I tipped over his stupid desk.'

The two of them exchange glances. The guy behind is much younger, skinny, armed with a large wrench. He shrugs.

The first one says 'We don't know any Trey. Now, I suggest you put that knife down, son, or you could get hurt.'

In your fucking dreams.

'What do you want?' says Ewan.

'It's been brought to our attention that you've been threatening two young ladies.'

'Don't know what you're talking about.'

'Our information is a snake was involved.'

Ewan stands stock still. There's a rushing in his head, but he's calm. Okay. This is her, his stupid cousin. She's finally got the message. She's sent them. But he's glad. Game on.

In the moments before combat, time slows to a trickle. Every soldier knows this. Elation replaces any fear. He tightens his grip on the boning knife.

Swift and strong.

The bruiser, smug bastard, is staring right at him. 'I can see you know what I'm talk—'

In a flash, Ewan raises his arm and slashes. But the bruiser is fast. He parries with the bat, knocking Ewan sideways. The knife goes flying and they crash into the hall table. As Ewan's head hits the wall, a fist slams into his gut, driving the air from his lungs, and he goes down.

Spots dance in his vision. The pain in his chest is sharp and makes him gasp. But he's been in enough prison yard brawls. He's used to getting hurt; you have to ignore it.

Stay down. Let him think he's won.

Ewan moans, making out he's injured. The knife has landed inches away under the smashed table. He can see it out of the corner of his eye.

The bruiser looms over him and sighs. 'That was a bit stupid, wasn't it?'

Ewan gazes up at him, paints on a pitiful look.

'I don't know what you want.'

'I want you to listen, son.'

Ewan's fingers edge towards the boning knife.

'Yeah, but whatever you been told…it's crap, I promise you.'

His hand closes on the knife. He takes a deep breath and leaps to his feet. This time he catches the bruiser off guard. He lunges, aiming for the ear, and rips the knife down across his throat.

The bruiser staggers backwards, clutching his neck, eyes bulging with shock, as the blood pulses between his fingers.

Fucker wasn't expecting that.

Nor was the other guy. He sort of half catches the bruiser as he collapses. Ewan rams the knife in the other guy's gut. Then yanks it out. The guy lets out a pathetic whimper as he goes down, landing on the bruiser, who's twitching as he bleeds out.

Ewan looks down. He has blood on his trainers which is a

annoying; they're brand new. Then he realises Jared is watching him from the lounge doorway.

'What the absolute fuck?' says his brother, hands on hips.

'They came steaming in here,' says Ewan. 'Kicked the door in. I had no choice.'

Jared shakes his head in annoyance. 'Shit, man, we need to get out of here. Like now.'

Ewan sighs. He's not wrong about that. And they haven't even seen the end of the movie.

32

Friday. 8.45am

Lexi queues at her favourite coffee shop on Baker Street. It's close to the office, but not too close, an upmarket indie with a relaxed ambience. They know her and greet her like a pal.

'Hey. How's it going?' Big smiles, music in the background. Dua Lipa?

'Fine.'

What else is she going to say?

This is their schtick: pretending their customers are buddies and bringing a villagey feel to this wealthy enclave in central London. But this morning their chumminess, however fake, is welcome.

The row with Beth kept her awake most of the night. She slept shortly before dawn, had the usual nightmare, and woke with a stress headache and a sense of doom. She was feeling bad enough about what she'd done to Kate Jessop before Beth added her little zinger.

Of all the brainless schemes Beth has come up with over

the years, and there have been a few, this takes the biscuit. But Lexi blames herself. As soon as she figured that her cousin Ewan could be behind the murder at Renfrew Hall, she should've taken it straight to the police. Her hesitation opened the door to Beth's lunacy.

But what now?

She's sinking deeper into a moral quagmire of her own making. What if Ewan turns up dead, which is likely. What then? How can she explain that away? The police won't believe anything she says. At best, she'll be an accessory to murder. At worst, she'll be charged as part of a joint conspiracy.

How did all this happen? And so fast. She didn't realise what was going on. The tsunami came from nowhere, seized her and swept her away.

She doesn't think about her childhood. She's worked hard to put all that behind her. Ewan was a casualty. She recognises that. But so was she. It wasn't all her fault, and she can't bear the responsibility for what he turned into; we all make our own choices. Ewan certainly made his.

The one that faces Lexi now is what to do about Renfrew Hall. And she's made up her mind. This is what she should've done all along: she'll tell Yildiz she can't do it and walk away. She may end up losing her job, but there are other firms. At least she'll salvage her integrity and self-respect.

She arrives at the office and finds it bustling with activity. Everyone is trying to appear busy. Then she sees why. Roger Cavendish is lounging in an armchair in his daughter's office.

He doesn't come in much anymore, but when he does, it's like a visit from royalty. All the younger brokers are hoping to get noticed.

Lexi is badly in need of the opposite, a day of respite

when she can slide unseen under the radar. Now that seems unlikely.

She's settling at her desk and swapping her trainers for heels, when Pia bobs up like an overexcited puppy.

'Gemma and Roger would like a word,' she says in tones of awe.

'Right,' says Lexi. 'Thanks.'

'Shall I…tell them you're coming?'

Shoe in one hand, Lexi looks up at her. The bright and blank expectancy on her face screams: pat me, give me a treat. If Pia had a tail, it would always be wagging. Tempting as it is to say something cutting, Lexi reins herself in. Being smart at Pia's expense is mean, and she doesn't need her own ethical standards to crash any further.

'Yeah. Thanks,' she says. 'I'll be right there.'

'Okay,' says Pia, and off she trots.

Lexi gets a moleskin notebook out of her bag. Look professional, look busy.

As she strolls across the room to the boss's corner office, she adopts an expression of serenity and calm.

Breathe. In for three, hold for four, out for five.

She taps politely on the door, although father and daughter have already turned towards her. And there's a tension between them, a distinct froideur, which is interesting.

'Morning,' says Gemma with a brittle smile. She's behind the desk, but if this is her attempt to establish authority, it's not convincing. Roger, all smiles, is on his feet and moving the other armchair for Lexi to sit on.

She smiles at him. 'Thank you.'

He inclines his head. Once they're all settled, he steeples his fingers, a typical Roger gesture, and says, 'Tell us about your lunch with Arif Yildiz.'

'The invite came out of the blue. He was very charming.'

'That's a first,' says Roger.

'As I told you, he's interested in Renfrew Hall, but at a knock down price.'

'The whole thing's ridiculous,' says Gemma. 'We should just walk away. I don't care about the money. We can't be seen to be pushy; a man's died. There's a criminal investigation. It's not worth the reputational damage.'

Easy for her to say.

Lexi looks at her. The way she raises her head and flicks back her hair; the snooty disdain. Yildiz is right about her. She is a charmless harpy, and without her old man's backing, she'd be nothing.

But she's also right. And you should agree with her.

'What's your view, Lexi?' says Roger.

Lexi is ticking with annoyance, and, at this moment in time, there's no way she can agree with Gemma Cavendish. All she wants, and she wants it with every molecule of her being, is to grind the self-important diva to a pulp. She wants to win.

She raises her eyebrows. 'Well,' she says, 'we need to be cautious, extremely cautious. But I have put out some feelers, as you suggested, Roger, and I've already made contact with Kate Jessop, Craig Jessop's wife.'

Roger grins and shoots a look of paternal benevolence at his daughter. Then he wags a finger at her. 'You see, Gem, I told you, Lexi is the one person I trust to bring to this deal the sort of finesse it needs.'

Gemma glares at him like a spoilt toddler on the brink of a meltdown. But she keeps her mouth shut.

Roger is looking smug. Of course he is. The reality of what's happened sweeps over Lexi, making her moment of triumph hollow. Once again, he's played them off against one another. If she succeeds, the firm makes money. Potentially a lot of money. If she fails, it'll be on her, he lets Gemma boot her out, and he finds another hungry and rash young broker to step into her shoes. For him, it's all an exercise in managing his delightful daughter.

She smiles her best smile, but her insides are a free fall. Besides being an awful cliché, 'go with your gut' is one of the worst pieces of advice on the planet. It also ignores what your gut contains and is preparing to expel from your body. Best not to dwell on that.

Lexi has broken her own cardinal rule: in business, check your emotions at the door. Never let them dictate your behaviour.

You did the opposite. Why?

How could she be so mind-numbingly stupid?

'Well,' says Roger Cavendish with his famously rakish grin. 'We're in your hands, Lexi.'

It sounds like a threat.

33

Friday. 9.30am

DCI Knight stands, arms folded, right next to Boden's desk, looming over her. She has a scowl on her face. Boden is forced to lean back in her chair and look up at her.

'I just don't understand this, Jo,' Knight says in a condescending tone. 'You take the witness to see Jessop's wife. You let them talk alone. And you don't question her afterwards. Why not?'

'I didn't think it was appropriate. Or useful.'

The DCI is frustrated and cross, and Boden is in the firing line. 'I always thought you were a smart officer, but apparently not. Do you even realise what we're dealing with here?'

'A murder?'

'This woman is a property agent. A villain involved in a multi-million pound property deal gets his throat cut. Hasn't it occurred to you that this could be the tip of a much larger iceberg?'

You hope.

Boden stares back at her. The belligerence, the aggressive stance, is a mask for her insecurity. Five days in and the case is progressing too slowly, but that's no excuse for the boss trying to bully her.

Sod this!

Scooting her chair back, Boden stands up. Now she has the height advantage. Knight takes an involuntary step back.

'Yes, that has occurred to me,' says Boden evenly. 'But I don't think that justifies putting inappropriate pressure on a witness. The way I was trained to be a detective is to follow the evidence.'

In the wider office it's eerily quiet, just the clack of the odd keyboard. But although Boden's colleagues are all glued to their screens or busily scrolling on their phones, everyone is listening.

'Oh, yes, I was forgetting,' says Knight, her voice dripping with sarcasm. 'Your superior training in the Met. I suppose we're all a bunch of country bumpkins to you.'

Boden meets her gaze. 'Hardly,' she says.

'So educate me, Sergeant. What would you do? If God helps us, you were in charge.'

'Okay,' says Boden. 'We've got two bodies now. Jessop and his sidekick, Liam Cox. I've encountered Cox before, came up as a street dealer. Tough, not an easy man to kill. So why was he taken by surprise? And why did this all happen at Renfrew Hall? We've got a caretaker, Mason Green, and he's clearly lying. He's the key to this. There must've been comings and goings to set up a hit like this. Is he just scared or was he paid off? Or both? I'd start by putting pressure on him. Then maybe we get some vehicles we can trace. As for Kate Jessop, that's a hiding to nothing. She's angry, she's grieving, and she hates the police. Whatever her solution to all this is, it won't include us.'

Knight is staring straight at her. Her face is blank and impossible to read. There's a heavy silence in the room.

Well, she asked.

A crooked smirk creeps over the DCI's face. She shrugs and says calmly, 'Welcome back to the team, DS Boden. Now we have your full attention, go and see Mason Green and get him to talk.'

What the…?

It's a bit like being slapped.

DCI Knight smiles, pivots on her smart kitten heels and marches off across the office. Everyone avoids her eye, concentrating on their screens. She disappears through the swing doors which flap shut behind her.

Conversation bubbles up again, as Boden sinks down into her chair. Chakravorty comes and perches on the edge of her desk. She's grinning from ear to ear. 'You've been sand-bagged,' she says.

Boden shakes her head and chuckles. 'I certainly have.'

How did Knight even know that her mind was not on the job? And the truth is, it hasn't been. She's been mooning about Cal, feeling resentful about the DCI's approach, and wishing she was somewhere else.

Not only did Rachel Knight notice what she was up to, she understands Boden's psychology well enough to know how to call her out about it.

She got you. You deserved it.

The DCI may be brutal in her methods, but she's sharp, observant and nothing gets past her. That's how she's risen so quickly through the ranks. Despite her recent fall from grace because of her husband's skulduggery, she's still good at the job.

Shaking her head, Boden smiles ruefully to herself. Then she stands up, puts her phone in her bag and turns to Chakravorty. 'Right,' she says. 'Let's get on with it.'

34

Friday. 9.35am

Beth unlocks the door to the apartment and slips in. She's kept her key, obviously. Coming back is strange and a bit sad, because the place had become like home. All this light and space. It hits you even before you get to the main room.

Of course, Lexi is long gone; Beth knows her routine. It's a shorter journey to work for Lexi from here, but Beth factored that in. She was up early and in the cafe across the road, consuming a bacon roll, when Lexi walked past.

Trainers on, striding out, Lexi looked fraught. Serves her right. Beth was tempted to run out and accost her. Lexi could've apologised and everything could've been sorted. But it's probably a bit soon for that. Lexi's a sulker; sometimes she finds it hard to let stuff go.

Beth finished her breakfast, did a bit of random scrolling, and messaged a few mates. A girl she's met a couple of times sent her a party invite. Then she strolled across the road and into the building. The concierge wasn't bothered. He gave her a friendly nod, and Beth was carrying her second Latte Macchiato, so he probably assumed she'd just popped out for it.

To be honest, she's not sure why she's doing this. Okay, there's the champagne and few other bits and bobs, which are definitely hers that she wants to collect. The perfume Damian gave her for starters; two hundred quid a bottle.

As she wanders down the hall and into the main room, she notices it's been vacuumed, and the floor in the kitchen area washed. Lexi has blitzed the place. She must've been up half the night doing housework. She's completely OCD. The kitchen work tops have been wiped and cleared of clutter. The sink smells of bleach. Beth opens the fridge; that's been cleaned out, too. The half-eaten pot of yogurt is gone, the cheese, the bag of salad, but her bottle of Veuve is in the door slot. Even Lexi wouldn't bin a bottle of vintage champagne.

Beth gets it out. She's tempted to open it and drink it. But that's because she's still feeling stroppy about the whole thing. On top of a bacon roll and two lattes, it wouldn't go down that well.

She drifts over to the window and gazes out. Such a great view. Looking out like this over the city transfixes her and slow her whirring brain.

Envy is a weird emotion. She figured that out at primary school. Every single kid in her class had it better than her; cleaner clothes, a packed lunch on school trips, a parent who wasn't a smack head. The only thing she had going for her was her looks. And that was a mixed blessing.

You can't avoid the fact that it's all a lottery. Some people are born into money and get to live in a luxury roost like this, where you can survey the city like a lord. Others have to hustle for every penny. She can't remember a time when she didn't have to hustle.

It's what you deserve.

Her mum OD'd years ago, but that was the only advice she passed on to Beth. You get what you deserve, and you pay for your sins.

Beth knows this is bullshit. Her mum grew up in a village in the west of Ireland and her parents booted her out when she got pregnant at fifteen.

Sin, rules, laws; you let all that garbage tell you how to live your life, you're stuffed. It was guilt that killed her mum. The smack was just the means. Lexi came with Beth to the crematorium. It was only the two of them. No service. They stood there, staring at the coffin and Lexi read a poem. Beth decided then and there: you do what you do, no point feeling guilty. Ever. Lexi feels guilty about Ewan, always has. Perhaps that's why she reacted so badly. But that's guilt for you. In the end it's lethal.

Tears well in her eyes. Nowadays she rarely thinks about her mum, but the stupid cow was still her mum. That never changes.

Pull yourself together.

She's checked into the Travelodge for a second night, but she needs a more long-term solution to her housing problem.

She remembers what Damian said. He did offer. And he's been texting her from his jail burner.

She gets her phone out and looks at it. Last night, around midnight, he sent her a string of texts.

we need to talk

babe, we really need to talk

beth?

She's been ignoring him because she suspects it's about Ewan, and, particularly after what Lexi said, she doesn't want to know.

But until she can sort things out with Lexi, she's in a fix. So, needs must.

Her thumbs fly over the keys.

sorry babe. crashed early. just got your message xx

She goes into the main bedroom, the one she was using, to find the bed stripped and the bed linen piled in a corner. This is upsetting, as if her friend was hell bent on erasing every trace of her. She checks the second bedroom; all Lexi's stuff is still in there. So it's not because she's changing rooms.

Her phone buzzes.

at last. Where you been?

She plonks down on Lexi's bed and thumbs her reply.

sleeping. doh!

marcus wants to talk to you

why?

dont argue babe. just give me your address

no address. lexi chucked me out

where are you?

travelodge but I need a place to stay

There's a pause. Using a phone in prison can be tricky. Strictly speaking, they're banned. But, according to Damian, more or less everyone has a secret burner stashed, and the screws turn a blind eye. It's an accepted part of the culture.

Beth waits. Now he knows she's homeless, he'll step up. She knows he will.

She waits a couple of minutes. Nothing. She jumps up, heads into the en suite, and finds her perfume. It's still in the bathroom cabinet where she left it. She goes back to the kitchen and pours herself a glass of water. She's never been patient, and having to wait makes her antsy.

Her phone pings with an incoming text.

which travelodge? Southbank?

She thumbs a reply.

near there

Okay. we'll find you somewhere. don't worry.

Thanks. She adds three hearts.

Marcus'll collect you with your stuff. Where can he pick you up?

Beth smiles to herself. It's a relief to know that he's still on her side. At least someone is. But, apart from the fact he got arrested, he's always been reliable.

She'd rather not be picked up by Marcus, but she doesn't want to argue.

She types her reply.

corner of union street and great suffolk street by the pub?

how soon?

say an hour?

Okay. Make sure you're there

I will be

I know you, babe. You lose track. Set the timer on your phone. Don't keep him waiting.

She replies with a laugh out loud emoji.

Things are looking up. She puts the champagne and the perfume in her bag. Maybe she should leave a note for Lexi?

Sod that! Let her stew.

As she heads back to the Travelodge, everything looks better, like a weight has been lifted. She wonders what sort of place they'll come up with. The flat she shared with Damian was in Camden and pretty cool until the cops wrecked it. She's fairly sure Marcus owns a number of properties; Damian has mentioned that.

Marcus is his older brother by some years; same dad, but different mums. Marcus brought him up. Beth has only met Marcus once. He looks nothing like Damian, but perhaps that's because they're only half-brothers. He's bald and stocky, with a bit of a gangster vibe going on. But Damian says this is just to scare people off so they don't give him any hassle. He's got a wife and kids, although Beth has never met them.

Back at the Travelodge, she packs her suitcase and heads out. It's not far to the meeting point, and she arrives early, feeling smug. Damian thinks she doesn't know how to keep appointments; well, he's wrong about that.

There's a row of wooden bench tables outside the pub, which hasn't opened yet. So she sits down, case beside her, and waits.

She's been there about ten minutes when a large black Range Rover Discovery pulls up kerbside. A young bloke gets out of the front passenger seat and opens the back door for her. She wheels her case towards the car. He gives her a nod, takes it, and puts it in the back.

As she climbs into the back seat, Marcus glances at her; he's texting on his phone. He's wearing a leather jacket, and she can smell the expensive aftershave. He doesn't smile.

'All right?' he says. 'Put your seatbelt on.'

'Where are we going?' says Beth.

'Don't worry,' he says. 'It's all sorted.'

He goes back to his text. Beth watches him as the car pulls away and heads up Great Suffolk Street under the railway bridge. The driver and the young bloke in the front are silent; the young bloke has earbuds in and is playing a game on his phone. Marcus sits beside her, texting and ignoring her. It's quite uncomfortable, as if they're pissed off with her, which doesn't make a lot of sense.

Why would they be pissed off with her? Blokes can be weird. And, in Beth's experience, the older they get, the worse it is. She decides to ignore it, look out of the window and enjoy the ride.

35

Friday. 10.50am

Lexi is on the phone to her third cleaning company. Getting someone to come and deep clean her flat, as a matter of urgency, and remove any traces of snake, is proving harder than she expected.

'Snakes are actually quite clean animals,' some pompous dipshit at the first company told her. She hung up on him.

What she wants more than anything is to go home and get her life back to normal. The rental client from Dubai has emailed about the apartment; and now she's got rid of Beth, he can move in as arranged, which is one less problem for Lexi to solve.

But the real issue, the elephant in the room, is her own idiocy.

What the hell were you thinking?

Roger left after their meeting ended. Gemma has remained holed up in her bunker, brooding, with Pia taking

195

her kefir shots and a Buddha bowl from a restaurant round the corner.

Besides calling cleaning companies, Lexi has been hiding away in her corner as she tries to process the triggers which led to her own emotional kamikaze.

Having taken a sensible and sane decision, she walked into Gemma's office and her good intentions flew out of the window. She may have come away with the win, but where does that leave her now? Even if she wants to make this deal work, it's highly unlikely that Kate Jessop will respond to her overtures and get in touch.

Hubris.

It's not a word that ever featured in Lexi's mother's vocabulary, but the sentiment did.

'What've you got to be so puffed up and pleased with yourself about?' That's what her mother said when she came home from school with the news that she was top of her year in the mock GCSEs. Instead of praise, Mum shook her head ominously and announced, 'You're riding for a fall, my girl.' There was never any pride in her achievements, only embarrassment and resentful silences.

Years later, when Lexi tried out some CBT for her anxiety, the therapist said to her, 'Maybe your mother was scared?'

'Scared of what?'

'Scared of what would happen to you if you reached too high.'

'That's bullshit,' Lexi replied. 'She was just being a bitch, which is her default setting.'

Money is all her mother ever worried about; keeping her head above water and paying the bills. When Lexi was little, Mum and Auntie Mari used to paw over old copies of Vogue they got from the hairdressers.

'When I win the Lottery, that'll be me,' that's what Mum used to say. Then the old man cleared out the bank account and did a bunk.

But perhaps the therapist had a point? Class, race, gender; they're still the determining factors. Lexi is an outsider. It's always been harder for her. She needs to be better just to compete. Behind the bitchy put-downs, was Mum just afraid she'd crash and burn?

You can't let her fear define you.

She told Yildiz she was the person who could make this deal work, and he's made it clear he admires her confidence. Roger Cavendish wants to use her, but Yildiz wants her to succeed, not just for the money, but because of who she is. Because they're alike. From the same background. Cut from the same cloth, that's what he said. He scares people, intimidates them. But he's shown her his softer side. If she can prove herself to him, she'll have his respect and support, and she won't need the Cavendishes.

It comes down to one thing. Have you got what it takes?

She kicks off her heels, pulls on her trainers, then grabs her raincoat and her bag. What she needs is to get out into the fresh air, move her body, get her blood and energy flowing. She thinks best when she's walking. That's how she'll come up with a strategy, not stuck in an office.

Outside, the morning is damp and overcast, with a brooding sky threatening rain. Turning up her collar, she cuts through the turnings to Gloucester Place and strides out in the direction of Hyde Park. She gets down to Portman Square and already she's feeling better. She waits at a crossing on the corner for the traffic lights to turn red, then she steps off the pavement. But when she's only halfway across the road, a motorcycle comes hurtling straight at her, ignoring the lights.

It happens in a split second. She flings herself sideways to get out of the way. The bike misses her by a whisker. She lands on her side, hand outstretched, in the middle of the crossing. Pain shoots up through her hip. The bike speeds up; the rider doesn't give her a backward glance.

'What the hell?' she screams after him. But he's gone.

A middle-aged couple standing on the far pavement rush to her aid.

'My goodness, are you all right?' says the woman. 'He could've killed you. Such recklessness.' The husband concurs. 'Bloody idiot. Should be reported to the police.'

The woman helps Lexi to her feet. Her left hip and thigh throb where she hit the tarmac. She's trembling, her legs like jelly. The suddenness of it. The bike came from nowhere.

'Should we call an ambulance?' says the husband. Several more concerned passers-by have stopped.

Lexi staggers to the pavement; the woman still has her arm and supports her. The sharp pain on impact is abating. She tries swinging her leg from the hip; it makes her wince, but it all seems to work. Her left palm is grazed where it hit the ground as she tried to break her fall.

'I think I'm okay,' she says.

The husband has picked up her bag and hands it to her.

'Thank you,' she says. 'I didn't see him. It's the shock of it.'

'Awful,' says the woman. 'We saw the whole thing. You were on the crossing and he rode straight at you. You could almost think it was deliberate.'

Lexi's pulse is pounding. She takes some deep breaths to calm it.

'Oh, it's typical London,' she says, brushing it off. 'Some courier in a hurry. I'm okay, really.'

'Let us get you a cab,' says the husband.

'No, I'm fine. I'll just walk a bit. But thank you for your help.'

She walks on to avoid further concern and conversation. Receiving help from complete strangers always makes her uncomfortable. She hates being the victim. But she's badly shaken.

Grand Georgian terraces surround the square; it's home to embassies, upmarket offices and a few luxury residences. Her firm recently sold a pied-à-terre here for silly money. The gardens are a tranquil haven of greenery with an overarching canopy of plane trees. She tries the wrought-iron gate, but it's locked, which is a pity. It would be great to slip in and sit for a few minutes to calm her jangling nerves.

She reaches the opposite side of the square, the traffic is queued at the lights, but she waits. More caution, more awareness of her surroundings; she's telling herself this as the bus in front of her pulls away.

That's when she sees him, parked across the road on a double yellow line. The same motorcycle? It can't be, can it? She's not sure. It passed her in such a blur. Has the bastard actually stopped to apologise?

Unbelievable.

As the column of traffic moves off, she gets a better view. The rider is in black leathers, sitting astride the bike, and appears to be looking in her direction. The size of him confirms it's probably a man. His arms are folded. The helmet has red flashes down the side, but the visor is up. He is looking at her, head tilted to one side as if it's all some kind of joke.

Part of her wants to cross the road and give him a piece of her mind. But she's unsure. Confrontation is not always the best move. She should cross the road the other way and avoid passing him.

But at that moment, he takes off his helmet. Young, dark beard, shaved head. Lounging on the bike with a macho swagger, he points at her, grins and nods.

An icy chill runs through Lexi's veins. Is it him? No! She hasn't seen him for years, not since he was a teenager, but he does look like her cousin, Ewan.

36

Friday. 11.15am

As far as Beth can make out, they're way out west somewhere, close to Heathrow. This is not a part of London that she's familiar with; a bit industrial, warehouses and factories, that sort of thing. They've been driving for three quarters of an hour. No one has spoken to her. Marcus has been on his phone, receiving messages, sending messages. Observing him out of the corner of her eye, she'd say he's definitely hacked off about something.

For the last few miles, she's been racking her brains to remember all the things Damian told her about his brother. It doesn't amount to much. She can pinpoint at least two occasions when Damian came home ranting about something Marcus had said or done. Other times there have been comments like 'he's a stubborn bastard.' Beth once asked Damian why he put up with this shit. Why didn't he just go out on his own? He was the one with the network of contacts in the clubs, and the kind of people he sold to would not be comfortable buying from Marcus. But Damian just laughed and said, 'You don't understand, babe.'

After sharing the backseat of a car with this silent neanderthal for an hour, Beth wishes she did understand. She's not stupid. Marcus runs a successful drug dealing operation. He's the business end, dealing with suppliers, rivals, evading the cops, so obviously looking like a thug helps.

She decides to take the bull by the horns. She turns to him, smiles and says, 'Is it much further? Cause I need to pee?'

He turns his bullet head to look at her, inhaling as he does so. 'Is that 'cause you're pregnant?' he says. 'Pregnant women need to pee more, don't they?'

Beth has no idea. But she smiles and nods. 'Yeah.'

'Five minutes,' he says, and returns to his phone.

They're on a dual carriageway, cruising in the fast lane, with signs to the M4. Patches of green punctuate the urban sprawl of west London between the hulking warehouses with their corrugated facades, the service stations offering meal deals, the billboards advertising getaways to far-flung destinations. It passes in a blur.

Beth is getting grumpy, and she really needs to pee. How the hell is she going to get into town if she's stuck out here in the boondocks? She hates the tube and getting an Uber home after a night out will cost a fortune. Or is this a ploy by Damian to stop her from going out? It's his stupid jealousy. He's inside, so he wants her tucked up out in the sticks, away from the fun, and other men. Well, she's not having it.

She's about to tell Marcus as much when the Discovery slows, takes a slip road off the main drag and turns into an industrial estate.

Marcus pockets his phone and looks at her. 'Right,' he says. 'You and me need to understand one another. I'm not

Damian, and the last thing you want to do is muck me about.
You got that?'

Beth meets his gaze. His eyes are small, almond-shaped
and muddy in colour. He blinks a lot, much like a tomcat.

She shrugs. 'I'm just looking for a place to stay.'

He harrumphs.

The car stops in front of a pair of heavy steel gates. The
driver taps a number into the keypad on the fence and the
gates slide open. They drive into a compound, a concrete yard
in front of a large industrial hangar. It looks like some kind of
delivery depot, but it's deserted, weeds growing up between
cracks in the concrete.

Beth has a bad feeling. None of this is right. She glances
over her shoulder at where the tall gates are clanking shut
behind them.

'Why have you brought me here?' she says.

Marcus ignores the question.

There's a two storey, brick built office block next to the
warehouse bit with a metal stairway up the side. The car pulls
up in front of it.

Be cool. Don't let them see any fear.

The young guy who loaded her case in the back opens the
door for her. She steps out and thanks him. Marcus has got
out the other side. He walks round the front of the car and
points at the stairs. 'You go first.'

'What is this place?'

'You'll see.'

'What about my stuff?'

'Brandon'll bring it.'

Marcus is taller and more solid than Beth remembers, and
his hands are large and meaty. She's encountered plenty of
club bouncers like this. They stand a bit too close so you feel
intimidated, but they move like lumbering elephants. It's easy

to outrun them. But here there's a high chain linked fence all round, so nowhere to run.

Beth makes a point of trotting up the stairs. She gets to the top way ahead of Marcus and lounges on the metal platform, waiting for him. He's forced to glance up at her above him; that should make it clear she's not about to take any crap.

He gives her a sullen glare. 'Go on in.'

There's a half-glazed door. Beth opens it and steps inside a small office reception area with a counter, but no other furniture. The place is dusty and unused. Behind the counter is another door. Whatever this is, it's not residential. Beth turns to face him.

'What's going on? This isn't a flat.'

Marcus is closing the door behind him. It's just the two of them. He sighs. 'Damian's a good lad. But he's a sucker for a pretty face.'

Beth has her bag hanging from her left shoulder, and inside there's a can of pepper spray. She lets her hand move slowly towards the zip.

But Marcus is watching her. He smirks. 'Don't get silly,' he says. 'We're just going to have a chat.' He calls out. 'Holly?'

The door to the inner office opens and a woman appears. She couldn't be more out of place in this dump. Chic, perfect hair and nails, casually dressed, but nothing she's wearing, including the Hermès scarf, costs less than several grand.

'This is my wife, Holly,' says Marcus.

Holly steps forward with a smile on her face. 'You must be Damian's girlfriend,' she says. 'Beth, is it? Lovely to finally meet you.'

Beth is confused and relieved in equal parts. Her manner is friendly and relaxed. She's well-spoken, bordering on posh.

How did a gorilla like Marcus land her? It must be the money.

'Good to meet you too,' Beth replies. 'Is there a loo?'

'Of course. Come this way.'

Holly leads her through the office at the back, which is piled high with cardboard boxes, and into a small galley kitchen smelling of fresh brewed coffee. At the end, there's a door.

'This is the bathroom,' says Holly, pushing the door open.

'Thanks,' says Beth.

Holly is still beaming. 'Oh, and while you're having a pee,' she says, 'perhaps we can get the formalities out of the way?' She picks up a box from the kitchen worktop and holds it up.

It's a pregnancy test kit.

WTF!

Beth stares at it and her heart sinks.

Holly is opening the box. 'I presume you know how to use these things?' She holds up the instructions. 'It's a while since I've needed to. After three kids, I persuaded Marcus to have the snip.'

That doesn't sound very Marcus.

Beth nods. 'Yeah. Course.'

Her brain is rapidly calculating. Three days since the insemination. What are the chances? Is it enough?

Be optimistic. Think positive.

Holly hands her the little plastic wand. Beth takes a deep breath to calm the rioting butterflies in her stomach. Two lines for pregnant, one line for not pregnant. She's done the test enough times before, usually in trepidation, willing it to be negative. Now she needs the opposite.

Two Lines. Pleeeeze!

Much as she wants to shut the door and lock it, Holly is

just standing there in the doorway. She tilts her head, still smiling. 'You don't mind, do you?'

Beth shakes her head. 'Course not.'

Unzipping her jeans, Beth perches on the cold porcelain and wills her tense muscles to relax. As the stream of warm urine hits the stick, she watches the blank oval window, hardly daring to breathe. The control line darkens to bright pink, confirming that the test is working. Beth's eyes remain on the stick, searching for any hint of a second line. But it remains stubbornly blank.

This is just too soon.

Holly can't see the stick from where she's standing, which is as well.

The seconds tick by and the space beside the control line remains empty. Holly checks the fancy Cartier diamond watch on her wrist.

'I think that's over two minutes,' she says. 'Can I look?'

Beth tears off some toilet paper, wipes herself, then lays the stick on a fresh piece. She holds it up for Holly to see. One line. Negative. Not pregnant.

Holly raises her sculpted eyebrows and nods.

'Perhaps it's not working,' says Beth. 'These things aren't a hundred per cent reliable, are they?'

37

Friday. 11.20am

Lexi makes it back to the office; both her hip and leg are sore. She'll have a massive bruise, but nothing seems to be broken, which is the only upside. Her own quick reflexes saved her.

It's not him. You imagined it.

He put his helmet back on and rode off. One glimpse from across the road. Maybe ten seconds, if that. It's preposterous. Just some moron trying to wind her up. He looked nothing like her cousin.

He pointed at you. Why?

It was such a brief moment; sometimes you think you know what you're seeing, but you don't. And Lexi's been here before, in this netherworld of doubt. Your brain wants answers; it demands them. But there are none, so you make stuff up. Is this what she's doing? Creating a dark fantasy?

She keeps going round in circles with this. What happened to her at Renfrew Hall was so shocking. Her mum says that he's been released on licence. But what does that prove? Nothing really.

Did he track her to Renfrew Hall and attack her client? The idea is ludicrous. How would he even do it?

Then this morning she was almost hit by a motorcycle. But is there any real reason to suppose it was Ewan?

You're being paranoid.

As she walks into the office, Pia gives her a startled glance, so she must be dishevelled. Avoiding her questioning gaze, Lexi heads straight for her desk.

She sits down and is removing her trainers when she sees Gemma approaching.

Here we go. Round two.

But Gemma pauses, hands clutched in front of her, right hand cradling her boney, bejewelled left fist. It's what she does when she's nervous. Makes her look like an old hag.

'Bit of a situation,' she says. 'I've just had a call from Jazzy Gupta.'

Jazzy Gupta runs a boutique concierge firm; her client list is unsurpassed. Only multi-millionaires to billionaires need apply. She once offered Lexi a job, but by then, Lexi was focused on getting back into property.

'Oh,' says Lexi.

'Has that client from Dubai moved into the Riverreach at Bankside yet?'

'No. Why?'

Lexi has an uneasy feeling. Has Gemma got wind of the fact she's staying in the flat? But how?

'Jazzy has a problem with the penthouse. That Chinese girl, I can never remember their name.'

They're a client, a major client. You should remember.

'You mean Gao Zheng Ming's daughter?' says Lexi. 'I think she's called Li Hua.'

'Yes, that's it. The Gaos. Well, apparently Li Hua and some student friends had a party. Got hold of some bad drugs or something. I don't know. They trashed the place completely and a couple of them ended up in A&E. It'll take at least a couple of days for Jazzy to sort the penthouse out. So she's wondering if we can put the brat in this other apartment. Of course, the girl's father owns it, so…y'know, awkward.'

Lexi inhales and nods. Clearing up after some rich kid's wrecking spree is a standard job in the concierge business. The entire penthouse might need to be refurnished to get it back up to spec.

Gemma paints on a conciliatory smile. 'I was thinking you could pop over there, talk to Jazzy, and sort things out.' She hesitates and adds. 'If you're not too busy.'

Gemma could do this herself, but luckily, she's too idle.

Lexi hails a black cab outside the office. Traffic is steady, a few hold-ups in the centre of town, but the driver is old school, he knows the back doubles. Lexi is on the lookout; she can't help it. There are plenty of motorcyclists weaving in and out of the vehicle queues, but none appear to be following them. The cab drops her at the front entrance to the Riverreach tower and she scurries inside.

The reception has a long marble desk to the right, with at least one person on duty 24/7. But to the left there's a seating area separated from the main hallway by a large blond wooden frame containing a massive stained glass abstract. The theme continues with paintings on the walls creating a cross between a VIP airport lounge and an art gallery.

Jazzy Gupta is sitting on one of the long sofas, texting on her phone. As soon as she catches sight of Lexi, she jumps to her feet. Five feet tall, a dainty elfin figure, she has the energy and bounce of a small terrier.

'My darling girl, such a pleasure as always,' she exclaims in her plummy tones with the vaguest hint of a Mumbai accent.

It's hard to air kiss someone so much shorter than yourself, but Lexi does her best.

Jazzy can speak faster than anyone else Lexi knows. Her small hands flap, her dark eyes sparkle as the words pour out of her. 'You are such a life saver. A silly situation, aren't they all? But these kids come to London—Li Hua is nineteen—all they know is the safety and privilege of the bubble they've grown up in, and they go wild. Wild, my dear. I'm not saying it's her fault. She's totally naïve, and I think she was targeted. 'Friends', aren't they all? Invited themselves round. Pills, coke, who knows what else? She comes to this morning, the place has been stripped. The art work, some furniture, watches, phones, laptops, anything with a designer label. What they couldn't take, they trashed. Two of Li's actual friends had to go to A&E.'

'Is Li Hua okay?'

'She'll survive, but of course she's petrified of her father finding out...'

'Next plane back to Shanghai?'

'Exactly.'

Jazzy gives Lexi a speculative look. It's impossible to guess her age; around fifty, perhaps. Behind the charm, she's a shrewd businesswoman, and someone Lexi has always admired. 'But,' she says with an extravagant sigh. 'That would be a pity. I think the poor girl's learned her lesson.'

Lexi nods. She understands Jazzy's thinking. The only daughter of a tech billionaire, being groomed and educated for a prominent role in her father's empire. If Jazzy bails her out now, she's made a friend, and that's a worthwhile investment for the future.

'Well,' says Lexi. 'I agree. No need to upset Mr Gao.'

Jazzy smiles. 'And of course we don't want the police poking about, but I have an insurance assessor who's friendly. The art is the problem; some expensive pieces. But I know the artist; I'm sure I can persuade him to paint me some replicas. The Gaos will never notice the difference.'

As Jazzy rattles on, they make their way, arm in arm, to the lifts, and Lexi wonders how on earth Jazzy is going to square this financial circle. The cost of restoring the place will be substantial. But that's her problem, and one she'll no doubt solve with her usual mix of astuteness and panache.

'About the flat,' Lexi says. 'No problem with Li Hua moving in, except someone has been staying there. Temporarily.'

Jazzy raises her eyebrows. 'Oh.'

Fortunately, Lexi has cleaned it. Erasing Beth's crap proved a good outlet for her anger. Her patience with Beth snapped. The lunacy of involving Damian and his brother in this is extreme, even by Beth's standards.

Jazzy is watching and waiting for her to say more. Lexi meets her quizzical gaze.

She'll smell a lie. She's way too smart.

Lexi gives her a sheepish look. 'Actually, it's me. I've been staying there for a few days. Problems with my flat. Obviously Gemma doesn't know.'

'Obviously,' says Jazzy sympathetically.

'But I can move out.'

'What sort of problems?' says Jazzy.

The stress has been taking its toll and Lexi finds it hard not to blurt out the whole sorry saga. But that would be unprofessional.

Jazzy's fingers brush her forearm, the lightest of touches, reassuring without being intrusive. 'Perhaps I can help,' she says.

Can she? If only.

Lexi shrugs. 'A foolish situation,' she says. 'Someone put a snake through my letterbox. To frighten me, I suspect. Just a stupid prank. Turned out to be a corn snake, not poisonous, but…'

Jazzy throws up her arms. 'My dear, how awful for you! There are some strange people about nowadays. Some kind of sick joke. Do you know who's done this?'

'Not for certain, no. There are…several possibilities.'

Lexi becomes aware of Jazzy's penetrating gaze. Then her eyes drift off, nodding to herself, calculating.

'Size of your flat?' she says briskly.

'It's a small one-bed in north London. Nothing fancy.'

Jazzy inhales. 'Okay,' she says. 'I have some chaps. They do specialist cleans for me. Anything from biohazards to bodily fluids. They should be able to sort you out in a couple of hours. Also, you'll need a new secure front door. I have some people who can do that.'

Lexi is taken aback.

'Jazzy, I didn't mean for you to—'

Jazzy raises a peremptory finger. 'I know. But we're helping each other here, aren't we? Give me your address and a key. It'll be done and dusted by the time you get home.'

Lexi could hug her. Instead she says, 'I'll reimburse you, of course.'

Jazzy shakes her head. 'You will not. Consider this a courtesy to a colleague. If we don't take care of our own, who will?'

Lexi is too relieved to refuse, although she should.

'I owe you,' she says.

And that's what she wants.

Jazzy's a fixer and a deal maker, and this is all about the trade in favours. Lexi is well aware of how this game is played; it's also how the wider world works. Eventually Jazzy will want something in return, a recommendation, or a heads up on a new property deal. Favours are worth hard currency; sometimes more than hard currency.

Jazzy smiles and squeezes her hand. 'Some jokes just aren't funny. Any more nonsense, I would take it to the police.'

Lexi smiles back. She's right.

'Now,' says Jazzy, beaming. 'Are you going to this shindig of the Yildizs this afternoon?'

Arif Yildiz is launching a new development in Battersea. Lexi and every other super prime listings agent in London will be there scrabbling for business.

'Maybe,' says Lexi. She was planning to give it a miss.

'Oh, do come,' says Jazzy. 'We can watch the shenanigans together. Better than monkeys at the zoo.'

Lexi grins. She's right about that, too.

38

Friday. 11.22am

Beth is surrounded by stacks of cardboard boxes. She wonders what's in them. They look innocuous, but isn't this how dealers hide their stuff, inside something else? Cleaning products? Teddy bears?

She's sitting on an old office chair; it's the sort that swivels and moving rhythmically from side to side is helping steady her nerves. They haven't tied her up or anything, but Brandon is standing several feet away, arms folded, watching her.

She can hear voices—Holly and Marcus—but not what they're saying. Holly will have told him that the pregnancy test was negative. But these things are never totally reliable. She hopes Holly is making that point on her behalf.

The problem is, even if she is now pregnant, it's not by Damian. Some women conceive and they reckon they know at once, even if it takes ages to show up in a test. But Beth doesn't have that sense. The insemination took place three days ago. The test is too soon. But then she was never expecting to get into this sort of tangle with Damian's brother.

Holly appears, but her expression has changed. She's not smiling anymore. Marcus is behind her; he doesn't seem happy either. But then what would happy look like on a bloke like him? He wears a permanent scowl.

'Well,' says Holly, 'you've put us in a difficult position.'

Jump in first.

'Yeah, listen, I know you're pissed because you think I lied to Damian. But it wasn't a lie. I was pregnant, then that night, after I went to see him in Belmarsh, I had a miscarriage.'

Holly sighs. 'And why didn't you say this before we did the test?'

'I was just…confused about what's going on here. Why you don't trust me?'

Marcus shakes his head and puts his hands on his hips. 'Oh, for fuck's sake!'

'I don't think that's true, is it, Beth?' says Holly evenly.

She sounds calm, unlike her old man, who's fidgety and angry. She's flexing her fingers and checking the ruby red nail polish which sets off three heavy gold rings.

'Let's try this again, shall we?' she says. 'This time you're going to tell us the truth.'

This is not going well.

Beth meets her gaze and smiles. She suspects Holly is the only thing standing between her and Marcus's fists, or worse.

'I want to do that,' says Beth. 'But, y'know, this is all a bit scary. I love Damian, and I think he loves me. It's depressing being in jail. I just wanted him to be happy and have something to look forward to. And I think we definitely will have kids together one day. That's the truth.'

Holly and Marcus exchange looks. It's a bit like Shrek and Princess Fiona, although Beth doubts Marcus has a heart of gold.

'You saying you lied to him to cheer him up?' says Marcus.

Beth nods.

Marcus inhales deeply. More of a huff. He seems to huff a lot, as if too many things annoy him. He's about to speak, but Holly places her long manicured index finger on his chest.

'Let us explain our problem to you, Beth,' she says. 'Then we can work out how you help us solve it. Okay?'

Beth puts on her most innocent face; it usually gets her out of trouble. 'Of course,' she says. 'I want to help.'

Marcus steps forward. 'You told my brother that some bloke was hassling you and threatening you. Some bloke you knew years ago. Who the hell is he?'

'Ewan. We…sort of grew up together.'

'Damian was worried. He's stuck in a bloody prison cell, and some nutter is hassling his pregnant girlfriend. That's what he told me.' He makes the word pregnant sound like an accusation. 'I sent a couple of guys round to have a quiet word.' As he speaks, he's going redder and redder in the face, like he's mad as hell.

Oh shit…

'Now one of them is dead, the other's in intensive care in the hospital. Two bloody good men. Your little childhood pal knifed the both of them. So, I wanna speak to this Ewan. Urgently.'

Beth's stomach plunges like a broken elevator. Her head spins. This is not good. Also, no way is it her fault.

'I did…tell Damian how dangerous he is.'

'Did you?' Those muddy cat's eyes are boring straight into her, and it's not a pleasant feeling.

'I swear to you, Marcus. I did explain.' The words spill out in a nervous gabble. 'Ewan stabbed a kid when he was fourteen, went down for it. He's only just got out. He followed Lexi and killed this client of hers that she was supposed to be meeting.'

'Who the hell's Lexi?'

'She's my best friend. Ewan is her cousin.'

Another huff. 'Wait a minute, let me get this straight. Is his beef with her or you?'

'He knows we're close. I was scared he'd try to get to her through me. And so was Lexi.'

'This isn't even about you, then?'

'Well, it is and it isn't. He is completely crazy. And I told Damian that.'

Marcus sucks the air in through his nose, so it makes a singing sound. 'Fuck me,' he mumbles under his breath.

Holly is watching, arms folded. There's a serenity and a detachment about her. Marcus is the opposite; he's full of explosive energy, pacing up and down.

He turns abruptly, leans right over Beth and the words fly out of his mouth laced with spit. 'This is worse than I thought. You are a fucking piece of work, y'know that?'

Beth wants to wipe his saliva off her face, but she daren't move. When blokes come at you like this, you make yourself small and meek. The more you cower, the less they hit you. That's been her experience, but only if they're sober. Fortunately, it's half eleven in the morning, and Marcus doesn't smell of drink.

He steps back, shoves his hands in his pockets, and walks in a circle.

Holly offers her a tissue. So this is how it's going to be. He scares the shit out of her. Holly pretends to be nice.

She wipes her face. And dabs her eyes. The tears are real.

'Okay,' says Holly. 'Your friend Lexi, we need to talk to her.'

Beth nods. Marcus picks up Beth's bag from where it got tossed on the floor. He flings it at her. She catches it; good reflexes. The only thing she wasn't crap at in school was sport. She once played in a cricket match, although she didn't understand the rules. They are weird.

'Phone her,' says Holly. 'Now. Tell her you need to meet.'

Beth opens her bag. 'She's probably at work. I doubt she'll agree.'

'Persuade her,' says Marcus.

Beth pulls up Lexi's number, rings it. It goes straight to voicemail. She shows them the screen.

'Leave a message,' says Holly.

Beth feels panicky. How is this ever going to work? Lexi's ticked off with her. Marcus looks like he could burst a blood vessel, and Beth is stuck in the middle.

This is not your fault.

She takes a deep breath. 'Hey babe,' she says. 'It's me. Bit of a sticky situation here. We really need to talk. ASAP. Please call me back. Love you.' She hopes that sounds desperate enough.

She hangs up. They're both looking at her.

Lexi will call her. However annoyed she is, she'll call. They have each other's backs, always have.

39

Friday. 11.25am

Ewan and Jared are having a great time. It's like they're in a movie. Riding round the West End on the bike, zigzagging in and out of the traffic, running a few lights; it's like they're the heroes in the chase scene. A taxi driver hoots them, as Ewan cuts him up. He's scowling like Vin Diesel, and shaking his fist.

Jared is loving it. He gives the guy the middle finger and laughs.

They walked out of the old man's house last night. Had no choice. Ewan chucked a few things in a couple of saddle-bags and threw them over the back of the bike. When the stupid old fool rolled home, he was in for a shock.

As they left, the second guy was crawling down the hall and begging for help.

'You got a phone, haven't you?' said Ewan. 'Ring a bloody ambulance.'

To tell the truth, deep down Ewan is teed off. The nerve

of these blokes. They actually kicked the door in! Who knows what their plan was? He didn't wait to find out. Attack is the best form of defence; Rusty taught him that. Don't give your opponent time to think.

But it proves what he's known all along. She sent them. This is the kind of bitch she is. Evil. She's fucked up his life once, and now she's trying to do it all over again. And a man has a right to defend himself.

Get the bitch before she gets you.

Parked outside the house, they found a big black Toyota pickup. Jared went back inside and filched the keys from the dead guy's pocket. He was in favour of nicking it, but Ewan said no. A stolen vehicle would be asking for trouble; anyway, he preferred the bike.

The good part was what they found in the glove compartment: one of these soppy man bags, but inside there were a couple of wraps.

On their way into town, they stopped off at a Maccy D's and got burgers and fries. Then they hit the john, Ewan chopped out a line and hoovered it up. He wasn't greedy. He knew he had stuff to do, but it gave him the bump he needed.

Since then he's had a couple of top ups and he's surfing the wave.

A bus is blocking their path and they're stopped at the lights on Regent Street.

'So what's the plan?' says Jared. 'You had her and you missed.'

Ewan swivels in his seat. This narks him, and it's typical of Jared.

'Two guys kicked the fucking door in, brother. And where were you? Playing with yourself on the sofa.'

'Didn't look to me like you needed any help.'

'I didn't.'

Jared folds his arms and huffs. 'Just asking, bro. You letting her off the hook?'

'No!'

'What's the plan, then? Cause I'm getting bored.'

The bus shifts forward with glacial slowness. Ewan flexes his fingers. The gloves make him hot and itchy, but he always wears them. Foolish not to. He always wears full leathers too. You come off a bike at speed, you'll be ripped to shreds. Rusty told him the story of a guy he knew…but he's had enough of stories.

He can hear a ticking noise inside his helmet. Tick tock. Tick tock. And it's getting louder. And his whole body feels itchy.

Fuck this shit!

Ewan opens up the throttle, swerves round the bus, mounts the pavement, narrowly missing some idiot family taking a selfie. They scatter. People are screaming. It's great. He veers back on to the road in front of the bus and roars off.

'You bored now?' he shouts over his shoulder.

40

Friday. 11.30am

Boden and Chakravorty are driving through a pall of rain. The wipers slap across the windscreen, barely clearing it. They've been hunting for Mason Green for half the morning. The sky is louring and ominous; the landscape is drenched. At the gatehouse they drew a blank. It was deserted, curtains half drawn.

'Could've done a runner,' said Chakravorty.

Boden wondered that herself. But where would he go? When they spoke to him three days ago, he was desperate, and scared of being made homeless. In Boden's opinion, he was also lying about what he knew. They should've followed up the next day. Boden knows she should've made the point more forcefully to the DCI, but she didn't. It was laziness. She hasn't been giving the job her full attention; unfortunately, the boss is right about that.

So far, they've visited two farms in the vicinity of Renfrew Hall. This is the third.

Chakravorty is driving, Boden sits beside her, sipping a lukewarm coffee and gazing out at the grey green patchwork of flooded fields.

The muddy lane opens out into a sizeable yard awash with black puddles. Chakravorty drives gingerly through them, as the car bucks over the ruts.

'I hate the country,' she mumbles.

At the far end there's a sturdy two storey farmhouse of weathered redbrick and beyond it a traditional, open-sided Dutch barn piled with bales of straw, with a clutch of smaller outbuildings next to it.

They park outside the house. Boden gets out, pulling up her hood and thinking about the boots they should've brought but haven't. She's wearing a new pair of Oxblood loafers, and her feet are going to get wet.

Even on a drab, rain soaked day, the place looks well kept. A neat porch, and next to it, propped on its side, a hand painted sign. Boden turns her head to read it. *Welcome to Jess's pumpkin patch.* There's a picture of an orange pumpkin.

She knocks on the door as Chakravorty, standing on the other side of the car, says 'Look!'

Boden follows the direction of her finger. Through the murky veil of rain, Chakravorty is pointing at three vehicles, an old Range Rover, a small hatchback and a white transit van, parked between the barn and one of the outbuildings.

'What?' says Boden.

'The other side of the van,' says Chakravorty. 'See it. Just the back of it. A canvas top.'

Boden peers. The DC's sharp eyes have seen more than her. It could be the beat up, olive coloured Land Rover driven by Mason Green.

'Gotcha!' murmurs Boden under her breath. Things are looking up.

She turns as the door to the farmhouse opens. A young woman, no more than a teenager, is surveying her. She wears overalls, her hair is pulled back in a ponytail, and she has thick grey boot socks on her feet.

Boden pulls out her warrant card and introduces herself and Chakravorty.

'We're looking for Mason Green,' she says. 'I think he works here sometimes.'

The girl gives her a surly look. 'Sometimes.'

A male voice calls from inside the house. 'Bring 'em in here, Jess. Bring 'em in here.'

The girl opens the door wider and motions them in with a jerk of her thumb.

Boden doesn't wait for her to change her mind. She and Chakravorty follow her into the house.

A short, tiled hallway opens out into a cosy kitchen with a large Aga belching out heat. Lily and Simba are sharing the rug beside the Aga with a sleepy Border Collie. Lily's watching a cartoon on a tablet. She doesn't give them a second glance.

On the other side is a man in his early fifties sitting in a motorised wheelchair.

'Morning, sir,' says Boden. 'I assume you're the farmer.'

'You've met the farmer,' says the man. 'My daughter Jess. I'm Brian Penrose.'

Boden dips her head towards the girl. 'My apologies for the assumption.'

Jess continues to scowl.

'What do you want with Mason?' says Penrose.

Boden scans him. Broad shoulders, capable, work-toughened hands, but his legs and feet are twisted and immobile. Some kind of accident?

'We just have a few questions for him,' she says.

'He may have been forced by circumstance to work for that villain, but that doesn't make him one.' The tone is polite but challenging.

Interesting.

Boden glances at Lily. 'Is he here?'

'He doesn't know any more than what he's told you,' says Jess. Her arms are folded and the tone is belligerent.

Brian Penrose exhales. 'Listen, I know you're just doing your job. He's working in the outhouse. But he's not going anywhere. He rarely lets this little mite out of his sight. She's in here because of the rain.'

Lily is in her own bubble, giggling at something on her tablet, and she's certainly better off in this warm kitchen than in her freezing cold home.

'Sit yourselves down and have a cup of tea,' says Penrose. 'I'm sure you could do with it.' He waves a hand at his daughter. 'Put the kettle on, Jess.'

Boden considers his change in attitude, which suggests they've hit on something here. Five days into the investigation and no one has visited the properties in the immediate vicinity of Renfrew Hall. This is an oversight in Boden's view, but it's the DCI's call. The tech takes priority, but it also pays to be patient and listen.

'That would be most welcome,' she says. 'It's a grim day out there.'

Jess frowns but picks up the kettle and puts it on the hot plate of the Aga.

Boden takes a seat at the long deal table and Chakravorty sits down next to her. The DC puts her phone in front of her.

'Do you mind if we record you?' she says.

Brian Penrose moves his chair forward to join them. 'Not at all,' he says. His hands grip the arms of his wheelchair. 'You're probably wondering why I called him a villain.'

'Who are we talking about here?' says Boden.

'Jessop,' he says. 'Isn't that why you're here? Someone knifed him.'

'We're part of the murder investigation, and obviously we're interested in any information you can give us relating to that.'

He nods. 'This used to be a dairy farm,' he says. 'We had a prize-winning herd of a hundred and fifty Friesians. But the supermarkets did for us. Even before my accident, I couldn't make it pay. So we've diversified. Got to change with the times. Jess has been brilliant at this. We do a pumpkin patch for Halloween, a Maize Maze in the summer, and we keep llamas. Kids love 'em. A few cash crops like oil seed rape. And we buy in young beef cattle and fatten them up. That's how I first met Mr Jessop. The new landlord.'

'You're tenant farmers?' says Boden.

'Three generations,' says Penrose. 'Jess is the fourth. My grandfather took the tenancy from Lord Orme between the wars. My father took it on, then me. I've worked this land for thirty years. After the Ormes sold up, the Hall was owned by some Russian billionaire. We never saw him, just some lawyer. Place was empty for a few years. Although they made a film there. Then he got sanctioned, and it was sold on again. All a bit dodgy if you ask me. That's when Mr Jessop appeared.'

Boden sits back. This is how cases are made, through good intel leading to solid evidence, and part of her would like to prove her point to DCI Knight.

'Flashy sort of bloke,' says Penrose. 'Plans to renovate. But he said we could continue to put our livestock on the fields at the front, because they made it look more like a proper English country estate. I assumed from this he'd be looking for a foreign buyer. Last summer, during the drought, we were glad of the grazing. Those big old horse chestnuts provide shade for our cattle. That's when I approached him about the tenancy.'

Jess is leaning on the bar of the Aga, arms folded. The kettle sings. She dumps a couple of tea bags in a large brown teapot and fills it with boiling water.

Penrose gives his head a sorrowful shake. 'And that's when I found out the kind of bloke I was dealing with.' He slaps the sides of the wheelchair in frustration. 'No bloody way on God's earth I wanted to end up like this.'

Jess is watching her father, brow furrowed, as she pours mugs of tea and places them on the table. There is both pain and solicitude in her expression.

'What happened, if you don't mind me asking?' says Boden.

'Problems with a tractor. I jacked it up to fix it. Jack failed and the lot came down on me, crushing my spine and pelvis.' He dismisses this with a wave. 'I asked him if Jess could take over the tenancy. She's young, but with me to advise…he wouldn't even consider it. Gave me a flat out no. Then I discovered he'd already applied for outline planning permission for a change of use of the land, got a bevy of lawyers on it.'

'He wanted to build on the land as well as renovate the house?' says Chakravorty.

'Yeah. Double, probably treble his money. Ruddy great housing estate is what he had planned,' says Penrose. 'Didn't even tell us. This is green belt, designated farmland. But we soon discovered that's no barrier to a bloke like him. Local politicians in his pocket, bought and paid for.'

'Wouldn't you be protected by the terms of your tenancy agreement?' says Boden.

Penrose shrugs. 'I thought we would be. I talked to a solicitor. But he reckoned the succession clause was weak. Advised me to negotiate with Jessop.' The anger and bitterness in his face is palpable.

'And did you?' says Boden.

He meets her gaze. 'Never got the chance.'

Boden wonders what's emerging here. A motive for murder?

Penrose seems to read her mind. He gives them a sardonic smile. 'I know what you're thinking, and no, I won't be shedding a tear. But it won't stop anything, will it? The next crook who comes along'll just pick up where he left off. His death'll make no difference to us. The writing's on the wall. It's all about money.'

His eyes are a watery blue; a tough man without an ounce of self-pity. It's hard not to admire him.

'Tell us about your relationship with Mason,' she says.

Penrose sighs. 'Not much to tell. Knew his dad. Good lad. Good worker. Things've been difficult for him, so we try to give him work when we can.'

There's a change of tone here; it's slight, but it's the only thing he's said that doesn't ring true for Boden.

He knows Mason better than he's letting on.

Boden finishes her tea. 'Okay,' she says. 'We should probably go and have a word with him. Thanks for the tea and for your time.'

Friday. 12.10pm

Once she's entrusted Jazzy Gupta's assistant with the keys to her flat, Lexi accepts a lift to the launch party in Battersea. There's no necessity to go back to the office, and rolling up in the back of Jazzy's sleek, chauffeured, black Mercedes is a far more regal way to arrive than just piling out of an Uber like everyone else.

The high-rise development is a collection of luxury apartments on Queenstown Road, next to Battersea Park. The launch is in the penthouse suite, with access to the podium garden, weather permitting.

'Have you read the details?' says Jazzy. 'The square footage is not massive. But I like the location and with a price tag under two million, they'll make an attractive pied-à-terre.'

Lexi smiles to herself. This is not Jazzy trying to sound snobbish. From her point of view, she's just stating the facts. This is the rarefied world she inhabits, where wealth is normal. Jazzy may well be as rich as some of her clients.

Roger Cavendish is. And Lexi aspires to be, one day. That's what it's all about.

For now, she gets to step out of a fancy car in her Louboutin heels, instead of changing into them in the loos.

Her phone is on silent, but during the short drive, it vibrates five times, all calls from Beth. Could she be any more petulant and annoying?

The best policy is to ignore her. They may have been friends for a very long time, but for Lexi, this is the last straw. It's time to get real. Beth is a liability she can no longer afford, and this time there will be no reconciliation.

Her focus this afternoon must be the event and cementing her relationship with Arif Yildiz. She needs to bring her A game.

Unfortunately, as soon as they get out of the car, she clocks Kenny Coin homing in on them. He makes it to the building's plate glass doors before them, but then stands back with a gallant sweep of his arm for them to go first.

'Ladies,' he says.

Lexi can feel his eyes. It's the sort of unsettling male gaze she hates. Not overtly sleazy, but laced with a knowing smile. He seems to be saying, 'I know who you are, what you want.' What she wants is to punch him.

As ever, Kenny is immaculate; tailored jacket, open-necked shirt, polished oxfords. His dark hair is slicked back with just enough of a five o'clock shadow on his chiselled jaw to make him hip; at least, that's clearly his opinion.

'Kenny!' says Jazzy, opening her arms. He envelops her in a light, professional hug accompanied by an air kiss. He's never too touchy-feely; he knows you can't do that anymore. Then he turns to Lexi.

'And here's the queen of super prime herself,' he says with a smirk.

'If I didn't know you better,' she says, 'I might think you meant that.'

He gives her his attempt at a boyish grin, which he probably thinks is attractive. 'I only speak the truth. Always a place for you in my shop, darling.' A hint of the Tottenham accent breaks the surface of his carefully crafted upper crust veneer.

Jazzy is already heading for the lifts, and Lexi is anxious to join her, but Kenny tags along.

Like many in the property business, Kenny started out flipping cheap flats in rundown areas, but his energy and ability to close deals others deemed impossible helped him climb the ladder, reinventing himself on the way up. Now his client base is Dubai not Dalston.

Following them into the lift, he paints on a serious face. 'That business at Renfrew Hall.' He shakes his head.

How the hell does he know?

'Terrible. Absolutely terrible,' he says. 'One reason I'd never send one of my agents to a property like that on their own. Especially not a woman. Roger should know better.'

Lexi shrugs. 'These things happen. And anyway, Gemma's in charge now.'

Kenny raises his eyebrows as if a rotting fish has just arrived under his nose. 'Ah yes, the lovely Gemma. We'll say no more.'

Mercifully, it takes less than thirty seconds for the lift to ascend and the doors to open at the penthouse floor.

'Well,' says Kenny. 'My door's always open. If you want a boss who'll take care of you, not to mention make you seriously rich.'

Lexi and Jazzy make their escape. Once they're out of earshot, Jazzy whispers, 'Does Roger know he keeps trying to poach you?'

'Probably. But I've told him no more times than I can count.'

Jazzy ponders this. 'Rejection takes people in different ways. And Kenny Coin strikes me as the kind of man with a warped sense of humour who might have an unhealthy interest in snakes.'

Lexi turns to look at her. 'Seriously?' she says.

Could it be him? Sour grapes?

'I wouldn't dismiss it,' says Jazzy. 'Is his name really Coin as in money?'

'Maybe it was Coyne originally. But he changed it before he figured out how tacky it would be. Now he's stuck with it.'

Jazzy Gupta laughs, a light jovial sound. 'You're such a smart girl,' she says, patting Lexi's arm. 'I need some champagne.'

As they gravitate towards the bar, Lexi notices their host, Arif Yildiz, and he's in conversation with Roger Cavendish.

Roger appears to have popped in from a polo match. A short-sleeved, collared shirt and white pants. Most of the men favour some kind of suit jacket, a concession to the weather, grey and damp, as much as anything. But Roger is displaying his tanned muscular arms, and he doesn't seem cold.

Lexi surveys the room, a large open-plan space with a wall of windows on two sides looking out above the treetops of the park. All these kinds of places use height to create a sense of superiority and escape from the bustle of the city below.

She's considering the psychology of high-rise blocks, when a woman she doesn't recognise approaches her.

'You look thoughtful,' the woman says, with a flick of her dark mane of hair.

'I'm just marvelling at how we accept luxury apartments

so far above the ground, when, the practicalities, not to mention safety considerations, outweigh the fantastic view.'

The woman smiles. 'Actually, I agree with you,' she says. 'Although I'm not sure my husband would. You must be Lexi. I'm Rania Yildiz.'

Shit!

Lexi has a sinking sensation.

Always figure out who you're talking to!

She laughs nervously. 'Now I feel a complete fool. You invite me to this lovely launch, and I say something stupid like that.'

'No,' says Rania. 'It's an honest comment. And they'll be too few of those here this afternoon. But to sell properties like these, you need to be aware of people's legitimate concerns. You'll need an answer for those questions, like is the cladding safe?'

'I'm sure everything here is top spec.'

'It is. But, if I were a buyer, I wouldn't want to think I'm being fobbed off, or worse still, lied to.'

'Property agents can have a terrible reputation,' says Lexi.

'My husband says you have a manner that invites trust.' She lets the emphasis fall on the last two words.

Her gaze is regal and penetrating, her simple jersey dress elegant but understated. To Lexi, it's the definition of class, but the whole encounter is making her uncomfortable.

Rescue comes from an unexpected quarter. Teddy Devereux, his topknot neatly plaited, approaches them carrying two champagne flutes.

'In a former life, I was a waiter,' he says in his cut glass accent. 'And I can't seem to help myself when I see two ladies in need of a drink.'

It's a slick intervention, Lexi'll give him that. And it forces her to introduce Devereux to Yildiz's wife.

Having offloaded the glasses, Teddy spreads his hands and a look of rapture spreads across his features. He could be looking at the Sistine Chapel. 'Your husband has such taste,' he declares. 'I'm in awe.'

Lexi catches Rania's eye and is rewarded with a wry smile.

Fifteen love to me, Teddy!

Wandering off to admire the view, Lexi ventures out onto the strip of soggy astroturf that constitutes the garden. She stares over the ornamental shrubs that line the balcony, and the treetops of the park, to the brown turgid line of the Thames beyond.

'I'm glad you could make it,' says a voice from behind her. The soft tenor with the hint of an accent sends an involuntary shiver of excitement up her spine.

She turns to face Yildiz, who is beaming benignly at her.

He's too old, too married, and this is business.

And yet she feels it; some kind of frisson. Is it the power he wields to make or break agents' careers? Or a potentially jealous wife scoping her out? Or the sheer fact that a man like this is interested in her, at least professionally. All of it adds up to something, although she's not sure what.

'Thank you for the invitation,' she says with a tight smile. 'I've just had the pleasure of meeting your wife.'

'I'm glad. She's so integral to all this, although she would never admit it. I rely on her taste.'

'Looking around, I'd say that's paid off.'

Compliments exchanged. There's a lull. Yildiz tilts his head. 'Renfrew Hall,' he says. 'Any progress?'

'I made contact with Mrs Jessop yesterday. But...it's a delicate situation. The poor woman is grieving and I would feel guilty if—'

'No, don't feel guilty, Lexi' says Yildiz sharply. 'You

must press her, and I'll tell you why. You're doing her a favour.'

'Am I? It doesn't—'

'Of course you are. In the midst of emotion and grief, how can anyone see what they need? Your job is to help her clarify. This is the place where her husband was murdered. Think about that for a moment. I would want to be rid of it as soon as possible, wouldn't you?'

'I suppose if you put it like that.'

'She may not want to think about it, but a quick sale will be far easier for her in the long run. Okay, we profit. That's business. But she walks away with a tidy cash sum to rebuild her life. Does she have children?'

'Two girls.'

He smiles. 'What would you want if you were in her shoes?'

'I'd want to escape.'

He shrugs. 'She'll thank you in the long run.'

Lexi considers this. He's right. Hard-nosed but essentially right.

42

Friday. 12.15pm

Boden watches Jess Penrose striding out across the yard in front of them. She splashes through the puddles in her green wellies. Boden's own feet are soaking; she feels envious and tetchy. Chakravorty brings up the rear, in a more sensible pair of trainers.

They're heading for one of the outhouses at the back of the farm buildings.

'What's he doing?' says Boden, as much to force her to slow down and engage.

'Butchering,' says Jess, over her shoulder. 'When we send the cattle to the abattoir, we always get a carcass back, which we cut up for the freezer.'

Boden and Chakravorty exchange looks.

Butchering?

'Isn't that quite a skilled job?' says Boden. 'How does Mason know how to do it?'

Jess stops at a wooden door and shrugs. 'Dad used to do it. He taught Mason years ago.'

Years ago?

This confirms Boden's suspicion that Brian Penrose was underplaying how well he knows Mason. An angry man in a wheelchair, his bolshy teenage daughter, and a man who wanted to help and protect them? Is that what they're looking at here?

Jess opens the door and the sharp metallic tang of blood hits them with a faint musky odour of animal fat. The smell reminds Boden of a crime scene more than a butcher's shop, but attendance at numerous postmortems has given her a strong stomach.

On top of an old, stone-topped table, there's half a beef carcass. The meat is a deep, almost ruby red, marbled with thick veins of creamy white fat. The bones, thick and sturdy, jut out where joints have been severed, their whiteness stark against the rich colour of the meat.

Boden catches Chakravorty's eye. The young DC is looking queasy.

On a wooden block beside the table, there's a selection of butcher's knives. A cleaver with a broad rectangular blade, a pointed boning knife, a long breaking knife with a curved blade like a Scimitar. Boden knows she and the DC are thinking the same thing: what are the chances they're looking at the murder weapon?

Motive and method.

But there's no sign of Mason Green.

'He must've popped out,' says Jess.

Boden curses under her breath. Tea and chats? Has she allowed herself to be duped by the Penroses? That would be annoying.

'Here's the thing, Jess,' she says with icy calm.

'Obstructing a police inquiry is an offence. How's your dad going to manage while you're sitting in a police cell, eh?'

A bit below the belt.

But it hits the mark. Jess reddens with embarrassment and blinks a couple of times. 'I didn't do anything to ob—'

Boden raises her finger. 'Stop before you make this worse for yourself. You saw us drive up, you texted him? Am I right?'

Jess stares at her boots. She's not a bad kid, and she's not used to lying, certainly not to a police officer.

She struggles with this for a moment, and then she blurts out, 'He saw you himself. He texted me, asked me to take care of Lily.'

'And give him time to get away?'

Jess nods.

'Why's he running? What's he done?'

'He hasn't done anything?'

'Did he want to help you and your dad?'

Jess shuffles from foot to foot, an inner battle going on, then she erupts. 'We're not stupid. We looked Jessop up on the net. All the stories about him and his family. They're drug dealers. Bloody drug dealers! You lot must know that. Says the police've been chasing him for years. He bought the Hall with drug money. And he's trying to buy us with drug money. He's the criminal here, not Mason, but you're ignoring that. All you lot are doing is trying to find someone to pin a murder on. I hope you like your job.'

She glares at Boden, full of righteous spite, but tears prickle on her lashes.

Boden sighs. 'When you say 'we' looked him up, you mean you and your dad or you and Mason?'

Now the tears flow. 'Dad thinks this is all his fault. That

we wouldn't be in this situation if it wasn't for his accident. But we would, wouldn't we? Mason was only trying to help.'

'By killing Jessop?' says Chakravorty.

'No! He'd never do something like that. That's just not who he is…'

'But you don't know for sure, do you?' says Boden.

'I know who he is,' says Jess through her tears. 'I know him. He's not…he's not a killer.'

Boden wonders how many times she's heard that. People aren't, until they are, until something tips them over that invisible line.

She tilts her head. 'Are you and Mason in a relationship?'

Jess hunches her shoulders; she's embarrassed. 'Not really. Just, y'know…hanging out, more like friends.'

'Then be his friend and tell us where he's gone.'

'I don't know.'

'Take a guess,' says Boden. 'Because running makes him look guilty. You must see that. And I do like my job most of the time. And we are well aware of Craig Jessop's history and connections.'

Little does she know the DCI is obsessed with this.

Jess wipes her face with the sleeve of her jumper. 'He's probably in the old grain silo. We don't use it anymore. I'll show you.'

'Good decision,' says Boden.

43

Friday. 12.20pm

Lexi has sipped her way through two flutes of champagne, which is her limit for these sorts of occasions. They went down too quickly, because she's quite tense, but there's a lot in play. It's tempting to accept a third glass from the tray being offered to her. Instead, she asks the server for some sparkling water.

Roger joins her. Hand slotted casually in his pocket, glass in hand; alcohol doesn't seem to ruffle him.

'Interesting chat with Yildiz,' he says.

Lexi can't work out if that's a statement, referring to his own conversation, or a question about her conversation.

'Yes,' she replies. The server brings her the sparkling water; she thanks them.

'He rates you,' says Roger.

'I'm flattered.' She takes a mouthful of water; the pop of the bubbles helps distract from her nerves.

'See that odd little fellow he's talking to now?' Lexi

follows the direction of his gaze. 'I have it on reliable authority that he's bankrolling this development.'

Yildiz is chatting to a shorter man, middle fifties, cropped grey hair and a well-cut Armani suit masking his pot belly. The man has a sallow face and a bland smile. And, as she observes them, she notices Yildiz's manner is subtly different. More deferential? This is someone he wants to impress.

'Who is he?' says Lexi.

'He's called Besnik Krasniqi,' says Roger with a shrug. 'As far as I can gather, no one has a clue who he is. I've looked him up. Quite a common Albanian name. I found a football player, a professor, various others. But he's a mystery.'

Lexi wonders what kind of response Roger is expecting.

'A grey money man?' she says.

'Probably,' says Roger. Then he adds abruptly, 'Renfrew Hall? Is Yildiz still pushing for that?'

'Yes,' she says.

Roger pulls a face, a cross between a grimace and a look of pained concentration. 'Let's not be precipitous,' he says.

Precipitous? What the hell's that supposed to mean?

He raises his eyebrows and smiles. 'Say this for Yildiz. He serves a decent.champagne. I need a refill.'

Lexi watches him meander away to the bar.

Understanding Roger's cryptic comments can be annoying at the best of times. He is the boss, ultimately, despite what Gemma might think. Why can't he give her a clear instruction? If he thinks this deal Yildiz is proposing is a bad idea, why doesn't he just say?

Maybe he is saying.

If she was stressed before, now she feels worse. Jazzy Gupta comes bustling across the room towards her.

'Had a text from Cosmo, my assistant. The cleaners are in

your flat sorting it out. Should be done and dusted within the hour, and he's sourced a new front door.'

Lexi forces a smile. 'Thanks, Jazzy. I'm more than grateful.'

Jazzy gives her a quizzical look. 'Sounds like a but there somewhere?'

Lexi sighs.

Just tell her.

'I'm sorry,' she says. 'I haven't been completely candid. I have a cousin who's done some crazy stuff in the past. I don't know if it's him, but…perhaps it is.'

The bearded young bloke on the bike has been preying on her mind. The more she tries to dismiss it, the more it seems like he could be Ewan.

'Cousins are the worst,' says Jazzy with a shake of the head. 'If you have a lot, as I do, then statistically one of them is going to turn out to be a sociopath.'

Lexi can't help smiling. Jazzy is so matter-of-fact about everything.

'Ewan was in prison until recently.'

'Is he dangerous?' Jazzy's gaze is direct and penetrating. 'What does he want?'

How can you answer that?

'He's been texting me, following me.'

Jazzy reaches out and touches her arm. 'You know what I'm going to say, don't you, my dear? It's a matter for the police.'

Lexi nods. 'I know.'

But that could be career suicide.

She has no chance to say more. A woman with bright red lipstick and white blonde hair is bearing down on them. Tall and angular like a model, she's impossible to ignore. She thrusts out her hand towards Lexi; the nails are red talons.

'My goodness, it's Lexi Harper, isn't it? Fancy seeing you here.'

Lexi is forced into a handshake.

Jazzy smiles. 'I'll leave you to catch up.' She retreats.

Staring at her 'friend', Lexi tries to mask her confusion. 'Sorry,' she says. 'I've got a terrible memory for—'

The woman is expensively dressed, but so is everyone in the room. There's something else about her. She fits in, and yet somehow she doesn't. 'Holly,' she says. 'Holly Stirling. A friend of Beth Nolan. Beth's boyfriend Damian is my brother-in-law.'

Lexi is thrown.

'Oh,' she says.

WTF? More bullshit of Beth's?

'You're a hard woman to track down. Beth has been calling you. You don't pick up. Why would you ignore a friend?'

Lexi is moving rapidly from surprise to irritation.

'I've been busy,' she says curtly.

'We went to your office, and a pleasant young woman called Pia told us where we might find you.'

'Listen, I don't know what Beth's said, but it has nothing to do with me. None of it. I didn't ask her to—'

'No. You listen, Lexi.' Her voice is quiet but emphatic. There's a hardness around the eyes. 'We have a situation here, and we require your help to resolve it. This is not a request.'

Lexi balks. 'I'm sorry, you can't walk into a private event and expect—'

'Can't I, Lexi?' Those red talons reach out and grip Lexi's wrist. 'Lots of curious eyes here. Think about your brilliant career, your lovely colleagues. You don't want a scene, do you? We just need a chat. Now.'

Lexi stares at her. The make-up is immaculate, but it's a

mask, a disguise. Damian's brother is a criminal. That much she knows. And the wife?

Inhaling, Lexi glances around. She's right; eyes will be on her. Roger? The Yildizs? Jazzy? Is there a lull in the chatter, or is she imagining it? She looks down at her captured wrist. Holly smiles and releases it.

'Okay,' Lexi says. 'I can spare you ten minutes. But I have colleagues here who will be looking out for me.'

Make it clear you're not intimidated.

Holly Stirling looks her up and down. The gaze is leisurely and dripping with disdain.

'It's just a chat,' she says.

Inside, Lexi is quaking. What the fuck has Beth got her into?

Friday. 12.35pm

Beth is in a trendy independent coffee shop, full of retro styling and reclaimed furniture, close to Sloane Square. In the heart of Chelsea, her favourite stomping ground, it's the sort of place she would love to hang out in normal circumstances. But sitting opposite Marcus Stirling is not a normal situation. It's like all the terrible dates she's ever had rolled into one.

Their table is on one side of a large room, with no other customers that near. The vibe Marcus gives off is enough to deter anyone. If you saw him, you'd keep your distance.

But there's a hot chocolate with marshmallows and cream in front of her, which is helping soothe her jittery nerves.

Marcus is glued to his phone; he's not a person for idle chit-chat. In fact, he has about as much charm as an XL Bully. She's made several attempts to engage him. She listened to bits of a podcast once about kidnappings, and the advice was to engage your kidnapper in conversation, so they relate to you as a human being rather than an object. But Beth doubts that Marcus relates to anyone.

His sidekick, Brandon, is seated next to her, effectively blocking any exit route to the door. He's a wiry lad in his twenties and a real foot-tapper. His right leg is turbo charged, jiggling up and down to a compulsive rhythm.

They're waiting. And it's been a while. She feels trapped in her seat, because basically she is.

Marcus looks up from his phone. His eyes are curious, and not in a good way.

'Drink your chocolate.' It's an instruction. Beth obeys.

Be cool. It'll be okay.

Then Marcus glares at Brandon. The foot-tapping abates. Beth gives him a sympathetic glance; she knows what it's like to have too much energy.

Finally, out of the window Beth sees the black Range Rover Discovery pull up kerbside. Holly gets out of the back seat, followed by Lexi.

Beth's heart soars.

She's come!

Her friend hasn't let her down. She's the one person in the world that Beth knows she can rely on.

Holly strolls into the coffee shop and Lexi follows. Beth wants to jump up and throw herself into her best friend's arms, but Brandon is in the way.

Marcus puts his phone in his pocket as his wife approaches. Beth beams and tries to make eye contact with her friend, but Lexi is scowling like a pissed-off teen and avoids her gaze.

Holly takes charge of the situation. She nods to Brandon, who vacates his seat and Holly motions Lexi to sit down in his place. Beth reaches out impulsively and touches Lexi's arm. But her friend stiffens and pulls away.

'I'm so sorry, babe,' Beth murmurs.

Lexi just exhales; she's staring at Marcus, who's glaring back at her. Holly sits down next to him, and steeples her fingers.

'Okay,' she says. 'This is really simple, Lexi. We need you to get in touch with your cousin, Ewan, and arrange to meet him.'

'What? How?' says Lexi. 'I haven't seen him since we were kids.'

Marcus chuckles. Well, more like rumbles deep in his barrel chest. 'Most people would respond by asking why,' he says. 'So I'm assuming that you're lying when you say you've had no contact?'

Lexi has a mulish expression. 'Whatever Beth's said to you, it's rubbish,' she says. 'She lies about everything. Surely Damian's told you that.'

Beth glances across at her. That's hardly fair.

'Water under the bridge,' says Holly. 'Suffice to say, two colleagues of ours paid a visit to your cousin. One was an old and dear friend. Your cousin...' She takes a breath. '...murdered him in cold blood, slashed his throat...'

Lexi gasps. Her hand flies to her mouth.

'...and stabbed his companion, putting him in intensive care.'

Everyone at the table is silent; they seem to be in a bubble, with the babble of voices around them in the coffee shop far away and separate.

Beth can feel Lexi trembling. Her friend's head dips and she puts her face in her hands.

'I can see you're shocked,' says Holly. 'Which is to the good. And your way out of this situation is clear. We have no interest in why your cousin is threatening you. All you need to do is set up a meeting and leave the rest to us.'

Lexi removes her hands. Tears are rolling down her cheeks. 'I can't just…I don't know…I…'

'But you can,' says Holly. 'Didn't you receive a text that you believed was from him?'

Lexi wipes her tears with her fingers. She nods.

'That's where we start.'

'It's for the best,' says Beth. 'He's crazy. Like some kind of mad dog, you know that, babe.'

Lexi ignores her. Her chest is rising and falling, her breathing laboured. They're sitting inches apart, but it seems like miles. Beth wants to comfort her. Hearing what Ewan has done must be a shock; it was a shock to Beth. But it fits with what he did at Renfrew Hall.

'And what you need to bear in mind,' says Holly, 'is we know where you live and work. It's in your interests to co-operate with us. You are the catalyst for this situation, Lexi, and therefore, you bear the responsibility for the outcome. As to the future, you will owe us a debt. We have funds to invest in property and you can help us facilitate that.'

Lexi shakes her head abruptly. 'That's not possible,' she says. 'There are laws, and my firm does not do business with criminals. You may think you can blackmail me, but you can't blackmail them.'

Holly and Marcus exchange a private husband-and-wife-smile. Beth finds this odd; perhaps he does have a soft side, which only his wife sees.

'You prefer a better class of villain, do you?' says Holly. 'That's amusing.' She looks at her watch. 'You have until six o'clock to make contact and persuade him to meet you. Give me your phone.'

Lexi stares at her, still belligerent. Holly waves her hand impatiently. Lexi gets it out of her bag and hands it over. Holly types in a number.

'This is the number you use to call us,' she says. 'And if you have any sort of notion to share this with the police, I would consider it carefully. Be sensible, Lexi. We all make mistakes, but do you really want to wreck your entire life?'

Holly places Lexi's phone on the table between them. She gets up and so does Marcus. They saunter towards the door, which Brandon is holding open for them. They head for the Discovery, waiting for them on the double yellow line outside, and in another moment they're gone.

Lexi has her hand over her mouth. 'I'm going to be sick,' she mutters.

'Deep breaths,' says Beth, putting a hand on her back.

Lexi inhales and exhales slowly. It seems to work.

'Have some of my hot chocolate,' says Beth, pushing the mug towards her friend. 'It'll help.'

Lexi turns to look at her. It's a hard and hostile scowl. She pushes her chair back to increase the distance between them.

'I know you're upset,' says Beth. 'But—'

'How do I know any of this is even true? You, Damian, the whole crooked bunch of you. Are you just setting me up, Beth, so I'll launder money for these people?'

Beth feels as if she's been smacked.

How could she even think that?

'No, babe, I'd never do that. All I wanted to do was help you.'

'Don't call me babe,' Lexi snaps.

She's turned away from Beth, hugging her arms around herself.

'I don't believe you,' she says. 'I don't know why I've put up with your scams for all these years. It's obvious what you are. You're scum. You're as much of a criminal as them. I don't know why I've ever trusted you.'

A desolate wave of anguish sweeps over Beth. Her eyes flood with tears.

She doesn't mean it. She's just angry.

'I know I've fucked up, but—'

'Your whole life is one long fuck up. You never learn, Beth. Nothing ever changes. You're just too stupid and too lazy.'

The words rip into her. Lexi has never talked to her like this before. Anyone else, it'd be no big deal. But not Lexi.

'I'm sorry,' she whispers.

'Sorry doesn't cut it. Even a moron like you should be able to understand that. You've put me in an impossible position.'

'What are we going to do?' says Beth.

'We? There is no we.'

Lexi stands up. She looks a bit wobbly on her feet and reaches out to the table to steady herself.

'You must do what Holly says or—'

'Or what? You won't get your pay off? How much have they offered you?'

Why is she saying this stuff?

'They kidnapped me and forced me.' Beth can't stop crying, and they're attracting some curious glances. 'This is the best option, and after what Ewan did to that client of yours too—'

'I don't believe you. And I don't trust you.'

'Can't we go back to flat and work out what to do?' pleads Beth.

'What? You're worried you've got nowhere to stay?'

'No. I just thought—'

'Don't come anywhere near me. Don't call me. I don't care if you're sleeping on the streets. I won't help you. You need to understand that. I never want to see you again.'

Lexi loops her bag over her shoulder and heads towards the door.

Beth watches her go. It's as if her guts have been kicked out. Plenty of people have hurt her over the years. Physically, emotionally, that's just part of life. But the realisation creeps over her, blokes are one thing, mostly it's just sex, this is what it's like to have your heart completely broken.

45

Lexi is shaking like a leaf. A maelstrom of thoughts is ricocheting round her brain.

Ewan? This is a lie, it has to be. They're setting you up.

She's walking in a daze down Chelsea Bridge Road towards the river, blocks of luxury apartments on her left, some of which Cavendish Cooper sold, and Ranelagh Gardens, part of the Chelsea Hospital grounds, on her right. She notices the branch office of a rival firm, one of the big corporate guys. It's hard to miss with its glossy steel and glass facade. Can she imagine herself working somewhere like that? She could end up having no choice, but would they even take her?

Not if you become the girl who got her client murdered.

The shoes are killing her; patent leather pumps with a spiky stiletto. They cost the best part of seven hundred quid, and she can feel a blister forming on her right heel. A black cab approaches, travelling in the opposite direction, but she waves at it furiously; the cabbie executes a U turn and pulls up next to her. As she gets in the back, she wonders if she should head back to the office. It's tempting, and she needs time to calm down and think. But wouldn't that look to Yildiz like she's bailed? Wouldn't that be rude? She can't afford to create a bad impression.

She gives the cabbie the address of the development. It's a short drive, only about five minutes, on the south side of the river.

Her phone has been vibrating in her bag. Beth, no doubt. More lies. More bullshit.

She pulls it out; she's on auto-pilot and checking her phone is a reflex action.

Five missed calls.

From Mum? Again?

She frowns at the screen. This is the most her mother's called her in years. Lexi has a sense of foreboding.

She clicks on the number and returns the call.

'Mum?'

'My God, Lexi!' exclaims a panicked voice on the other end of the line. 'Why do you never pick up?'

'Are you all right? What the hell's happened?'

'Are you all right? Have the police been in touch?'

'In touch about what?'

'It's Ewan…he's…he's…' she's frantic. 'Some blokes came round to the house. Debt collectors, the police say. Ewan attacked them with a knife, killed one, put the other in hospital. The police are looking for him.'

Lexi opens her mouth to speak, but no words come.

Not a lie then.

'Lexi?' says her mother.

Breathe. In for three, hold for four…

She can't hold her breath. She splutters. Her heart is beating too fast and won't slow down.

The taxi draws up outside the development.

'Lexi? Are you still there?'

'Mum, I've got to go. I'll call you.'

'Wait Lex—'

Lexi hangs up. She swipes her card on the handset to pay the cab fare, and steps out.

Standing on the pavement, she struggles to gather her thoughts. She has to bring some order to the chaos in her head. But if it's true about Ewan, the police will get him.

What if they don't?

Kenny Coin comes strolling out of the main entrance to the building. He sees her, beams, opens his arms, and walks towards her.

'Hey, Lexi. You really, really should let me buy you lunch —' His smile turns to a frown. 'Are you okay? You seem really—'

'Do I really, Kenny? Really, really?' she snaps.

She strides past him and into the building, ignoring the pain in her heel. He flings out his arms and says something. But she's out of earshot. The burst of temper gives her the adrenaline punch she needs.

She takes the lift up to the penthouse floor. There's a bathroom to the right as you enter the suite, and she's praying it's unoccupied. From the babble of chatter floating down the hall towards her, she concludes the party is still going on. With luck, she'll slip back in unnoticed. How long has she been gone? No more than twenty minutes? If anyone has noticed her absence, she'll say it was an important client call she had to take.

It'll be fine.

Reaching the bathroom, she tries the handle, but it's locked.

Sod it!

Her right shoe is killing her. She glances down, easing her foot out. The heel is red raw and bleeding.

As she examines it, the bathroom door opens and Arif Yildiz appears.

There's a moment of awkwardness.

He grins. 'Lexi,' he says. 'Are you okay?'

'Fancy heels!' she replies with a shrug. 'The more you pay, the worse they are. These are brand new, so it's my own stupid fault for not breaking them in.'

He peers down at her foot. 'Oh my goodness,' he says, his voice full of concern. 'Let me get you some medical attention…'

'No seriously, Ari. That's not necessary. I've got some… plasters in my bag…'

A white lie.

He's scrutinising her and tilts his head. She must look like crap, because he takes her arm gently and shepherds her towards another door.

'Come in here,' he says, 'and let me get you some proper help and another more comfortable pair of shoes.'

His tone is tender and paternal, which takes her by surprise; this is not a reaction she was expecting.

'Ladies and their shoes,' he says, shaking his head. 'I say to my wife and to my daughter, why would you walk around in something like that?'

Lexi allows herself to be guided, and relief courses through her.

How great would it be to have him for a father?

There have been too few times in her life when she's felt cared for; she learned early on to take care of herself.

He smiles at her. 'Don't look so worried,' he says. And the tone is soft and soothing, the way you might speak to a child. It touches her to the quick and the dam inside her breaks. The tears come and she can't stop them. He steers her into the room, which turns out to be the study, and closes the door behind them.

'I'm so sorry...' she blubs.

'Sssh,' he says, guiding her towards the desk chair.

She sinks into the soft leather. He squats down beside her and inches the shoe off. She winces.

'You're bleeding,' he says. 'I think a doctor should be called.'

'No, that's ridiculous,' she says. 'It's just a blister.'

He looks up at her. 'It must be painful because you seem very distressed.'

She turns away; she doesn't want him to see her like this.

'This is so unprofessional,' she whispers. 'I'm so sorry.'

'Hey,' he says. 'No apology necessary.'

She meets his earnest gaze. The concern is genuine. She can feel it. Whatever his bullying reputation, this is a glimpse of the man beneath, and he's full of compassion. Are they crossing a line here between business and friendship?

'I'm just...I can't explain,' she says. 'I've been speaking to my mother.'

He doesn't comment or question; he waits.

'It's family stuff...'

He stands up. 'Ah, families,' he says. Then he sits down on a stool next to her, close, but not too close. 'They can be complicated.'

Leave it at that.

She wants to, but she can't. The strain and pressure of the last few days is choking her. She probably has some kind of

PTSD. His kindness is as overwhelming as it is unexpected. Would it be so wrong to respond to that?

'My cousin,' she says. 'He was in prison until recently. And I've just heard from my mother that he's committed another murder.'

An expression of horror spreads over Yildiz's features. 'Oh my good God, Lexi! How terrible for you.'

Now she can't seem to stop. It pours out. 'He's… unhinged. His childhood was terrible. He stabbed another boy at fourteen.'

Yildiz is frowning with concern. He gives his head a sorrowful shake. 'That's awful.' He reaches out and touches her hand. The physical contact with him is consoling.

And talking to him is so easy; she doesn't want to stop. She can't stop.

'But that's not the only problem,' she says. 'I think…well, maybe, that he's been following me, stalking me. He sent me some texts.'

'That's horrible.'

'And…he might've followed me to Renfrew Hall.'

Yildiz's brow furrows with perplexity. 'What are you saying, Lexi?'

'I think it could've been him who killed my client, poor Mr Jessop. But I've got no proof. Only a feeling.'

He inhales sharply and doesn't speak. She can hear his breathing.

Her hand flies to her mouth. 'I feel so guilty. The notion that this could've happened because of me.'

You've done it now. It's all fucked.

But telling the truth is a release. The knot in her chest and in her belly unwinds. His face is inscrutable.

What the hell is he thinking?

He folds his hands and says, 'Listen to me carefully, Lexi.

The first thing you have to know is this is not your fault. You are not responsible for the actions of your cousin.'

'I'm not sure everyone's going to see it that way. Roger'll sack me. No one goes to a firm that gets their clients killed.'

Yildiz gives her a sardonic smile. 'Well, it's not the best look for your brand, I'll give you that. But what matters is what you do now. Have you spoken to the police?'

'Not about this. I was interviewed about what happened. But I haven't shared my suspicions because…well, they're just that.'

He stands up and slots his hands in his pockets.

'However crazy this sounds, that's what you must do. Tell them, immediately. Firstly, because it's the right thing to do. Secondly, because it's imperative to lessen any reputational damage to yourself.'

'I know you're right. I don't know why I've hesitated.'

'Five days ago you witnessed a brutal death that left you reeling. But when did you learn your cousin has murdered someone else? Today?'

She nods.

'Then, provided you speak to the police now, at once, having just learned this from your mother, no one can reproach you for your actions.'

'You're right. Thank you.'

'And if Roger is foolish enough to let you go, Cavendish Cooper not the place you should be, is it?'

Yildiz stands in front of her, solid and reassuring.

He's right. Of course he's right.

Relief courses through Lexi. This cuts through all the confusion, all the nonsense with Beth and Damian's gangster brother. She'll tell the police about that too.

They'll get what's coming to them.

'I'll phone the DS that came to see me,' she says. 'I've still got her card.'

Yildiz nods. 'It's the right thing. And the police will catch him, Lexi. Then you'll have nothing else to worry about.'

She reaches out to him. 'Thank you,' she says. 'You put everything in perspective.'

He squeezes her hand. 'Don't let this wrong-foot you,' he says. 'Remember who you are. You're a winner. Keep your eye on the prize.'

'I will.'

46

Friday. 1.20pm

Boden is standing in front of the boss's desk. Knight leans forward on it, pivoting her swivel chair from side to side with a coiled tension, as she stares at her computer. On screen is the live feed from the interview suite. Mason Green has been cautioned and brought in. He sits listlessly on a chair, staring at the wall in front of him.

Boden and Chakravorty found him hiding in the disused grain silo. Jess Penrose led them right to him and Boden's impression was that he was relieved.

'You think he's our killer?' says Knight. She sounds disappointed.

'I'm not sure,' says Boden. 'The knives have all gone to the lab. One of them might be the murder weapon. We've got a motive of sorts. But do we believe he was capable of taking on Jessop and Liam Cox?'

'He could've picked them off separately. Cox then Jessop. Young man, looks pretty fit and strong.'

Ever since she arrested him, Boden's doubts have been growing. He sat in the back of the car, gazing out of the window with a blank expression. Lily has been left with the Penroses, although social services will need to be informed.

'Takes real rage to cut someone's throat, unless you're an out-and-out psycho,' Boden says. 'Has he got that? I'm not sure.'

'Well, let's see what he has to say for himself,' says Knight. 'If we can get enough out of him to take it to the CPS, that'll be a result.'

Boden knows that the DCI's preferred option would be to tie the murder to Craig Jessop's criminal past, but to crack it in five days will still be a good outcome for her, and go some way to repairing her tarnished reputation.

Knight gives her a chilly smile. 'Get me enough to charge,' she says. 'A confession would be good.'

Boden nods and heads for the door. The DCI's attitude annoys her. She understands it, but that still doesn't make it any easier to swallow. Results and statistics make careers. That's probably why she's still a sergeant.

Chakravorty meets her in the hallway and offers her a filled roll wrapped in cling. 'Hummus and salad. All they had left,' she says.

'Thanks,' says Boden.

Chakravorty bites into her own roll as they walk. Boden sighs. She doesn't feel like eating. She's been here before and she doesn't like it. Being pressured by a boss to push a suspect into a confession. Is Mason Green vulnerable? There's something about his silence and despair that bothers her. Knight would argue that it's guilt. But guilty of what? Two brutal murders? A team has been dispatched to search the gatehouse for evidence. Whoever killed Jessop and Cox would've ended up covered in blood.

.   .   .

Boden and Chakravorty face Mason Green across the narrow plastic table in the interview room. But Mason's demeanour has changed now the tape is running. He's nervous and hyper.

Leaning forward in his chair, he says, 'I want to tell you what happened.'

Perhaps Knight'll get her confession?

'Okay,' says Boden. 'First, I need to caution you again.'

As she recites the caution, she can feel his leg tapping under the table. He's decided to talk; now he's impatient and on edge.

'And,' she says, 'you may want to reconsider whether you want a lawyer to be present.'

'No,' says Mason bitterly. 'What use are bloody lawyers? They didn't help Brian.'

'And you wanted to help Brian, didn't you?' says Boden.

Mason nods. 'Look, I knew when they turned up that it was an opportunity.'

'Who turned up?' says Boden.

'Two of them,' says Mason. 'But only one spoke English.'

Where is this going?

'Two of them?' says Boden.

Mason sighs. His eyes dart around as he tries to order his thoughts. 'Jess asked me to help her. I've known her since she was a kid. I'm ten years older. But Brian and my dad were mates for years. Played darts, went to the football.' He frowns. 'His accident should never have happened…if I'd been there…a beat-up old tractor. He tried to fix it himself, on his own, because he had no choice.' He speaks rapidly, and Boden notices he's sweating although the room isn't warm.

'Because of the cost?' says Boden.

'While he was in hospital, I helped on the farm as much

as I could. Jess was brilliant, loads of new ideas. The pumpkin patch really took off. She promoted it on Instagram and people loved it. Then Jessop turned up. Where did he get the money to buy Renfrew Hall, eh?'

'Where do you think?' says Boden.

'I don't think, I know. My girlfriend's brother got three years for dealing. Y'know what he told her, you grass, they'll kill you. You know who he worked for? Liam Cox. Cox runs all the networks round here.'

'What was his name, your girlfriend's brother?' says Boden.

'Matt Horner. Check it out. He's in Birmingham, Winson Green. I'm not lying.'

'Two men?' says Boden. 'Tell me about them.'

'They just turned up one day. Driving a Mercedes, a Black Series Coupe. Leather jackets, fancy watches, sounded Eastern European. They were friendly, sort of. But they had that edge, y'know.'

'What sort of edge?'

'They could do stuff, hurt you, if they needed to.'

'Did they threaten you?'

'No, just asked a load of questions. About the Hall, about Jessop, when he would be there. I figured, what do I owe him? He doesn't pay me on time, he's trying to boot the Penroses out. They're all just villains. What do I care if some other thugs come asking questions about him?'

'When did these men turn up?'

'First time was back in August.'

'They came back?'

'About three weeks ago. They gave me a phone number. Offered me five grand to phone them when I knew Jessop was likely to be there.'

'And did you?'

Mason closes his eyes and swallows. His chin quivers.

'Yeah, I took the money and made the call.' He shakes his head regretfully. 'I didn't…know what they'd do. What they wanted with him. Maybe I should've guessed. But, I was broke. And I didn't care.'

'How did you know when Jessop would be there?'

'He phoned me two days before and said a property agent would be coming from London. Told me when. Wanted me to go up to the Hall and switch the electricity on. Last six months, it's been off when no one's there. I go up and switch it on if anyone's coming.'

'You phoned this other number when?'

'After Jessop phoned me.'

'Two days before he and Cox were killed? What did you tell them?'

'I said Jessop was coming to meet a property agent. Monday. Four pm.'

Boden leans back in her chair. 'Mason, how do I know these men even exist? Did anyone else see them or know about them?'

'No. Well, Jess knew vaguely.'

'Vaguely?'

Boden watches his face; he's close to tears, but she knows she has to push him.

'Is this a story you've made up?' she says.

'No.'

'You sure? You haven't made this up because you murdered Craig Jessop and Liam Cox?'

'No! Christ no!' His body shudders with the visceral release of pent up tension. 'What kind of fool do you take me for? You think I could creep up on a bloke like Cox with a knife?' His shoulders slump. 'I could lie to you. I could say they threatened me, threatened Lily. But I'm telling the truth.

You got my phone. The call's right there. I was desperate, so I took their fucking money. Don't you think I'm gutted enough and ashamed of what I've done?'

His tears drip onto the plastic tabletop. He wipes his face with the back of his hand.

'Where's the money?' says Boden.

He gives her a remorseful look. 'In a pink Peppa Pig backpack, upstairs under Lily's bed.'

'Five thousand pounds in cash?'

He nods.

'Let's take a break,' says Boden. She glances up at the wall mounted camera, and imagines what the DCI must be thinking. If this is true, then her ambitions for a broader OCG inquiry could be reborn. 'Do you want anything, Mason? Coffee? Water?'

He shakes his head.

Chakravorty switches off the recording and they both leave the room. They head off down the corridor.

'Do you reckon he's telling the truth?' says Chakravorty.

'I'll believe it when we have the evidence to back it up,' says Boden. 'The forensics team should find the money.'

'A Black Series Coupe?' says Chakravorty. 'That should help with the ANPR.'

Boden's phone buzzes. She glances at it and frowns. Lexi Harper?

She answers. 'DS Boden.'

47

Friday. 1.30pm

Lexi is in the study of the penthouse in the luxury development in Battersea; Yildiz has left her alone to make the call to the police. The launch party is winding down and she can hear people in the hallway outside as they leave. Snatches of laughter increase the hollowness she feels inside. Despite Yildiz's reassurances, she can't escape the fact that she could be responsible for a man's murder. Who is ever going to forget that? Hasn't she got enough guilt in her life?

DS Boden answers immediately, brisk and professional, which is both reassuring and intimidating at the same time.

'It's…Lexi Harper here, the…property agent.' Her voice is quaking.

'What can I do for you, Ms Harper?' says the cop.

'I…just…I'm not sure where to begin.' It's harder than she thought. What do you actually say?

'Take your time.'

'I think…well, I'm not sure, but I might know, that is, I suspect I know who might've killed Mr Jessop.'

There's a moment of silence on the other end of the line.

'Okay,' says Boden. 'Where are you?'

'At an event, a property launch in Battersea.'

'Do you feel able to tell me about this on the phone, or do you want to meet in person?'

Lexi sighs. 'I need to tell you now, urgently…well, you'll see why.'

'Okay,' says Boden. The cop has a way of saying okay that sounds provisional, as if she's agreeing but reserving judgement. It's probably a police thing, the way they train them to sound detached.

Lexi takes a deep breath. Where the hell does she begin?

The detective can obviously hear the hesitation in her silence because she says, 'Take a breath and tell me who and then tell me why you think that.' And now she sounds more sympathetic.

'It's my cousin,' Lexi blurts it out. 'His name is Ewan Burns, and I think he's been stalking me. I think he might've followed me to Renfrew Hall. He recently got out of prison. His sentence was for murder. He stabbed another boy when he was fourteen. But my mother just phoned me and told me he's killed another man, stabbed him and wounded someone else. And the police are looking for him.'

'Where did this recent attack take place?' The cop sounds businesslike.

'He's been back home, living with my uncle in Luton. I think it happened there.'

'Luton. Is that where your mother lives?'

'Yeah, it's where I grew up.'

'Have you any idea why he's stalking you?'

'No, not really. I haven't seen him since before he went to

prison and that's over ten years ago. But I was nineteen. I'd already left home, so I'd hardly seen anything of him for years before that. It was probably one Christmas the last time. We're not a close family.'

'When you say he's stalking you, have you actually seen him?'

'Well, I'm not sure. I saw this boy on a motorbike that could've been him. And I've received a threatening text.'

'Saying what?'

'Don't ignore me. That was on Tuesday.'

'The day after the murders?'

'Yes. And then on Wednesday evening, I came home and found a snake in my flat. Someone had put it through the letterbox.'

'A snake?' The cop sounds genuinely surprised.

'Apparently, it was a corn snake. Not poisonous.'

'Scary enough, though. Okay, listen. My colleague is contacting the team who are looking for your cousin. But my concern is for your safety, if he could be targeting you. You certainly shouldn't go home or anywhere he might find you.'

'I know.'

'Is there a friend you can stay with?'

'I've been…using another flat. Yeah, I'll find somewhere.'

'And you're with other people currently?'

'Yes.'

'I'm going to ring off and speak to my colleagues. But, listen to me Lexi, be cautious, but don't panic. If he's wanted in relation to other serious offences, we will find him. Once I have more, I'll come back to you. Any sighting of him, any suspicion that he's near, ring me or call 999. Are you going to be okay?'

'Yes. And…thank you.'

'We will find him. I'll call you.' The cop hangs up.

Lexi feels a weight has been lifted. She realises her hands are shaking.

You've done the right thing.

The police will catch him and, whatever the fallout, she'll deal with it. She's wondering if she should bite the bullet and tell Roger now when the door opens a crack and Jazzy Gupta pops her head round.

'I was wondering what'd happened to you,' she says. Then her expression changes. 'My dear, are you all right? You look as if someone's died.'

Jazzy steps into the room as Lexi puts a hand to her mouth. More tears, but of relief.

'Oh my dear girl!' says Jazzy. She sits on the stool vacated by Yildiz and places a comforting palm on Lexi's shoulder.

'I'm okay,' says Lexi. 'But I'm wondering, have you moved Li Hua into that apartment yet, because I really need to…it's complicated…and—'

'I gather the cousin issue has not gone away.'

'No,' says Lexi.

'You must stay with me,' says Jazzy. 'You'll be far safer.'

'But I don't want to put you to—'

'I insist. Have you seen the size of my driver, Carl? Ex-military. He'll see anyone off.'

Lexi smiles at her friend. Surely she can call her that now? She's always been guarded in terms of professional relationships, but the kindness these people have shown her in her hour of need has floored her. Yildiz, now Jazzy, where would she be without them?

48

Friday. 1.35pm

Beth has stopped crying, although she's still shellshocked and nauseous. They're on some road next to Battersea Park, standing under a dripping tree next to the railings. Brandon offers her a cigarette. She shakes her head; that would definitely make her puke.

As soon as Lexi left the coffee shop, Brandon came back in carrying a motorcycle helmet. He insisted she put it on. He had his instructions from Marcus. They were to follow Lexi. At first Beth flat out refused, but he just stood there.

'You got no choice, have you?' he said, although he sounded vaguely sympathetic.

Beth felt so desolate she didn't know what to do. She could've made a scene, accused him of harassing her, got him chucked out. But where would that have left her? She's skint. Marcus has all her stuff, Lexi hates her. She hates herself, if she stops to think about it. It was easier to do what she was told.

Brandon has one of these nippy trail bikes that scream when you accelerate; the sort used to ride up behind people and nick their phones. This is probably why Brandon got it.

Riding pillion felt precarious. She didn't want to hold on to him, but as soon as they set off, she seized him round the waist out of sheer panic. They'd caught up with Lexi as she was getting into a cab.

Brandon kept his distance, and they travelled in a slow convoy over the river and down the road to a block of luxury apartments next to the park, where the cab dropped her. She talked to some bloke before disappearing inside. Oddly, once she was through the door, this bloke gave her the middle finger. Not a friend, then.

Brandon had removed his helmet. 'Nice gaff,' he said. 'This where she stays?'

The place looked brand new and there were all these flags outside advertising apartments for sale.

Is he thick?

'Probably work,' Beth had muttered. 'She sells flats.'

They'd set up camp across the road. Brandon sent a text, presumably to Marcus. Then they hung around, trying not to be too conspicuous.

It's a good half hour, perhaps more, since they arrived. And it's cold and damp. Beth is shivering; all she has is a denim jacket. But she'd be miserable wherever she was right now.

There's a steady flow of traffic separating them from the block, but it seems to Beth that when Lexi comes out, she'll see them.

Brandon is on his third fag, bit of a chain smoker.

'Those things kill you, y'know that, don't you?' says Beth.

'Yeah, but not 'til I'm old and knackered, and who wants

to be old?' says Brandon, grinding the cigarette end into the pavement with his foot.

He's got a point. Why worry about something in the future? This chimes in with Beth's philosophy. Enjoy yourself as much as you can. Getting from day to day with a smile on your face is hard enough.

Lexi'll come round. You have to believe it.

'You an optimist?' says Beth.

He screws up his face. 'I dunno.' Then he sniggers. 'What kind of stupid fucking question is that?'

They lapse into silence. Beth gives him a sidelong glance. He's not bad-looking, bit of a mullet haircut. She notices his hands; he bites his nails, which reminds her of Lexi. Except he's not secretive about it. He can't keep still, fidgets continually. Beth wonders if this is him or if he's taken something. Could be either. Or both.

'How long you worked for Marcus?' she says.

'Couple of years.' He lights another cigarette and twiddles it between his fingers.

'Good boss?'

Brandon shrugs.

'Where you from?'

He glares at her. 'What the fuck d'you care?'

Beth sighs. 'I'm just making conversation. Since we're stuck with each other.'

His arms are folded across his chest, as if he's hugging himself, and he's leaning against the railings. He draws on the ciggie and shoots a glance at her. His eyes are his best feature, with long dark lashes like a girl. 'Sorry,' he mumbles.

'I try to get on with people,' says Beth defensively. 'It's in my nature.'

He doesn't reply, but he is looking at her now.

'Basildon,' he says.

'Okay,' says Beth. 'You got family there?'

He shakes his head. 'Grew up in care.' He hesitates, and adds, 'Got a brother, but we lost touch.'

'Hard,' says Beth.

'I don't give a monkey's,' says Brandon with a shrug.

Across the road, a sleek, high-end black Mercedes with tinted windows pulls up outside the apartment block. The kerb is down several steps from the neatly paved area that fronts the block, so it is possible to see through the plate glass doors of the entrance beyond.

Brandon sees her first.

'Put your helmet on,' he says sharply. 'Think that's her.'

Two women are coming through the doors. One is tiny, but the other does look like Lexi. Recognition brings a wave of distress, but Beth swallows it down, and turning away, she pulls the helmet on. Brandon is already astride the bike and starting it up.

Lexi and the other woman are walking towards the Mercedes. The driver gets out and opens the back door for them to get in. Her friend's head is dipped to listen to what her small companion is saying. She doesn't look in their direction at all. And she appears to be limping.

It's those silly Louboutin heels. You told her not to buy them.

Beth climbs onto the back of the bike behind Brandon, and he swings it around to join the flow of traffic as the Mercedes pulls away.

Keeping up with it is no problem. There's a slow-moving stream of vehicles as they head north back across the Thames, and Brandon makes sure there's a couple of cars between them and the Mercedes.

Beth wonders where they're headed and what the hell will happen next. Surely, Lexi will have the good sense to do what

Marcus has asked. It would be mad to ignore him. And perhaps once this is all sorted out, and things have calmed down a bit, Lexi will realise that Beth only ever meant to help her.

She will. She has to.

Beth holds on tight as the bike speeds up across a changing traffic light to keep up. She can't even imagine what her life would be like without Lexi. It's an outcome she refuses to consider. Somehow, this has to work.

49

Friday. 2pm

Boden and Chakravorty are speeding down the M1 to a rendezvous with DI Tom Roscoe, the SIO of the team hunting Ewan Burns.

The investigation has veered off in a different direction, as often happens. And to give the boss credit, when Boden told her about the new intel they'd got from Lexi Harper, Knight took it onboard without any resistance.

The information Mason Green gave them needs verification. Did he really speak to some potential suspects two days before Jessop's visit to the Hall? It's only one line of inquiry.

What Lexi Harper's saying sounds more plausible to Boden.

They pull into the London Gateway services, where they find Roscoe in the car park, leaning on an unmarked vehicle and scrolling on his phone. Roscoe is so tall and lanky he's always lounging on something. Boden has worked with him before, when he was deputy SIO to her former boss. They also went on an awkward date once. It was at a time when she was isolated and lonely, and she agreed to it out of desperation, which is hard to admit to herself now.

'Afternoon, ladies,' he says with a grin. 'Welcome to the A team.'

Still trying to be Mr Charming.

Boden smiles, although for a terrible moment, it looks like he's going to hug her, but he thinks better of it.

Chakravorty is watching with a wry smirk. She knows about the date, unfortunately.

'Well, let's get a coffee and I'll fill you in,' he says. 'We've been tracking our man's bike on ANPR and the last hit was in Central London.'

They walk towards the Starbucks franchise.

'That fits with what our witness is telling us,' says Boden. 'She believes he's stalking her.'

'And Ewan Burns is her cousin?'

'Yes. I asked her why he's stalking her. She says she doesn't know. But if he followed her to Renfrew Hall, slipped in and knifed her client, not to mention his sidekick, he's certainly making a point.'

Roscoe nods. 'You think she does know why?'

Boden shrugs. 'If so, she's not telling us.'

They reach the coffee shop, and Roscoe insists on ordering and paying.

As they wait for their drinks, Roscoe stands, hands in trouser pockets, with his trademark slouch.

'I'm surprised the powers that be have given this to Knight,' he says airily. 'Bad luck for you, that you have to work with someone like that.'

Like that?

The office politics, the rumours. Boden's been on the receiving end of enough toxic gossip herself to hate it. She feels Chakravorty bristle beside her. The DC is a straight shooter, and she's loyal. Boden ignores the hook; whatever her private opinions about Rachel Knight, she's not about to share them with a player like Roscoe.

Always friendly, never intimidating to colleagues, that's his MO, and it's made him popular with both the junior and senior ranks. Boden doesn't buy it. He's rabidly ambitious, but, as far as she's concerned, he and Knight can scrap it out over who takes credit for this case.

Collecting their coffees, they move to a table away from other customers.

'First up,' says Boden. 'I'm worried about my witness. I need to call her and reassure her.'

'Absolutely,' says Roscoe. 'Here's what we know about Ewan Burns. Convicted of a gang-related murder as a juvenile. Released on licence and has a job as a vehicle mechanic. We're talking to his employer. Since his release, he's been living with his father. Yesterday evening, two men went to the house. He slashed the throat of one who died at the scene and stabbed the other who's in hospital.'

'Our victims both had their throats slashed.'

'That matches then,' says Roscoe. 'We've been told that the men he attacked were debt collectors, but we have our doubts. The one who died was a thug with a record as along as my arm, and quite a tough customer. The survivor is in intensive care; we haven't been able to talk to him yet.'

'So Ewan Burns is seriously dangerous?'

'Oh yeah. He finished his sentence in adult nick. Big guy, heavily into weight training. Probation service thought he was doing okay, but they would say that. Sounds to me like this is another gang he had some sort of beef with.'

Roscoe's phone buzzes. He answers immediately.

'Roscoe.'

He's focused and he's on it, which Boden finds reassuring.

'Thanks, mate. Cheers,' he says, hanging up.

He turns to Boden and Chakravorty. 'He's been riding round Central London. Met have put a drone up. Last sighting is in the City ten minutes ago, then he went off the grid.'

'Must've parked up somewhere,' says Boden.

'Yeah, but we've got it down to a pretty tight area. Lots of CCTV round there. He won't get far.'

Boden nods. She gets out her phone and rings Lexi Harper's number. It's answered on the third ring.

'Lexi,' she says. 'It's DS Boden. Where are you?'

'I've just arrived at a friend's house in St John's Wood.' The property agent sounds nervous.

'You okay?'

'Sort of.'

'Try not to worry. Stay there. Stay inside. Text me the address. I'm going to come round.'

'Oh,' says Harper. 'Is that really necessary? I don't want to upset my friend, if you see what I mean. She's been extremely kind.'

Boden knows exactly what she means. A posh address, a rich friend who won't want police in her house.

'Lexi,' says Boden. 'Have you told your friend this is a serious situation?'

'Of course. I've put her fully in the picture.'

She's lying.

'Okay, well. We need to know your whereabouts, so could you text me the address?'

'Happy to.' She doesn't sound it.

'If he contacts you, call me immediately. Okay?'

'Do you know where he is?' says Harper.

'We're narrowing it down. Just hang on in there, and I'll get back to you soon.'

'Thank you.' Her voice is small and subdued. She sounds scared.

Boden hangs up and turns to her colleagues. 'She's tucked up at a friend's house in St John's Wood. Not too shabby, eh?'

'So is that posh?' says Chakravorty.

'Yeah. Somewhat,' says Boden. 'So posh she doesn't want us to go round.'

'We're in the wrong job,' says Chakravorty. 'Can't be that hard to sell houses.'

Boden grins. She could be right.

50

Friday. 2.40pm

Ewan wipes his mouth with the back of his hand. He's just demolished the last bite of his double cheeseburger and he licks his fingers. He hadn't realised how hungry he was. Half the fries are still left. He offers them to Jared.

His brother scowls at him. 'You always cover them in ketchup. I hate ketchup.'

'Since when?' says Ewan.

'Since forever, you moron.'

Some grumpy old geezer three rows in front of them turns round and goes shush. Jared gives him the finger. They're in the expensive seats at the back of the auditorium. The cinema is fancy and empty, except for them and the weirdo in the mack.

They'd been riding around for quite a while, and Jared got fed up and whined about being cold. Fair play, the weather is pretty pissy. The leathers and helmets keep you dry, but even through his thick gloves, Ewan's fingers were getting numb.

So he'd found this underground car park where they could leave the bike and rest up for a bit. It turned out to be in the Barbican, a part of the City that neither of them knew.

While they were wandering around this huge concrete maze, Ewan saw a poster for the film. It was a Samurai movie, in Japanese with subtitles, but Ewan didn't give a stuff about that, or the fact it was halfway through.

He loves Samurai movies and watching these guys swinging their amazing swords round their heads. He would love a proper Katana. You can buy them on the net, but they're not cheap.

With the fries gone, Ewan moves on to the bucket of popcorn. The film is winding up to the final confrontation between the good guy and the bad guys. The music is loud and banging. They start this epic fight, long swords in one hand and shorter knives in the other. The good guy chops up a couple of the opposition straight away. A boot in the gut, then slashing from side to side, but it's elegant and skilful, the clash of steel ringing on steel. Ewan wonders what it would be like to be a proper swordsman, a true warrior, like these guys. The training, the discipline, he would've been up for all of that. But he was born in the wrong place and the wrong time.

'Fucking brilliant,' he whispers under his breath, turning to his brother for his agreement. But the stupid sod has fallen asleep. Anyone who can't appreciate the beauty of a movie like this has got no soul.

Now the hero is down to his last opponent. And the bad guy is defeated and on his knees. But the hero pauses. He doesn't just hack off his head as he's perfectly entitled to do. He puts up his sword and bows. And the bad guy bows back. Respect between warriors, which is the only mark of true nobility.

But what comes next is the best bit. The vanquished fighter gets his own dagger, pulls up his robe and rips open his own stomach. He's committing seppuku; he has to because he's accepting the shame of defeat. The hero bows in deference to such courage, then raises his sword and lops off the guy's head.

Ewan has seen this in Samurai films loads of times before, but it always moves him. No one dies with honour anymore; it's all bombs and guns and drones. Not proper hand to hand battle. And what's the point in winning if your opponent doesn't acknowledge it and bow to you in shame?

And she will. You'll make her bow.

That's what Ewan wants, what he needs. To savour his victory, he needs to look into her eyes and see her shame.

The end credits on the film roll and the lights come up. He nudges Jared and they wander out of the cinema into the fading afternoon light.

As they saunter back towards the car park, Ewan feels light and floaty, moving along in a bubble. Jared is quiet too. That's the bond between the brothers. They don't need words. Never have.

The car park is one level down and accessed via a flight of bare concrete stairs. When they get to the bottom, there are a pair of double swing doors which Ewan shoulders open.

He freezes in the doorway. Across the other side of the low-ceilinged parking garage, there's a police car with flashing blue lights; and it's stopped in front of Ewan's bike. There are two cops in uniforms walking round the bike. One of them is talking into his radio.

Ewan shoves his brother back through the door, then grabs it so it doesn't bang and draw attention to them.

'Fucking CCTV,' says Jared. 'Saw it when we drove in.'

Ewan had too, but he thought they had time, that the cops

would be twiddling their thumbs. It irks him he was wrong. And this is down to her again, sending those goons after him.

You didn't deserve that.

'Always some bastard keeping tabs on you wherever you go,' says Jared glumly. 'None of us are free.'

Ewan exhales. 'Don't matter,' he says. 'It's time, anyway.'

The endgame. The battle.

Jared smiles at him and clenches his fist. 'Yeah,' he says enthusiastically. 'Bring it on!'

'Yeah,' says Ewan, and they bump fists.

51

Friday. 3.30pm

Lexi is perched on a leather bar stool in Jazzy Gupta's sumptuous kitchen in St John's Wood, and it all feels rather uncomfortable. She's never been good at accepting help. Now she's doubly in Jazzy's debt. But the cops have told her to stay put and wait. She hopes she's stopped them from turning up on the doorstep.

The house is an elegant white stucco villa, semi-detached but over five floors, with a spacious excavated sub-basement. This is where the kitchen is located, with large sliding doors onto the garden. It's what agents would describe as excellent family accommodation. Lexi gazes out at the neat patio lined with well-manicured shrubs in planters and the generous lawn beyond. This size property in this part of town goes for big bucks.

Jazzy is arranging crudités, olives, and cheese on a platter.

'I'm a nibbler,' she says. 'Big meals, seven course tasting menus, I simply can't do it.'

Lexi smiles. 'That's how you keep so trim.'

Jazzy pats her stomach and laughs. 'You think? You're lucky to be tall. Being short is a curse, always looking up at everyone.'

She bustles about with such energy, and although she's tiny, her huge personality can dominate any room. Lexi can't help envying her, the way she's turned what she perceives as a disadvantage to an advantage. That's confidence.

And she's so easy to talk to. They could almost be two old friends relaxing in a kitchen and catching up on all the gossip.

You need a proper friend like this.

The rollercoaster of the last few days has left Lexi beleaguered and isolated. There must be twenty years or more difference in their ages, but she's always wanted an older woman friend; someone smart and worldly-wise, who she can talk things over with. Someone who can give her sound advice.

Jazzy goes to the wine cooler and selects a bottle of Cloudy Bay. 'The problem with champagne at lunchtime,' she says, 'is that when I get home, I always want another drink.'

At Yildiz's launch, the champagne was flowing, but Lexi noticed that although Jazzy always had a flute in her hand, she never did more than sip. Lexi suspects the wine is for her.

Jazzy opens the bottle and pours. She hands Lexi a glass. 'Just to take the edge off,' she says with a grin.

Lexi raises her glass. 'Thank you,' she says. 'For…well, for everything.'

As they chink glasses, Jazzy's daughter comes stomping in with a scowl on her face and dumps her backpack angrily on the counter.

'You're not gonna believe this,' she says to her mother, ignoring Lexi.

'Darling, where are your manners? We have a guest.'

The girl turns her pouting gaze onto Lexi. She's about fourteen, with her mother's dark, watchful eyes, but taller and leggy like a faun. Lexi can see immediately that she has the makings of a beauty. 'Sorry,' she mumbles.

'Lexi, please excuse her atrocious manners. This is my daughter, Zara.'

'Bad day at school?' says Lexi. 'I remember it well.'

Zara manages a smile. She's wearing a smart maroon blazer with a blue ribbon trim and a pleated grey skirt, the sort of old-fashioned school uniform that only comes with an expensive private school. How difficult can her life be Lexi wonders? What she wouldn't have given for a private education. In her own school, the battle was to get through a lesson without someone throwing a chair. Teachers came and went. After GCSEs, she got out and went to college, which was marginally better.

'So?' says Jazzy, raising her eyebrows with maternal authority. 'This is Beatrice again, is it?'

Zara's eyes fill with tears. 'She's just with Mia all the time now, Mummy. And she says she wants to share a room with her on the ski trip, and not with me.'

'That is tough,' says Jazzy, drawing her daughter into a hug.

Lexi sips her wine and watches enviously, as Jazzy strokes her daughter's hair. So much in life is determined by the luck of birth. From what she knows about Jazzy, she was born to money, and her husband Sanjay is successful in IT. She's also mentioned a son at Oxford and staying with her sister, who lives in the Hamptons.

Jazzy is rocking her weeping daughter gently. 'The thing

is,' she says, 'friends can be fickle. It's a fact of life, my darling.'

'It's so not fair,' says Zara. 'When Issie's gang was being so horrible to her last year, I stood up for her.'

'I know,' says Jazzy. 'You were a loyal friend, and this is how she repays you.'

Wise up, kid. It's your best friend who's most likely to shaft you.

As Lexi listens, she wishes she had someone to moan to about Beth, her lies and machinations. But it would be too shocking for Jazzy; she'd never understand why Lexi had held on to such a morally dubious friend for so long. Yildiz, maybe he'd understand? He's probably got people who he's had to discard along the way, as he moved up from one social milieu to something better. It's not snobbery; it's just practical necessity. These people would not accept a friend who shoplifts. And worse.

Lexi has her phone on the counter in front of her; it buzzes with an incoming text. She glances at it intending to ignore it, but the words jump out at her.

Fuck this shit. Told U not to ignore me. We need to talk.

She takes a large mouthful of wine to cover her shock. Is this him? Is it Ewan? It could be Marcus. It could be…

She inhales. Jazzy is scanning her; she doesn't miss a trick.

'Everything okay?' she says.

'Yeah,' says Lexi. 'Just something I… need to deal with.'

Jazzy flaps her hands. 'I'm sorry,' she says. 'I should've done this before. Let me show you to your room, so you can have some privacy.' She gives her daughter a comforting pat. 'Have some juice, darling,' she says, and she heads briskly towards the kitchen door.

Lexi follows her upstairs to the second floor, and a smart

double bedroom overlooking the back garden. High ceilinged, stylish, colour coordinated, Jazzy points out the door to the en suite and then discreetly disappears.

Sitting down on the bed, Lexi stares at the phone. She's left her wine in the kitchen, now she wishes she hadn't. She remembers DS Boden's instructions.

If he makes contact…

But is it even him? She needs to be sure.

She hesitates for a moment. Then her thumbs fly over the keys. In her head is the sick sense of guilt she's always had around her cousin, the heavy burden of responsibility she carries for his broken life.

Is this Ewan?

She waits. Outside, the November afternoon is darkening. She can see into the lighted windows of the house backing on to the Gupta's, another cosy enclave of comfort and wealth.

The phone in her hand buzzes.

No its fucking father christmas

She feels her stomach muscles tighten.

What do you want?

U cant shut me up. Send all the blokes you like. Im still here.

Lexi's palms are sweating.

I didn't send any blokes. I swear.

U still a fucking liar

Panic is engulfing her, but she has to think clearly. She needs to find out where he is so the police can get him.

Okay. You want to talk? Where? You in London?

There's a pause. With luck, this has wrong-footed him. If he gives her a location, she can give it to Boden.

Meet me?

Yes. Tell me where.

A couple more minutes tick by and Lexi's wondering if she's scared him off. Then another text pops up.

Go to front of St. Pauls. I see U on yr own I text instructions from there

When?

U got 1hr

Her body is rigid with fear, but the only way she can solve this is to agree. It's a half hour taxi ride, but she needs to give the police time.

It'll take me an hour to get there

U got 1hr

She wonders what she's going to tell Jazzy. Her friend already knows she's been speaking to the police about her stalker, but not any of the details. Perhaps she should have allowed DS Boden to come round? It was just a knee-jerk reaction. Her years in super prime property have taught her one thing: rich people have an odd attitude toward the police. They prefer private security.

But the priority now is to alert them. She scrolls her phone to find DS Boden's number.

52

Friday. 3.45pm

Boden and Chakravorty have been relegated to the back of the control room. Roscoe is in his element, prancing around and talking to the operational commander from the Met. Their turf, their job now. But it's hard not to feel like a spare part.

Chakravorty is watching wide-eyed; it's her first time witnessing a large operation like this. But for Boden there's an awkwardness bordering on embarrassment. It's some time now since she transferred out of the Met, and it's hard to forget the circumstances. Her boss at the time made it crystal clear there was no place and no future for her there and she had to go.

But as she looks around the control room now at the sea of faces, none of them are familiar. This is a big organisation and Cal keeps making the point to her that personnel have changed, and her old boss is long gone.

The Gold Commander in charge is female and younger

than Boden would have expected in that role. She looks surprisingly calm considering they've got a knife man on the loose, somewhere in the City, as the homebound rush hour is about to start and with the added complication, it's a wintery afternoon and already getting dark. Instructions are being issued, teams are being deployed.

Ewan Burns' motorcycle has been found in an underground garage in the Barbican. CCTV for the entire complex is being scrutinised, with one confirmed sighting of him outside the cinema.

Boden's phone vibrates in her hand with an incoming call. She looks down at it. Lexi Harper.

She answers. 'Lexi. How's it going?'

'He's…he texted me. Wants me to go to the front of St Paul's and wait for more instructions.'

This is a game changer.

'Okay, when exactly was this?'

'Just now. Like a couple of minutes ago. He's given me an hour to get there.'

Boden puts her hand over the phone, steps forward and calls out, 'Excuse me, ma'am! I've got the cousin on the line. He's texted her. Wants her to go to the front of St Paul's and await further instructions.'

As Boden speaks, every head in the room swivels to look at her, and the Gold Commander holds up her finger for silence. 'What else has he said?'

'He's given her an hour to get there,' says Boden.

She uncovers the phone. 'Lexi, can you read me the whole exchange you had with him?'

Harper sounds flustered. 'All he said is he wants to meet me and talk. And I've got an hour to get there.'

'He's saying he just wants to talk?'

'I don't know what he wants. It's a couple of texts.' The

tone is tetchy and Boden wonders about that. But Harper is jumpy and undoubtedly scared; the priority is to calm her down.

'It's okay, Lexi,' says Boden. 'Just to confirm. He wants you to go to the front of St Paul's…'

'And he'll text me more instructions.'

'When you get there, he'll text more instructions.' Boden repeats this so her colleagues can hear.

The Gold Commander is saying something quietly to her number two. In the background, people are moving around, but Boden focuses on her phone.

'Listen to me, Lexi. He's dangerous, so you do nothing. Stay where you are and wait to hear from me.'

'Yeah.'

'Are you going to be okay?'

There's a hesitancy, then Harper says, 'Of course. What will you do?'

'We're putting a tight net around the area. We'll apprehend him. Stay put. Any more texts, call me immediately. Okay?'

'Yeah. Okay.'

Boden hangs up.

'Where is she?' says the Commander.

'At a friend's in St John's Wood. She wouldn't let us go round there. Possibly bothered by what the posh friends would think. But it also feels like there's some element here that she's holding back.'

The Gold Commander nods. 'Like what?'

'She wouldn't read the whole text. Maybe she's nervous. But I don't know. Just a sense.'

'Have you got the address?'

'Yes. I made her text it to me.'

'You know her. Go with armed back-up and get round

there. I don't want him turning up and causing mayhem. DS Boden is it?'

'Yes, boss.'

'Good work.' The Gold Commander flashes her a smile.

'Thank you.' Boden beckons to Chakravorty, and they head for the door.

53

Friday. 4pm

Lexi, arms tightly folded, stands by the window peering out. From this vantage point, the garden below is long, with a serpentine path winding between the dark, overhanging trees and shrubs. On a wintery afternoon, it's already full of patches of blackness.

She's waiting to hear from DS Boden. It's hardly ten minutes since they spoke, but her nerves are in shreds. Exchanging texts with her cousin, and having the confirmation that it's him, has completely unmoored her. He's out there somewhere, not so far away, hiding and waiting for her. A cat strolls across the lawn, triggering a security light, and she almost jumps out of her skin.

What does he want? What the hell does he expect?

That young bloke on a motorcycle, almost running her down, then sitting astride his bike, grinning at her as if it were all some sick joke.

Was it really him? A grown man with a beard?

The thought, the reality of him, sends an icy chill right through her. And it's driving her back into the past, to a place she doesn't want to go, to memories she's tried to shut away.

She attended his trial, because her mother forced her to go. And in her head, that's still Ewan, a skinny teenager, sullen but defiant. She remembers how he kept staring across the courtroom at her. When the guilty verdict was handed down, he didn't react. Her mother sobbed, although Lexi told herself at the time it was just self-pity.

Now she's not so sure. It was easy to make snap judgements back then. Her aunt sat beside her mother, gaunt and desperate. She was dying of cancer, and Mum nursed her. She died a few months later, and everything imploded. Lexi had focused on herself and the escape plan that would get her as far as possible from her train wreck of a family.

It's not your fault. It was never your fault.

And yet, she knew her mother blamed her. They never spoke of it, but the accusation was there in her eyes. Mum watched her sister die. She watched her nephew go to jail. And her seething anger she directed at Lexi.

Lexi had to leave. She had no choice. It was the only way to survive.

The phone is on the bed. It buzzes. Going over and picking it up, Lexi is hoping for a message from the police. But it isn't them.

Tick tock

She texts back. What can she say? She can only lie.

On my way. Bad traffic

U setting me up?

No

You owe me

She starts to type: *I don't understand what you want from...* Then she deletes it.

Whatever he wants, he's right about that. She does owe him. He's the one who suffered, she's the one who escaped. Why? Because she was older? Maybe it was as simple as that.

In her mind's eye, she can still see the fragile little boy he was before he got swept up in the gangs. He was so broken and confused. Nothing would comfort him. The guilt rises up inside her in a torrent threatening to engulf her.

It is your fault.

She paces the room. None of this is any good. She can't alter the past. She has to get her head straight. He's a killer and extremely dangerous; she must leave him to the police. But what if he's cornered? What will happen then? The police will be armed, obviously they will. If he won't give up, if he threatens them, they'll shoot him.

The thought of that is unbearable. She's lived through some bleak times, but that really would be her fault, and there's no escaping that.

You setting me up? He knows.

But the stalking and the snake, even what he did at Renfrew Hall, these things were all designed to upset and unnerve her. Surely if he wanted to kill her, she'd already be dead?

She comes to a decision. There's no way she can just sit in Jazzy Gupta's plush guest bedroom and wait for the police to call her and tell her they've shot her cousin dead.

Scrolling on her phone, she orders an Uber. Then she returns to the thread of messages and types a new text. He's got things he wants to say to her, and that's the window of opportunity. If she can use this to talk him into surrendering, she must at least try.

I am coming. I promise you.

She presses send. It's the right thing to do, to try to save him. If it all turns out badly, which it probably will, at least she will have done that.

54

Friday. 4.45pm

Lexi's Uber hustles its way through the impatient, snarling rush hour traffic and drops her at a bus stop on Cannon Street near the front entrance to St Paul's. She adds in the extra tip she promised the driver and steps out onto a busy pavement slick with rain.

She'd slipped out of the house without a word; Jazzy and her daughter were still in the kitchen. It seemed simpler. But once in the cab, she sent her friend an apologetic text promising to explain later.

Would there even be a later?

Nervously, she turns her raincoat collar up against the drizzle. An umbrella would've been sensible. But there's nothing sensible about what she's doing now.

She walks slowly towards the front of the cathedral, as a steady stream of bustling pedestrians weave around her. Her cousin isn't stupid; he's chosen a busy place at its busiest time. Crowds of hurrying people are flooding out of their offices, shoving the milling tourists aside as they make for their buses and trains. If he's out there, a face in the dark, scurrying crowd, it would be impossible to identify him.

Her phone buzzes.

Go round right of building up to Cheapside to tube station

She stares at the text and the cold reality of it hits her. He's here, somewhere in the crowd, watching her. Should she reply? If he's watching her, it isn't necessary.

Crossing the road, she walks along next to the black iron railings of the cathedral grounds. His instructions aren't that explicit, but she knows this part of the City well enough. She turns left up New Change. It's dark now, with a sea of garish lights refracting in the rain. The congested pavement is packed with pedestrians and umbrellas. Putting her head down, she walks.

She stops just past St Paul's tube station to avoid the throng heading straight for it. It would be tempting to join them. Lose him, get out of here, text Boden.

But her phone buzzes again with further instructions. These direct her up King Edward Street towards St Bartholomew's Hospital. The crowd thins and the street is more sombre, fewer streetlamps, light leaching from windows, all punctuated by blinding headlights on the passing vehicles, glittering in the rain. It leaves her giddy, but perhaps that's fear.

Then she sees him. He's standing on the other side of the road in the gateway of what looks to be a small garden between the buildings. He's grown tall and broad-shouldered. A large man with a shaved head, a thick, dark beard and a leather biker's jacket.

He beckons to her, then turns and walks into the small park.

She hesitates. Whatever feelings and guilt she has about

that fragile little boy she used to babysit, this is not who she's dealing with now.

Walk away. Call the cop.

Even as she crosses the road and follows him, she is well aware this is madness. But she has no choice. This day was always going to come. She knows that. In her heart, she's always known it.

55

Friday. 5.05pm

Beth is soaked to the skin. The rain has gone through her denim jacket and plastered her T-shirt to her back. Her legs are numb with cold; the thin material of her leggings no protection when riding pillion on a motorcycle through the steady drizzle. She has her arms firmly round Brandon's waist, as much for the warmth from his body as anything else. They've been dodging in and out of the traffic for what seems like an age. All the stopping and starting, Beth is dizzy with it.

They're somewhere in the City. Beth's not sure where; she's more of a West End girl. The bike brakes sharply and he says something over his shoulder, but Beth can't hear. She can't see much either and flips up her foggy visor as he points.

Lexi, in a smart trench coat, is crossing the road about ten metres in front of them. She looks wet and cold too. But on the other side of the road is the gateway to some sort of public garden, and Beth glimpses the back of a big bloke in leathers walking away from them and down the path into it.

Brandon has his visor up too. 'I think that's him,' he says. 'He beckoned her. She's following him.'

Ewan? That's him!

Beth's heart leaps into her mouth. This is mental. Lexi shouldn't be going to meet Ewan on her own. She jumps off the back of the bike, but her limbs are so cold and stiff, she catches her foot in the process and lands facedown in the gutter.

Brandon looks down at her. 'What the fuck?' he mutters.

Beth scrambles to her feet. Fear for her friend overrides the grazes on her hands. Should she call out? Let Lexi know she's here. But Lexi has disappeared through the gateway and out of sight.

She turns to Brandon. 'Where's Marcus? Hasn't she called him?'

Brandon shrugs. 'Not far as I know.'

This is so fucking Lexi!

Beth has watched her friend march through life, a one-woman band thinking she needs no-one. It's just plain stupid.

'Well, call him then!' she exclaims.

Brandon glares at her. 'Chill,' he says. 'I'm about to.'

It's hard not to panic. Lexi has just followed a killer into a shadowy death trap nestled among the trees and bushes, away from the safety of the street and other people. No good can come of this. And the size of him, too. The only memory Beth has is of a skinny half-grown teen. But the bloke she caught sight of must be over six feet, and he dealt with Marcus's two guys with ruthless violence.

He'll kill her. You can't let this happen.

There's no time to think. Beth knows what she must do. She has to get in there and back-up her friend. He'll think twice about knifing both of them. Or maybe her sudden appearance will throw him off for long enough for them to run.

She has to wait for a gap in the traffic before she can cross the road. Brandon has got his phone out.

She scoots behind a black cab and breaks into a trot.

'What the fuck are you playing at?' shouts Brandon after her. But she ignores him.

Through the gateway, she finds herself on a slippery flagstone path. There's a soggy patch of grass with a border of shrubs, some trees ahead of her, and buildings either side. An old-fashioned streetlamp fixed on the side of the building throws an eerie light on the path. But up ahead are deep shadows from the overhanging trees and she catches a glimpse of Lexi. Then she's gone from sight round a corner.

Beth breaks into a sprint. Most things in her life she's been useless at, but she can run, usually away from store detectives or bouncers. What she's running into now is probably not good. But she has only one thing in her mind: get to Lexi.

56

Friday. 5.07pm

The gardens open out into a small central paved square with flowerbeds and wooden benches set in a semi-circle. As she walks, Lexi tries to calm herself by letting her gaze scan the surrounding buildings. Some older than others, four or five storeys, they encircle this small green enclave. On one side, there's the back of an old church.

But in front of her is Ewan. He turns to face her. She stops. There's enough light to see his face, but he just stands there staring at her. Not a kid anymore. A large, inscrutable man. A blank, strange expression.

'I can't believe it's really you,' she says, with a tremor in her voice.

He lets out a sigh, or perhaps it's more of a huff, tilts his head to one side, about to speak, but something catches his eye. He glances off to her right, where someone is running at full pelt down the path towards them.

She turns to look. A jogger? An office worker about to miss their train? Then recognition dawns.

WTF!

Beth comes to an abrupt halt beside her, leans forward, hands on her knees, gasping for breath.

'Fuckin' told you to come on your own,' growls Ewan.

'I did. I promise you,' says Lexi.

She's floored. A cascade of thoughts rush through her brain. If Beth's here, then Marcus is not far behind, and this could turn ugly very quickly.

She looks at her. 'Why the hell are you following me? I don't want you here.'

Beth inhales, but she ignores Lexi. 'Remember me, Ewan? Beth?'

He nods. 'Yeah. Another fucking bitch,' he says. 'You were there too that day.'

'I was, and I can tell you, it wasn't Lexi's fault.'

He glances to his left and points. 'You need to tell that to Jared, not me.' He pauses and nods, as if he's listening to someone, then he adds, 'Yeah, Jared says he wants to know.'

What? Who's he talking to?

Lexi looks at Beth, who's equally astounded.

Is he talking to his brother? Lexi is not sure what she was expecting, but this is another level of lunacy.

'Ewan,' she says. 'Jared is dead. He drowned when he was five years old. He fell in the river. No one knows how. Don't you remember?'

He doesn't reply. He tilts his head up and frowns, half closing his eyes, but the tension is zinging off him and the stillness of a beast preparing to pounce. This man is a killer. If she hadn't grasped that before, she does now. He's not the boy she remembers.

Run. Get back to the street and call Boden.

But she can't. And she's not sure why. Perhaps she's weary of carrying this burden.

Ewan inhales, and Lexi realises he has tears running down his cheeks. He looks off to his left again. Is he actually seeing his dead brother? He's seeing something. He's psychotic, he must be. His head dips abruptly and his hand goes to block his mouth as he lets out a muffled howl. It's desolate, a cry of pure pain. He squats down on his haunches, face in his hands, his body wracked with sobs.

Lexi stares at him, then she looks at Beth. She has no idea what to do. Part of her wants to comfort him, but who knows how that would be received?

He rocks on his haunches. 'Course I remember,' he says sorrowfully. 'I'm not mad. I'm not. I know he's…I know he's…You grabbed me and stopped me from going in after him. I could've…'

He clenches his right fist, lifts it up to his mouth, and bites down on it as he fights the tears. This is what he always did as a little boy. Lexi remembers it. He bit his own fist to stop himself from crying, when that bastard beat him.

She takes a tentative step forward. 'Ewan,' she says. 'I'm so—'

'No!' he shouts.

And he erupts. Jumping up to his full height, he bunches his fist and launches it straight at her. Lexi sees it coming, but she can't move fast enough. The blow misses her chin by inches and lands on her left shoulder. The force of it sends her flying backwards. She hits the ground, knocking the wind out of her.

And he's screaming at her. 'You don't get away with this. You bitch! You let him die! Everyone knows that! I could've saved him! You let him die!'

He's looming over her, and he hasn't finished. Gasping for breath, Lexi tries to scramble to her feet.

He's insane! He's going to kill you..

But Beth steps forward and somehow puts herself between them.

'Ewan,' she says, with surprising calmness in her voice. 'Lexi saved your life that day. You were only seven. You could hardly swim. The river was deep and fast flowing, and dangerous, because of the weir. She stopped you drowning too.'

He's shaking his head and scowling. His fist is still clenched, ready for the next blow.

'Don't you remember the weir?' says Beth.

'I could've saved him.' His voice cracks.

'You would've been swept away too,' says Beth.

Ewan is still shaking his head. But he turns away and bites down on his knuckle. He walks in a circle. Has she got through to him? Maybe?

Beth grabs her arm, pulling her up. She sways, legs trembling, she has to lean on Beth.

He spins round. 'Dad said I was a coward and I let my little brother die. All my life, he's blamed me. Because you of you!' His face is screwed up with fury.

Lexi knows she should run, but would her legs even carry her? She doubts it.

'Listen to me, Ewan,' she says. 'Just listen. Your dad's a bully and a self-pitying drunk. Always has been. He beat up your mum, and you, and Jared. He blamed everyone else for everything that went wrong in his life. He's a monster.'

Ewan's looking straight at her, but is he hearing her? It's impossible to know. She must get him to listen.

Just tell him.

'But you're right,' she says. 'What happened to Jared was

my fault. We should never have gone there that day. We were supposed to take you and Jared to the park for a kick-about. But it was so hot, too hot to play football. And some other kids were going to the woods down by the river. I decided we'd go there too. I knew we weren't supposed to. I knew about the dangers of the weir. But we went.'

Beth is still holding her arm, supporting her. She knows it's true. The innocence and stupidity of a childhood decision that led to this terrible tragedy.

'It's the truth, Ewan. And I've blamed myself every day since. But when we got there…'

A rush of memories comes flooding back. The panic she felt as she ploughed through the stinging nettles and jumped down onto the shingle bank beside the water. And Jared's head was just visible, bobbing along in the fast-flowing current. It was too late. He was way down stream out of reach. She grabbed Ewan's arm and hauled him back.

She glances at Beth. 'We should never have been there. I was twelve. My mum had drummed it into me. Don't go near the river. It's dangerous.'

Ewan has lowered his fist, but he seems far way inside his own head.

'He dared me to go in,' he whispers. 'Said I was chicken.'

'You mean Jared dared you?' she says.

Ewan looks at her.

There's no chance to say more. A motorcycle comes screaming down the path towards them. It halts with a screeching sideways skid and the rider raises his arm.

Beth shrieks, 'Brandon, no!'

A volley of shots ring out, and only then does Lexi realise the rider has a gun.

He shoots Ewan at a range of a couple of metres, too

close to miss. And as Ewan reels backwards from the force of the bullets, he spins the bike round and rides off.

Ewan lands flat on his back. The left side of his head is blown apart. His right eye is vacant and staring. He's dead.

Lexi's heart is thudding. Beth is clutching her arm.

'Oh shit,' Beth murmurs.

Suddenly all Lexi can hear is the background hum of the city: traffic on the street, the wailing of sirens. She looks at Beth. It's impossible to work out whose idiocy spawned this, Beth's or her own.

You should've left it to the police.

'Listen to me,' she says. 'Get out of here now, before the police arrive. You were never here. Never part of this. Got it?'

'But—'

'Don't argue, Beth. You don't want to go to jail.'

'I never meant—'

'I know that. Just go. Find somewhere to hide. And don't go anywhere near Damian or Marcus. And don't contact them.'

Beth nods. 'I'm so sorry,' she mumbles.

Lexi points to the opposite exit from where they entered the park. 'Go that way. Walk fast but don't run. Collar up, head down, like you're a commuter.'

'Will I—'

'Go, Beth. Now!'

57

Friday. 5.30pm

By the time Boden and Chakravorty arrive, an armed unit has secured the scene. It's a small public garden in the heart of the City; a hidden oasis during daylight hours, but a labyrinth of shadows at night.

It looks to Boden like a carefully chosen rendezvous. But who made the choice? Lexi Harper or her cousin? And why did she agree to meet him without telling them?

Ewan Burns's body is still lying on the wet flagstones. The paramedics have covered it. He must've been dead when they arrived. The message that came through on comms said he'd been shot multiple times. Random shooter on a motorcycle. There was a call to the emergency operator from Lexi's phone.

Lexi Harper is sitting in the back of the ambulance wrapped in a foil blanket. As Boden approaches, the paramedic with her gets out.

'Her cousin, apparently,' says the paramedic. 'She's unhurt, but she's in shock.'

'Thanks,' says Boden.

She climbs into the back of the ambulance and sits down opposite Lexi.

'Are you okay?' she says.

Lexi looks up at her. 'I couldn't let you just shoot him,' she says. 'I'm sorry.'

'It might not have come to that,' says Boden.

'Oh, I think it would,' says Lexi.

Boden decides not to argue the point. The skill of the specialist armed units is in de-escalation, and their aim is always not to shoot anyone. Mostly that works; it's only when it doesn't that it hits the news.

'The main thing is you're all right,' says Boden. 'Can you tell me what happened?'

'We exchanged more texts. I went to the front of St Paul's and he texted me further instructions, which led me here. I wanted to persuade him to hand himself in. We'd just started to talk and suddenly, out of nowhere, this man, I assume it was a man, rides up on a motorcycle and shoots Ewan, four possibly five times, I'm not sure, at close range. Then he rode off.'

'Any idea who the assailant was?'

Lexi shrugs. 'I've got no idea.'

'Can you describe him?'

Lexi shakes her head. 'I don't know, leathers, helmet. I don't know much about motorbikes. I couldn't say what sort. It all happened so fast.'

Boden nods. 'Another really horrible experience for you. You've been through the mill, haven't you?'

Lexi gives her a sardonic look. 'Tell me about it.' She's

wrung out, a tremor in her hands which she has clasped in her lap.

It all sounds plausible, and yet, there's something here that Boden can't quite put her finger on. An omission? The whisper of a lie?

You're being a jaded cop.

She reminds herself that often things are as they seem. This woman is not a suspect. She's a witness to two brutal murders that could be linked, but how?

'He was shot. Then what happened?' says Boden.

Lexi has a desolate, faraway look. 'He…it was obvious he was dead. I called the emergency services on my phone. And waited.'

The tears in her eyes spill over and run down her cheeks.

Boden pulls a tissue from a box on the shelf in the ambulance and hands it to Lexi.

They sit for a while. Outside the rain has eased up. Boden gazes out of the back of the ambulance.

Opposite them, overshadowed by the modern building behind, is a long wooden loggia with a sloping tiled roof. It has ceramic plaques on its back wall, which, if Boden remembers correctly, commemorate acts of heroic self-sacrifice carried out by ordinary people. It was erected by some Victorian philanthropist.

Why would Harper put herself on the line for a cousin who was a violent criminal?

'Why do you think he was stalking you?' Boden says. 'Why did he do all this? Did you find out?'

Lexi dips her head. 'Yes,' she says. 'Well, I sort of knew.' She blows her nose. Boden observes the tension in her jaw, the puckering of the brows, evidence of some inner battle going on inside her. This must be what Boden can sense, the thing she doesn't want to reveal.

Balling up the tissue in her hand, Lexi looks Boden in the eye. 'When we were kids,' she says, 'I used to babysit him and his little brother. One summer holiday, when it was very hot, we went to the woods. I was twelve, Ewan was seven, and his brother, Jared, was five. The thing was the woods ran down to a fast-flowing river. There was a weir, quite a drop in the water level, and it was dangerous. I knew we weren't allowed to go there, but it was a hot day. Somehow, Jared ended up in the river; he was swept away and he drowned. His parents, mainly his father, blamed me. And so did Ewan.'

Boden nods. 'You were held responsible for this child-hood tragedy? That's harsh.'

'Yes,' says Lexi. Her eyes are glassy, but they hold Boden's gaze. Her chin is quivering. It's delivered as a matter-of-fact explanation, but it's raw and has the ring of truth.

'And you think your cousin held a grudge for all these years?' says Boden.

Lexi sighs. 'Stuff got complicated. My aunt died of cancer a few years later. Ewan went off the rails and got involved with a County Lines drug gang. I got out.'

'Okay,' says Boden. 'Well, I'll get my colleague to come and record your statement.'

Lexi gives her a feisty look. 'You mean I've got to say it all again?'

'We're primarily interested in what happened here this afternoon, while it's fresh in your mind.'

'Right,' says Lexi with a shrug.

'Then I'll get someone to drive you to wherever you want to go. Back to your friend's?'

'I'd rather go home to my own flat.'

'No problem.'

Lexi is looking out of the back of the ambulance at the

body; she's lost in her own head. It'll take her a while to come to terms with all this. Boden knows from her own experience, the shock subsides over days, the deeper trauma takes years. The shadow of it never leaves you.

Stepping out of the back of the ambulance, Boden meets Chakravorty coming towards her.

'They've got the shooter,' says Chakravorty. 'Picked him up on ANPR running a light and brought him down with a stinger.'

'Great,' says Boden. She tilts her head towards the ambulance. 'I don't think she knows anything about it. Guilt based on past family stuff. That's what brought her here. Thought she could save him. Let's just record a statement, then she can go home.'

'You staying in London tonight?' says Chakravorty.

This hasn't occurred to Boden. 'I don't know,' she says. The prospect of a night with Cal slinks into her mind and she smiles. 'Maybe.'

58

Friday. 6.45pm

Lexi fumbles with the new key. The size, the shape, is all wrong, and she nearly drops it before finally unlocking her new front door. But the door is steel, in a smart metallic grey with a narrow satin glass panel down the centre, and reassuringly impenetrable. Jazzy Gupta has been as good as her word; her people have 'sorted things out'. It's what they do.

The interior of the flat has a different and distinct smell, not unpleasant. It reminds Lexi of the diffusers you find in expensive hotel rooms. Dumping her bag in the hall, she wanders into the kitchen. It's only been a couple of days since she fled from the snake, but it feels so much longer.

All the familiar objects are in place. The row of matching ceramic jars, the coffee machine, the kettle, the salt and pepper grinders.

Lexi picks up the pepper grinder; it was a birthday present from Beth a couple of years ago. Polished steel, perfectly curved to fit the hand, designed by Georg Jensen. Lexi looked

315

the pair up at the time; Selfridges were listing them at a hundred and fifty quid. Beth was vague about where she got them. Lexi suspected she'd shoplifted them. It's how she acquired most things unless she had a man in tow who'd let her loose with his credit card.

Just thinking about Beth produces a welter of clashing emotions. Lexi sighs. Beth has always stretched their friendship to the limit, and beyond, yet it's odd without her. Talking things over, listening to her eccentric views, chastising her. And she also stepped in to protect Lexi from Ewan. If she hadn't…

Did you do the right thing?

Beth is a thorn in her side, but when it came to it, she couldn't turn her in.

Be honest. It wasn't just that.

It all happened in an instant. Lexi went into survival mode. She needed Beth out of there. It was a selfish move, a knee-jerk reaction to avoid awkward questions from the police. The shooter must be connected to Marcus. Beth knew his name. Somehow, they must've been following her.

Lexi's thoughts are spiralling downwards into panic. The what-ifs are piling up. What if the police arrest the shooter and that leads them to Marcus? But the blame, the blame is clear. Her aim was to save her cousin, and the result was she led his killer straight to him.

She can hear her mother's scathing words. 'You're so bloody arrogant, Lexi. Think you know it all. Well, you don't.'

Your fault! Back then. Your fault now.

The bile rises in her throat and she can't stop it. She lurches over to the kitchen sink and vomits. Not that she has much in her stomach to expel. She retches several times more, and once the impulse passes, she staggers into the sitting room.

The sofa looks fine, cushions plumped. No scaly traces of the orange snake. But she's beyond caring. She flops down, spreads her arms out and tips back her head.

Closing her eyes, all she wants is to escape into the oblivion of sleep, preferably a dreamless sleep. The day has exhausted her, drained every ounce of emotional energy, and left her battered and beaten.

As she drifts, she becomes aware of a buzzing sound. It's her phone, which is in her bag in the hall. The temptation is to ignore it. But habit kicks in. You never ignore a phone call, not in her business.

She gets wearily to her feet, goes out into the hallway, picks up the bag and extracts the phone.

Unknown caller. Excellent. But what if it's the police?

She answers tentatively. 'Hello?'

'Is that Lexi Harper?' says a female voice. The tone is cold, businesslike, but familiar.

'Yes. Sorry, who's this?'

'Kate Jessop. You said you can help me. I need to find a buyer for Renfrew Hall. I'll be in London tomorrow morning and I was hoping we could meet up.'

Lexi reels as her scrambled brain struggles to process this. 'Yes, of course…I'm sorry. I'm just quite surprised to hear from you. But yes, of course, I'd be happy to help.'

'I can be at your office by ten if that's convenient.'

'Well, yes, that's fine.'

'I'll see you then.' She hangs up.

Lexi stares at the phone.

Shit! If you can deliver this for Yildiz.

Her rational mind snaps into action. She needs a hot

shower and some food. She has until the morning to prepare herself for a meeting that could change everything.

59

Saturday. 9.30am

Boden is at her favourite coffee shop in Soho with a large, black Americano and a croissant in front of her. Cal was on an early shift, so he was up at five. Some state visit from a foreign dignitary. But he'd cooked her dinner, and they'd spent a cosy evening in his flat like some old married couple.

Could it ever be that? Her and Cal long-term?

Don't bank on it. These things never work out.

Boden sips her coffee. The thought of him, the memory of his touch on her skin, can still make her shiver even this morning. The longing for him permeates her body, but it's not just sexual. He understands. He knows about the broken parts of her, the mistakes she's made, and it's okay. They have fun. They laugh.

You need to get your head straight.

However fantastic he makes her feel, it's casual, no strings. They agreed. If she lets herself slide into foolish hopes and expectations, she'll end up getting burnt. Why spoil what they've got?

Her phone buzzes. Chakravorty on FaceTime.

She answers. 'Hey, Prish.'

The DC is grinning knowingly at her. 'Good morning,' she says. 'How was your evening?'

Boden smiles. Despite their age difference, the young DC has turned into the nearest thing to a best friend, or at least, a best work mate.

'Very nice. Thank you for asking,' says Boden. 'Is the boss on my case?'

'No, your absence has passed under the radar. Too much going on.'

'Okay. Bring me up to speed.'

'Knight hauled in Kate Jessop yesterday and tried to put the screws on her about the ownership of Renfrew Hall.'

'Bet that worked,' says Boden, taking another sip of coffee.

'You're right. It didn't. She came lawyered up and just stonewalled. Renfrew Hall is owned by a shell company of an overseas shell company and so on. Untraceable.'

Boden takes a bite of her croissant. 'Craig Jessop hired himself some smart advisers, including, it has to be said, the DCI's former husband.'

'Anyway,' says Chakravorty. 'In other news, in a search of the gatehouse, five grand in cash was found in a kid's backpack.'

'So Mason Green could be telling the truth?'

'It's checking out. We've done a thorough trawl of ANPR and we've got a Mercedes Black Series Coupe with cloned plates and two guys, entering the area at the time Mason says they came to see him, and then again, just after two pm on the afternoon Craig Jessop and Liam Cox were murdered.'

'They were there, waiting for Jessop.'

'Yep. The DCI is even more convinced it's OCG related, and she's asking the powers that be for a wider remit for the investigation.'

'That always was her preferred option,' says Boden.

'When are you coming back?'

'Later. I'm meeting Tom Roscoe to wind things up here. And if it's looking like Ewan Burns is not our killer, I think I should talk to Harper. It's only fair she knows.'

'Are you running that by the DCI?'

'Not necessarily. Why bother her? I'll see you later, Prish.'

She hangs up.

Boden savours the rest of her croissant and licks the flakes off her fingers. Working for a boss with a self-serving agenda offends her deeply. But there's little she can do except try to do the job according to her own ethical standards.

She's finished her coffee and is wondering about ordering another when Tom Roscoe finally appears. Shoulders hunched, head dipped, he ducks through the doorway, his eyes darting from table to table. Boden raises her hand, and he weaves through the maze of chairs and customers towards her.

'Sorry to keep you waiting,' he says. 'But I've got some good news and some bad, well, bad from your point of view.'

He lowers his lanky frame into the chair opposite her.

'I'll take the bad first,' says Boden.

Roscoe grins. 'Of course. Instincts of a good detective.'

Boden gives him a tepid smile. She can do without his flattery.

'Well,' he says. 'I'm afraid Ewan Burns is not your man for Renfrew Hall. We've been speaking to his former employer, Trey Robinson. Burns has an alibi. He was working as a vehicle technician at Robinson's car dealership at the time of the murder. There's also video evidence of him being there. Robinson gets his technicians to make videos for his customers explaining the work they've done on their cars. Burns was a hard worker. He clocked up three that day.'

Boden shrugs. 'I'm not surprised. Anyway, looks like we've got some alternative suspects in the frame. What's the good news?'

'The hit on Burns looks gang related. We picked up the shooter, but he chucked the weapon. He's just been going no comment all night. His name's Brandon Ford, twenty-two, record as a juvenile, and intel is suggesting he works for a North London firm headed by Marcus Stirling.'

'What are you thinking, then? Ewan got out of jail and somehow he stepped on the toes of this gang?'

'Yes. The man Ewan killed is a known associate of Marcus Stirling. So, it's arguably a revenge killing. But if Brandon keeps schtum, takes the rap, we won't have the evidence to charge Stirling.'

'Do you think he'll crack?'

'Doubt it. Probably not the first hit he's done for the gang. And he knows what'll happen if he implicates Stirling. He'll take his chance with a not guilty plea.'

'Without the weapon, it'll be a hard case to make anyway.'

Roscoe shrugs. 'It's the Met's problem, not mine. I'm headed home. You want a lift?'

'Thanks, but I'll take the train later.'

Roscoe gets up and gives her a wistful smile. 'Good to work with you again, Jo.'

Boden paints on a smile. 'Yeah, you too.'

As she watches him walk away, she envies his detachment. Job done. On to the next.

60

Saturday. 9.45am

Lexi has been in the office for over an hour. She's revved up
on caffeine and adrenaline. When she arrived, it was just Pia.
A few of the other agents have been trickling in; fortunately
there's no sign of Gemma. But it's Saturday morning and
Gemma takes weekends off.

The plan that Lexi's formulated, through a long sleepless
night, is to aim for maximum surprise on all fronts. Don't
give any of them any time to think. She'll broker the deal
with Kate Jessop. Gemma will have no option but to back her.
It will all be presented to Roger as a fait accompli, and he can
shove his cryptic comments.

This is your time.

The firm's commission on the deal, even at a knock-down
sale price, not to mention her own, will still be substantial,
and Lexi will have cemented her relationship with Arif
Yildiz. In future, when it comes to Cavendish Cooper's high-
end clients, she'll be on point.

Checking the time on her phone, Lexi finds Yildiz's number. She wanders into the conference room as it rings and closes the door for privacy.

He comes on the line. 'Good morning, Lexi,' he says brightly. 'How's your poor foot?'

'Oh, it's fine. And I think it could be a very good morning,' she replies. 'I have some news. I'm expecting Kate Jessop in the next ten minutes. She's coming to discuss the sale of Renfrew Hall.'

She can hear him chuckle. 'I knew I was backing a winner,' he says. 'Well done.'

'I was hoping to discuss what you're prepared to pay. The ballpark figure, really.'

'Considering her... situation, and the fact it needs an extensive refurb, which will be expensive, my offer would be no higher than three.'

Lexi was hoping for a little wriggle room, but that sounds unambiguous.

'She may well think three million is a bit low.'

'She may. But you'll persuade her, Lexi. I have every confidence.'

'I'll let you know the outcome.'

'I'll put some champagne on ice. Or, actually, let's meet for lunch. I'll book a table.'

'Perhaps we should wait and see what she says?'

'No need. You'll persuade her. Oh, and did you speak to the police about that other matter?'

She takes a breath to steady her voice. She was expecting this, and she's prepared.

'Yes, and...it's resolved.' She can't bring herself to say more, and there's no need. But he'll probably see it on the news and put two and two together.

'Good,' he says. 'Very good.'

Hanging up, Lexi feels a rush of relief. After a week of absolute horror, things could be about to change.

You bloody well deserve this.

She notices Teddy Devereux staring through the glass wall of the conference room at her. Sneaky little toad has sussed that's something's afoot. She's asked Pia to make coffee and get pastries from the deli-bakery on the corner.

As Lexi strides out of the conference room and crosses to her desk, he intercepts her.

'Who are we expecting?'

'I don't know, Teddy. Who are you expecting?'

'Oh come on Lex, share. We're all colleagues here.'

Lexi wonders when the last time was that Teddy Devereux shared anything. It's not in his nature.

At that moment, Kate Jessop walks into the reception area. She looks elegant and expensive, although her face is still pale and drawn. Her trouser suit is nipped at the waist. Prada? Dolce & Gabbana?

Beth would know.

A cheesy grin spreads across Teddy's face. He's about to step forward, but Lexi grabs his arm.

'Fuck off, Teddy,' she whispers. 'This is mine.'

He catches her fierce look and backs off.

Lexi strolls across the room, hand outstretched and an expression of concern. 'Hello, Kate. It's great you're here, but, y'know, I could've come to you.'

Kate Jessop accepts the handshake, but she doesn't smile. None of this can be easy for her. Lexi shepherds her into the conference room. 'Can I offer you coffee? Or we've got herbal teas.'

'I'm fine. Let's do this. I've got a plane to catch.'

'Oh,' says Lexi. 'A change of scenery is probably a good idea. Somewhere nice, I hope.'

Kate gives her a spiky look, puts her bag on the table and sits down. 'What are they offering?'

This strikes Lexi as an odd attitude, even if she is stressed.

Lexi sits opposite her and opens her notebook. 'Well, I do have several prospects in mind, but first—'

Kate huffs. 'Let's cut the crap, shall we? I know who the buyer is.'

How?

'Do you?'

'Besnik Krasniqi.'

This is out of left field, and the surprise must show on Lexi's face. The man Roger pointed out talking to Yildiz at the launch?

'Don't look so innocent, Lexi. You telling me it isn't?' There's a frosty hostility emanating from Kate Jessop.

Innocent? What is this?

'Well, why do you think—'

Kate laughs cynically and shakes her head. 'Seriously?' she says. 'You don't even know who you're working for, do you? And I thought you were smart.'

Lexi is speechless. What is this about? Is this a move on Jessop's part to get leverage and force up the price?

'You know who Krasniqi is, don't you?' says Kate.

A grey money man?

'I'm not sure I do. But I can assure you—'

'He's a gangster. Runs the Albanian mafia. Craig only discovered this after he outbid Krasniqi when we bought Renfrew Hall.'

This is ridiculous. A gangster? Lexi tries to picture the bland little man she saw at Yildiz's party. But she's sure of one thing, someone of Arif Yildiz's stature would not do business with criminals. He encouraged her to go to the police about Ewan.

Kate Jessop is staring across the table at her. Her expression is hard to read. Seething bitterness?

'Drugs, human trafficking. You name it, Krasniqi does it. He's made millions. And he wants Renfrew Hall. Wants to live there. Suits his ego, I suppose.'

You have to get in front of this.

'Then why didn't your husband sell it to him?' says Lexi.

Kate exhales. 'It's more complicated than that. Craig bought the Hall to develop it himself. He never intended to just sell it on, and certainly not for three million, which is what Krasniqi offered him.'

The same as Yildiz's offer?

Lexi dismisses the thought. There's no connection. It's an amazing house, but it needs a considerable amount of work. Three million is a low but plausible offer.

Kate slaps her palm on the table. 'Come on, you know what a property like this could be worth on the open market! Craig had costed it, half a million to do the makeover, and he could sell it for twenty.'

'That's a low estimate for the makeover. To sell for twenty it would need to be ultra high spec,' says Lexi.

This is not how she expected this meeting to go. But she can see this is a ploy. Craig didn't have the cash to do it. That's why he decided to sell. Kate's using this outlandish story to jack up the price.

'Your husband came to us,' says Lexi. 'What made him change his mind and decide to sell?'

Kate Jessop drums her nails on the table; she seems frustrated and impatient, because she's not getting what she wants.

'Krasniqi,' she says. 'These bastards don't give up. Once

Craig figured out he was dealing with the Albanian mafia, he decided to get rid of the place. He just wanted to recoup his investment. That's what he was trying to do.'

Recoup his investment. That's the figure she's going for.

'All I can tell you,' Lexi says, 'is the potential client I've been speaking to is certainly not an Albanian gangster. He's a respectable property developer. We're very scrupulous about—'

'You still don't get it, do you?' Kate shakes her head. 'Krasniqi gets what he wants. At the price he wants. When people cross him…You were there. He had my husband…' she inhales to steady herself, 'he had my husband murdered to make it clear to me I must accept his offer of three million. That's who you're dealing with here.'

Lexi stares at her. Kate has tears in her eyes.

It was Ewan. But she doesn't know that.

She's grieving. Perhaps she even believes this is true. But the police will put her right.

Lexi sighs. 'That's a startling allegation. Perhaps you should speak to the police about this.'

Kate is glaring at her. All this talk of the mafia. She won't do that, and Lexi knows why. She's seen the media reports on Craig Jessop. He's the criminal here.

Kate brushes a tear from her cheek with a finger. 'Okay,' she says. 'Tell your respectable property developer I get the message. I'm assuming three million is still his offer. Is it?'

'Well, yes…' says Lexi, 'but that's because it reflects—'

'Then we have a deal. I want this to be over and my children to be safe. My lawyers'll be in touch. I want a speedy resolution. You owe me that.'

What?

She stands up and marches out without a backward glance.

Lexi sits, staring at the chair Kate Jessop has vacated. The pastries are on the table untouched, the silver coffee flask and ceramic mugs are still on the tray. What just happened here?

This is some kind of nonsense; it has to be. Yildiz is working for an Albanian gangster? They had a man murdered to get the deal they wanted?

But then she accepted the three million?

Why would she do that? It makes no sense. Lexi pours herself a coffee. If Craig Jessop had criminal connections, perhaps it's no surprise that his wife's assuming another criminal murdered him. If she believes that, and she's frightened, of course she'll accept the deal. That doesn't make the story true.

How did she know the offer was three million?

It's a co-incidence; it has to be. But a deal's a deal. When she finds out Ewan killed her husband, she's not going to be very pleased. In that regard, the sooner this is done and dusted, the better.

She picks up her phone and writes a text to Yildiz.

Good news. Three million agreed.

Her thumbs hover over the keys. She could call him. But she hesitates. There's something here that niggles. Perhaps it's Kate Jessop's chilly manner? Or what? A slither of doubt?

No! Ewan did it. This is bullshit.

61

Saturday. 11.30am

Boden arrives on the dot. She's arranged to meet Lexi Harper on the southern side of Marble Arch at the entrance to Hyde Park. The persistent rain of the last few days has blown over and a watery sunshine is filtering through the thin canopy of russet leaves still clinging to the trees.

Standing by the black spiked railings, Boden sees Lexi at a distance, crossing the road at the traffic lights and walking towards her. She has yet another coat, a stylish mid-calf camel coat with long lapels. It swings as she walks. Boden glances down at her own jacket, shabby by comparison, bought for warmth and durability. Sometimes in the job it's hard not to be envious.

Lexi joins her. 'I hope you don't mind this,' she says. 'I wanted to get away from the office.'

'Not at all,' says Boden. 'Shall we walk?'

They head into the park down a broad avenue of trees. The grass around the trees is carpeted in fallen leaves and the exposed winter wood forms a stark lattice of branches above their heads.

Lexi opens her bag, takes out a pair of sunglasses and puts them on.

Boden studies her as unobtrusively as possible. Lexi seems contained and detached, frozen almost. Hiding behind the glasses? The fact she's even back at work surprises Boden, but it's a coping mechanism she can identify with. You just get on with the job.

'How are you doing?' she says.

Lexi shrugs. 'I would say fine. But I don't think you'd believe me, would you?'

Boden smiles.

Lexi is gazing out across the park into the middle distance. 'You said on the phone you've got something to tell me.'

'Yes,' says Boden. 'We've received information about your cousin. Did you know he was working for a car dealership as a technician?'

'No.'

'Well, we've spoken to his employer, and it's clear he has an alibi for the day of the Renfrew Hall murders. He was working at the garage all day. We've confirmed that.'

Lexi stops in her tracks. She sways a little.

She turns to face Boden. 'It wasn't him?'

'No.'

'So he didn't follow me there?'

'Not that day.'

'You're sure?'

'Yes.'

Lexi, inscrutable behind the sunglasses, stares up at the sky through the skeletal trees. Boden waits.

It seems to her that what she's delivered is the worst

possible news, whereas she was expecting this to bring Lexi Harper some relief. What's clear is that it hasn't.

'Are you all right?' she says.

Lexi doesn't answer at once. She's standing stock still, but her body is charged with tension.

Finally, she says 'Do you know who did it then?'

'Our inquiries are ongoing,' says Boden.

'What's that?' says Lexi. 'Cop speak for you don't know or you won't tell me?'

Lexi's eyes are hidden behind the sunglasses, but there's an unmistakable hostility in her stance, and in her shoes Boden would feel the same.

What did Mason Green say? They're all just villains. And it's probably true. A dispute between OCGs? But ordinary people like Lexi Harper become collateral damage.

Doesn't she deserve the truth?

Boden makes a snap decision. Sometimes the moral obligation takes precedence.

'I shouldn't tell you this,' she says. 'But…well, I'm going to assume you'll keep it to yourself.'

'I'm not going to broadcast it on social media,' says Lexi with a cynical smile.

'We've identified two suspects and there's an organised crime component, so it was most likely a professional hit.'

Lexi inhales. 'You mean…some sort of gangsters killed Mr Jessop?'

'Probably, yes.'

Lexi nods. The hand resting on the strap of her bag trembles.

'Do you know why?' she says.

'Not as yet. The investigation really is ongoing.'

'Will you catch them?'

Boden shrugs. 'That's our aim. But to be frank, in these

kinds of cases, a professional killer is often brought in from Eastern Europe, and they'll be long gone. If we can confirm their identity, we can pursue them with an international arrest warrant.'

'But don't hold your breath?' says Lexi.

'It can be a lengthy and frustrating process,' says Boden.

Lexi turns and faces Boden. She takes off the glasses and holds out her hand. 'I am glad it wasn't Ewan. Thank you for taking the trouble to come and tell me in person, Sergeant. You must be busy, and I appreciate it.'

The formality of this puzzles Boden.

But she shakes Lexi's hand. 'I hope this in some way resolves things for you. You don't need to feel responsible.'

Lexi doesn't answer; she just nods. Then she says briskly, 'I have a business lunch, so I need to find a cab.' The sunglasses go back on.

Boden watches her walk away with a determination in her stride but also a whiff of fragility, as she heads off towards Park Lane.

There's a lot here that doesn't stack up, and Boden wonders if she's done the right thing.

It felt like her cousin's alibi was not what she wanted to hear? Why didn't she ask about the man who shot him? True, it's been all over the news, and difficult to ignore. So perhaps she knew already. But some cases you never get the full picture. Lexi Harper is a witness to the crimes of others, and it's not Boden's job to get to the bottom of her psychology. It seems as if she wanted her cousin to be guilty of the Renfrew Hall murders, but why?

Let it go. You've done your job.

Boden gets out her phone. She thumbs a text.

Done. What about you?

Cal texts back. *Yep. Can't wait to see you.*

She smiles. *Flatterer.*

What can I say? I'm missing you.

Really?

Really. We need to live in the same city.

Boden stares at her phone screen and smiles. Perhaps he's right. This is where she wants to be. Maybe it is time to let the past go and move on.

62

Saturday. 12.15pm

The restaurant is in Belgravia, a side street near to Sloane Square. As Lexi steps out of the cab, she observes her own foot touching the grey kerbstone with a surreal detachment. She's not sure how she got out of Hyde Park and into the taxi. Somehow her limbs carried her, despite the howling panic ripping through her brain. But that has morphed into something else. A numbness. Something inside her has switched off. Her brain is still processing, but there is no emotion.

An organised crime component? A professional hit?

Is it possible that Kate Jessop was telling her the truth? They had a man murdered to get the deal they wanted. And Yildiz was a party to this? Maybe he didn't know? That's possible, surely?

There are plenty of disreputable types on the fringes of the property business, but Arif Yildiz is a major player. That's what earned him the nickname the Big Fish. There could still be other explanations for Craig Jessop's murder. Other criminals.

Why was he so insistent you went to the police about Ewan?

Lexi stands outside the restaurant and she can't seem to move.

You know why. You just don't want to believe it.

The doorman is holding open the heavy, plate-glass door for her. She wonders why she's here. She should've texted with an excuse, gone home, given herself a chance to…to do what? Did they really have a man murdered for a property deal? Killed so his wife gets the message? What sort of person thinks like that? Not Yildiz, surely not him? Behind the facade he shows the world, he's charming and kind. She's seen it. He helped her with her shoe.

What if you've been played?

The idea slinks into her mind and explodes.

'I knew I was backing a winner.' That's what Yildiz said and she lapped it up.

The sycophantic flattery delivered with such ease and charm. All the tools of the salesman's trade. And Yildiz is a master. Did he draw her into the charmed circle of wealth, knowing her ambition, her desire to be one of them? Did he see her weakness and exploit it?

No, it just can't be!

The doorman is smiling at her and waiting. The foyer is empty. The maitre d' is at his lectern, and beyond the restaurant has only a smattering of tables occupied. It's still early. Is he even here yet?

Lexi has to move into the foyer in order to see. The maitre d' steps forward to take her coat, and as she turns to let him remove it, she catches sight of Yildiz, at a corner table, looking straight at her and smiling.

She smiles back; it's a reflex.

What the hell are you going to say to him?

There are several ways this could go, but none are good. She could just drink his champagne and say nothing. Why not? What difference would it make? One set of villains murdered another villain over a ridiculous piece of real estate. She could take her commission and move on. Who would know?

You would.

The maitre d' escorts her across the room and pulls out her chair for her. A young female server unfurls her linen napkin and lays it across her lap. It's all just an absurd ritual to make an overpriced lunch feel special.

'Well,' says Yildiz. 'You are an absolute star, Lexi Harper. I raise my glass to you.' He's drinking an apéritif in a heavy-bottomed tumbler loaded with ice.

The maitre d' hovers waiting to take her order.

'What can I offer you?' says Yildiz.

'A sparkling water,' says Lexi. 'I'm not feeling that grand.'

Yildiz's brow puckers with concern. He is good at this. 'I'm sorry to hear that,' he says. 'Do you need anything?'

Let it go. Have lunch. Play the game.

She can't.

'Can I ask you a question, Arif?' she says. 'Are you a proxy for this deal?'

His gaze slides away and he takes a slug of his drink. 'Depends what you mean.'

'Are you buying Renfrew Hall for Besnik Krasniqi?'

'Who told you that?'

'Kate Jessop.'

He nods, gives her a pensive look, which turns into a sad

smile. 'You're a smart girl, Lexi. You'll go far, but you need t—'

'No, I'm a very stupid girl, or rather woman, considering my age.'

His eyes narrow. 'Meaning?'

He flatters, then he patronises. She's not having that. The irritation tempers her nerves.

'I let a charming older man, a substitute father-figure, gaslight me with his attention and flattery, and manipulate me into doing his bidding. I didn't ask the right questions. I was grateful for the opportunity. My ambition blinded me.'

She's said it.

He sloshes the ice round in his glass and drains the liquid. 'That is indeed a depressing state of mind to be in,' he says.

'It is.'

She waits. She's standing her ground, and that's good.

He puts the glass down and laces his fingers. 'Perhaps I can reframe the situation for you.'

The ease with which he greeted her has gone. There's a steeliness behind the smile. But she doesn't care.

'How?' she says evenly.

'Do you read Balzac? He wrote something like: Behind every great fortune there is a crime. It's an interesting idea and, in terms of the super prime property market, a useful thought. Old money, new money, most of it's tainted on some level. We all swim with the sharks. It's the business we're in, Lexi.'

Is this his convoluted way of admitting that he knows Krasniqi is a criminal?

Don't let him distract you with bullshit.

'The school I went to, we didn't get much into French literature,' she says. 'So here's what Kate Jessop told me.

Krasniqi offered her husband three million, and when her husband turned him down, he had him murdered to make her take the deal.'

Yildiz huffs. 'That is an outrageous accusation.'

'But is it true?'

'Of course not. Don't be ridiculous.'

The server brings her sparkling water and is about to offer them menus. But Yildiz wags her away with his index finger. It's the aggressive gesture of a man who expects instant obedience.

He's pissed. There's no going back now.

'I've just spoken to the police. My cousin had no involvement in what happened at Renfrew Hall. The police think it was a professional hit associated with organised crime.'

Yildiz shrugs. 'Who knows what sort of connections Mr Jessop had? He upset the wrong people. And you have to consider his wife's motives. She's a grieving widow looking for someone to blame. She was probably also hoping for a better price.'

'She didn't argue about the money.'

Yildiz sighs. 'I don't know what you expect me to say.' The tone is tetchy.

'You haven't answered my question about Krasniqi.'

His gaze hardens. 'No no, Lexi. You don't get to come here and interrogate me. That's a private matter.'

He's not denying it.

'Don't I have a right to know if I'm implicated in a crime?'

The question hangs in the air. She knows she's crossed the line, but the adrenaline is flowing. She's not letting him off the hook.

He's looking right at her, but there's something in his

manner, a stillness, a coldness. The man she thought she knew has vanished. It dawns on her if he is involved, this could all turn out to be a gigantic mistake.

The restaurant is filling up. A noisy party of four is settling at the table next to them.

He leans towards her and lowers his voice. 'Think carefully about what you're saying. You're jumping to a lot of conclusions here. I've done nothing wrong. All I asked you to do is broker a deal.'

'I know but—'

He raises that intimidating index finger again and points it at her. 'There are no buts. Now let me give you some advice, and I suggest you take it. You've had some horrific experiences this week and you're clearly not yourself. Take some time off. I'm sure Roger will understand. Then I think you will realise the absurdity of what you're suggesting.'

Is that a threat? Feels like it.

Lexi meets his gaze across the table. His eyes have narrowed to inscrutable slits, boring into her. Who is he? A chill runs through her, and she realises how naïve it was to confront him like this. Now the connection with Krasniqi feels real. He's a property developer working for a gangster, but prepared to see a man murdered in order to improve his profit margin. If she isn't scared of him, she should be.

You need to get out of here.

'You're probably right,' she says. 'I've been under a lot of stress. I shouldn't have come.'

He smiles and leans back in his chair. 'I am right. You need to take care of yourself.'

She stands up. 'I'll bring Gemma up to speed with the deal. I'm sure she'll expedite matters to your satisfaction.'

He inclines his head. 'I'm sure she will.' Then he gives

her a chilly smile. 'Don't do anything foolish, Lexi. You've got a great career ahead of you. Cavendish Cooper is lucky to have you.'

Anything foolish? What would that be?

She manages a thin smile before turning and walking away across the restaurant. The maitre d' scurries to fetch her coat, and moments later she's out of the door.

Lexi strides out. She's moving on autopilot. Her thoughts are vague and muted, her brain is numb. She passes Sloane Square and finds herself heading down King's Road. The shops are full of enticing clothes, from sportswear to couture, accessories for every outfit, paraphernalia for the home, items of every description that you never knew you needed.

And she's reminded of Beth. Beth loves King's Road. A girl from a dead end estate, her aspiration in life was always to be a Chelsea girl. They first came here as wide-eyed teenagers skiving off school for the day to come to London.

If only she were here now.

The longing for her friend is sudden and intense. Lexi imagines her popping her head out of a shop doorway, a genuine friend, and in her own wild and wacky way, incredibly loyal.

You never thought you'd miss her this much.

The rawness of Ewan's death is something Lexi has banished from her brain, using her drive to get Yildiz his deal to block out everything else. But now? She's in some kind of mental free-fall; her limbs disconnected.

Yildiz is right about one thing, to have witnessed two murders in a week is a trauma by anyone standards. She hasn't eaten anything of any substance for days. Last night, in preparation for her meeting with Kate Jessop, she tried to eat some pasta, but it made her nauseous. It ended up in the bin.

She wonders idly if she's having a mental breakdown. Finding a bench on the edge of a tree-lined square, she sits.

The times she chastised Beth for her petty villainy, her scams, and always from a position of moral superiority. This feels hollow and arrogant now.

We all swim with the sharks.

It turns out that Lexi's gullibility and naivety are far greater than her friend's. And Beth's wretched, feral childhood gives her more of an excuse.

'You think you're so smart?' That was always Mum's gibe. But perhaps it was a warning born of fear, not a bitter accusation. The guilt Lexi carried for Jared's death fuelled her desire to escape and the relentless drive to succeed. Making money was the answer to everything. But deep down there was always the corrosive doubt: are you good enough? Will you ever be good enough? Yildiz saw that and used it.

And Roger Cavendish knew, or at least suspected, that Yildiz was working with Krasniqi. He used her too, to distance himself from wrongdoing, and to have a fall guy for his firm if the truth came out.

Lexi sits on the bench watching people passing by; a parade of strangers busy with their lives, none of them give her a passing glance.

And where is Beth now?

She takes out her phone and calls Beth. A recorded message plays: 'The number you have dialled is no longer in service.' This is predictable. Beth is a survivor. She's vanished, and if she's got any sense, ghosted her old life and cut all ties. Lexi has no way of contacting her. Beth could ring her. But will she? The things Lexi said to her seemed justified but they were cruel.

She won't come back.

An icy wind whips through the square, bringing down a few of the remaining leaves from the trees. Lexi shivers; she needs to move. She turns up her coat collar, gets to her feet and, unsure where she's headed, she walks away.

EPILOGUE

Eighteen months later.

Lexi is returning from her yoga class in the spring sunshine. Every Saturday morning, she does yoga. She has a schedule and she sticks to it; it keeps her on an even keel.

She turns the corner, approaching her block, and sitting on a wall, rocking a baby buggy back and forth, is the last person she expects to see. She stops in her tracks and stares.

Beth?

A welter of emotions wash through her, from relief to incredulity. The instinct is to swallow them down, but as her therapist would say, let them come. Beth hasn't seen her yet. She's talking to the baby in the stroller, so Lexi has a moment to just stand there and adjust.

For months, she searched high and low for her friend. She went to all the clubs and bars she knew Beth used to frequent, asked around, left messages. No one had seen her. In the end, she gave up. Beth had vanished.

Beth looks up and smiles. 'Hey,' she says, a little nervously. 'There's someone here I'd like you to meet.'

Lexi approaches. The baby is chuckling and making a grab at the cuddly rabbit that Beth is holding in her hand.

'This is Fleur. Fleur meet my friend Lexi.'

Lexi squats down beside baby and touches her tiny fist. Her hair is dark, but she has her mother's cornflower blue eyes.

'She's gorgeous,' says Lexi.

'You were right,' says Beth. 'When I found out I was pregnant from the surrogacy deal, I couldn't just give her away. And as soon as she was born, I was convinced of it. They were a bit snotty, but I hadn't taken any money. I quoted the law at them and they backed off.'

Lexi is still stunned.

'How have you been managing?' she says.

'A girl I used to go clubbing with had a baby on her own. She moved to Brighton. And I looked her up. She works in a bar, so she needed someone to do childcare for her in the evenings. I moved in with her and looked after her little boy.'

'The party girl staying in every evening?'

Beth shrugs. 'It was okay. When Fleur was born, we set up an arrangement. She looks after the kids during the day while I work, and I do nights.'

Lexi has imagined many things in the last year and a half, mostly bad, and including her friend dead in a dumpster. But not this.

'Where do you work?' she says.

'Well, I loved looking after Benji. And sometimes I took him to nursery. They were short-handed, so I helped out. And now I'm training to be a nursery nurse.'

Lexi stares at her in disbelief.

Beth beams from ear to ear. 'Just being with the kids all

day is great. They're fascinating. Full of energy like me. It's such fun. I love it.'

Lexi sits down next to her on the wall. 'I looked for you, y'know. Why didn't you call me, babe? I'm sorry I was so—'

Beth holds up her palm. 'No. It was justified. You were right about me. I knew I couldn't see you again until I could show you I wasn't a complete fuck-up. I made some stupid, moronic decisions.'

Lexi shakes her head. 'Trust me. Not as bad as mine.'

'I can't believe that. You're too smart.'

'Turns out I'm not. Not one bit.'

'You told me to steer clear of Marcus and Damian. But I did text Damian once. Don't worry, I did it on a burner. I found out that Brandon was on remand for killing Ewan. But in or out of jail, it's more than his life's worth to rat on Marcus. I just needed to know the police wouldn't be on my trail. Now I've got Fleur, I've cleaned up my act, no more dodgy stuff. I can't risk it. I've got to be here for her.'

The tears well in Lexi's eyes. 'It's so brilliant to see you.'

'I'm glad you feel that way. I thought you'd probably tell me to fuck off.'

'Never.'

'Oh, and I need to give you this.' She hands Lexi a credit card. 'It's yours.'

Lexi looks at it. Her old business credit card from Cavendish Cooper? 'I thought I'd lost it.'

Beth is awkward and embarrassed. 'No, it was me, and I'm sorry. I only used it once.'

Lexi shakes her head. 'I could not give a stuff. It's just money.'

Beth smiles. 'Anyway, why are you still living here? I thought you'd have got the penthouse apartment by now.'

'I left Cavendish Cooper. Long story. I was a wreck, had to take a few months off.'

'What are you doing now?'

'I started my own business a year ago. A property finders firm. We work with individual buyers to help them with their property search, give them objective advice and help them through the acquisitions process.'

'Is this still high end stuff?'

'Not necessarily. Our clients have all sorts of different needs. Maybe they're downsizing and want a retirement property in the country, or they're moving back to the UK from overseas, or they need a bigger family home. Most people don't have the time or the skills to find what they want.'

'Brave to set up your own business.'

Lexi shrugs. 'I enjoy running my own show.'

Beth grins. 'You always were a control freak.'

Fleur's little face puckers and she lets out a plaintive cry.

'I think someone's feeling ignored,' says Lexi.

'She's hungry.'

'Well, come inside. You can feed her.'

'You sure?' says Beth. 'Haven't you got stuff to do?'

'No,' says Lexi. 'And anyway, this takes precedence over everything else. Come here and give me a hug.'

She opens her arms and Beth steps into them. She clutches her tight. 'I've missed you,' she whispers. 'I was such an idiot.'

'Not as much as me.'

'I'm so glad you've come back. Both of you.'

A MESSAGE FROM SUSAN
PLUS A FREE BOOK TO DOWNLOAD

Thank you for choosing to read *What It Takes*. If you enjoyed it and would like a free book to download, plus keep up to date with my latest book releases and news, please use the address below.

susanwilkins.co.uk/sign-up/

**Your email address will never be shared, and you can unsubscribe at any time.*

Or scan QR code to go to Susan's sign up page

Do get in touch and let me know what you thought of *What It Takes*. I love hearing from readers. You can message me at:
susanwilkins.co.uk/contact

Or scan QR Code to go to Susan's contact page

LEAVE A REVIEW

If you feel like writing a review, I'd be most grateful. The choice of books out there is vast. Reviews do help readers discover one of my books for the first time.

Scan QR code to review What It Takes

tiktok.com/@susanwilkinsbooks

bookbub.com/authors/susan-wilkins

facebook.com/susanwilkinsauthor

instagram.com/susan_wilkins32

x.com/SusanWilkins32

BOOKS BY SUSAN

The Detective Jo Boden Case Files:

It Should Have Been Me

She's Gone

Her Perfect Husband

Lie Deny Repeat

See Me Fall

You Left Me

What It Takes

Other Books by Susan:

Buried Deep

Close To The Bone

A Killer's Heart

The Shout - Free when you sign up to Susan's newsletter

ACKNOWLEDGEMENTS

Huge thanks to Colin Liversage and Graham Bartlett for their expert advice on how the police would proceed. Some things have been altered slightly in the interests of drama.

In my career as an author, I've received the help and support of too many people to mention. The community of crime writers is friendly, welcoming, and nowadays global. Learning from those who have gone before is essential for any writer.

Thanks also to Jenny Kenyon for her unwavering support.

Last, but not least, thanks to Laura Wilkinson for her sharp editorial eye on the manuscript and her many suggestions for improvements.

But getting the books out into the world would be impossible without my partner in crime, Sue Kenyon. I just write the books. She does everything else.

My special thanks goes to all my newsletter subscribers. Your reviews really help. Your emails cheer me up and make me laugh. You also make me realize that, thanks to technology, I'm now reaching a global audience of readers.

Published by Herkimer Limited in 2024
Summit House
170 Finchley Road
London NW3 6BP

Scan QR code to go to susanwilkins.co.uk

ISBN 978-1-7392493-8-0